Men & Dogs

Men & Dogs

Katie Crouch

BLOOMSBURY
LONDON · BERLIN · NEW YORK

First published in Great Britain 2010

Copyright © 2010 by Katie Crouch

The moral right of the author has been asserted

Bloomsbury Publishing Plc
36 Soho Square
London W1D 3QY

www.bloomsbury.com

Bloomsbury Publishing, London, New York and Berlin

A CIP catalogue record for this book
is available from the British Library

ISBN 978 0 7475 9372 0
10 9 8 7 6 5 4 3 2 1

Printed in Great Britain by Clays Ltd, St Ives plc

Mixed Sources
Product group from well-managed
forests and other controlled sources
www.fsc.org Cert no. SGS-COC-2061
© 1996 Forest Stewardship Council
FSC

www.bloomsbury.com/katiecrouch

To Dad, who always hears me, especially when I'm out at sea.

I can't look at everything hard enough.

—Thornton Wilder, *Our Town*

Men and Dogs

1

Saturday

TWO DAYS BEFORE Hannah's father disappeared, he took her out in his boat.

It was an aluminum boat, flat and small with a pull-operated motor. Before they left, her father checked the gas and oil levels. Hannah held Tucker, the dog, on a leash.

Hannah was still small then. Eleven years old. Her hair was streaked with green from afternoons spent in the neighbor's pool.

She wasn't pretty. She had her father's powerful features, and they were too large for her face. She wore a long T-shirt and red sneakers. Her bathing suit snaked up in bright lines around her neck. She wasn't unhappy. She's always been good at waiting.

There was no plan for the day. There never was.

The Legares were a family who navigated by the outlines of Buzz's whims. The children had become excellent at collecting information. It was a survival tactic. They eavesdropped, they spied. Hannah's brother taught her how to open and reseal mail over a pot of steaming water.

That morning there had been a fight. Hannah listened to the dull murmurings of it through the bedroom wall, the voices spiking in volume, then falling flat to silence. Shortly after, Buzz stepped out into the hall.

I'll take Hannah, he said.

His voice through the door.

Her mother's laugh.

Take her to China if you want to, she heard her mother say. I don't care.

Hannah sat up. It was time to go.

Hannah, now thirty-five, remembers some details perfectly clearly, as if they happened just a moment ago. They bounce in her head, meaningless shards of color and sound. When she is ordering coffee. When she is in line to get on a plane.

Other things she knows she should recall — large events and happenings — now somehow eradicated. Sometimes she squeezes her eyes shut and scrapes her mind, trying to get to them.

She still has this list. Items she and her father took on the boat trip, written in an eleven-year-old's cursive on Hello Kitty paper, carefully folded and stored.

1 jug of water
3 bottles of Coke
4 cans of Budweiser
2 bologna sandwiches

1 net
1 package chicken necks
1 portable radio
1 fishing pole
2 hats
1 bottle of sunscreen, SPF 15
1 dog

When they were ready, Hannah untied the bowline and waited on the dock while her father pulled the cord. The engine sneezed, rumbled slightly, and died.

Damn it, Buzz said.

He looked up at his daughter and smiled.

Don't tell your mother.

She nodded. There were going to be many things she wouldn't tell her mother.

The boat started. Buzz steered them away from the Boat Club and turned the engine knob all the way to the right. Hannah stared at the shrinking land.

Always nice to leave, isn't it? her father said. Where should we go? China?

I don't know.

China.

No!

We'll send them a postcard.

No!

You're right, no postcard.

Hannah...

Yeah?

How many bones are in the body?

Two hundred six.

Hannah's father was a doctor, and she planned on being one, too.

How many cells?

One hundred trillion.

One hundred trillion, her father repeated, looking out at the water. He took a swallow of beer.

He was tall and, at forty-one, still lean from runs around the Battery. People remembered him as the high school track star. Buzz Legare wasn't staggeringly handsome, but he was disarming. People wanted to be near him. Men pointedly used his first and last name in conversation. Hannah noticed that waitresses lingered after taking an order, even when her mother was there.

Aren't you going to crab? he asked. We brought all of these chicken necks.

Hannah sighed. She didn't want to crab. She wanted to read about Kirk Cameron.

Pretty soon a day on the boat with your dad will be the last thing you want to do, he said. Pretty soon, it'll all be about makeup and boys.

OK. I'll crab.

Buzz turned on the radio. He always sang. He'd start out with

6

a hum, and then would become overwhelmed with the desire to perform. He never knew the words. He didn't care.

Wake me up before you LA-la

Go-go, Hannah said.
What?
Go-go.
Are you sure?
I learned the words so I can lip-synch them.
Lip what?
Lip-synch.
Buzz cocked his head.
We pretend to sing them. My friends and I. Like on a show.
Who pretends? he said, casting his line.
Everyone. It's a show.
Do me a favor, kid. Don't pretend. Just sing.
She looked at him, mouthing, *Wake me up before you—*
Out loud, he said.

It was midday, and men, both black and white, were sitting out in the sun, legs spread, fishing poles in their hands. They stayed on separate docks, but their children spilled into the river together, floating side by side on Styrofoam boards. Some of them waved. Hannah waved back.

Suddenly, a scream cut through the sound of the motor. Hannah jerked her head toward the shore. On one of the docks, people were running and gathering around something lying flat.

Kevin! someone shouted.

A woman was crouching, shaking a boy's shoulder.

Kevin! Will someone —*Kevin?*

Hannah's father knocked about the boat like a large caught fish, swearing as spray lurched up behind with sick, slapping sounds. They slammed into the dock.

A boy had been stung by a bee. He was in shock. His throat was swollen, and his tongue was the size of a pickle.

I'm a doctor, Buzz told the boy's mother. He always stood up a little taller when he said this. Hannah, get my doctor's bag. Center console, in the flare box.

Hannah ran back to the boat, found the flare box, and retrieved the bag, a perfect leather triangle that opened and closed with a reassuring snap. Inside, set rows of neatly arranged syringes, bottles, and rubber tubes. One of her favorite things to do was to put her hand inside. It was always cool, as if it required its own separate air.

Later, Hannah looked up what would have happened if her father hadn't stopped to help that day. The bee venom was almost as lethal as cyanide for the boy. When the tip of the stinger pierced his skin, an army of histamines split from the heparins and flooded his body. Water was released from the cells, causing his skin to strain against the liquid. He would have turned blue and choked on his own tongue while his mother watched.

Afterward, a party. The boy's father brought out another cooler of beer, and the neighbors came, carrying plastic folding chairs and bags of potato chips and a great bowl of pink, curling shrimp. Candy-lipped mothers rushed back and forth with more food. The afternoon poured away.

We have to go, Buzz said after a while. Thank you for the good time.

So we'll come see you, Doc, the boy's mother said. She was leaning into him slightly. You're our doctor now.

Buzz looked down at her and squeezed her shoulder. There was a pause, then he broke away and began running. Hannah and the others watched, openmouthed, as he did a cannonball off the dock.

He's swimming! the boy screamed. The doctor is swimming!

He ran after Hannah's father and flung himself in the water. Now people all over the dock were following Buzz. They jumped in with huge splashes, showing off awkward half dives in their shirts and shorts.

Come on, Hannah! her father yelled. He spouted water through his lips.

No, that's OK, she said. She was worried about her hair. She'd sprayed it up, a proud open lily.

Hannah! Swim!

She shook her head. The boy's mother was swimming near her father. She gave him a little splash.

Hannah, he called. How many times a day does a human breathe?

Twenty thousand.

How many heartbeats?

A hundred thousand.

Come on, sweetie.

No.

Scared?

No.

Come on, honey.

Why?

Because.

Why?

There won't always be a why.

They were all waiting. Her father, the not-dead boy, his mother, the strangers. It was April 6, a day she would come to circle in red each year and label: DAD. 1985. What was happening? Hannah Legare can tell you. It was the year of New Coke. The number one song was "One More Night." Christa McAuliffe was slated to ride the *Challenger*. Ronald Reagan was sworn in for a second term. As for the Legares—they were still a family. Hannah, eleven; Palmer, thirteen; Daisy, thirty-six; Buzz, forty-one.

On April 6, Hannah was a plain sixth grader with a bad perm. She was a bit scared of the water, and was shivering on a dock. She closed her eyes and listened to her heart, then held her breath to try to make it stop. It didn't, so she jumped, because her father told her to.

2
Hannah's Fall

WHEN HANNAH OPENS her eyes, she knows something is wrong. She sits up slowly, orienting herself. There is a ripping sound as her skin parts from the hammered-leather couch. It's not the sort of couch she would ever buy; nor would she purchase anything resembling the fluffy, synthetic white rug spread across the concrete floor, nor the enormous plasma TV and entertainment system complete with Wii, nor the oversize, framed sci-fi movie posters. But, having been turned from her home, Hannah is currently subletting an overpriced, furnished loft in San Francisco's South of Market district. The place is cavernous. The ceiling is twenty feet high; the gray walls yawn past the gleaming kitchen to a cold bedroom housing a large closet filled with old computers and an S&M-worthy wrought-iron bed. Though many, she knows, would be impressed by the loft's Trekkie-esque grandeur, Hannah can't help but see it as a very expensive, geeky prison — pretty much where she deserves to be living right now.

She sits up and takes a reluctant lap around the space. Her husband must have carried her up, dumped her on the couch, and left. She sits on the kitchen stool and rubs her eyes. Clothes are strewn on the floor, dishes and take-out containers litter the stone countertop. She is still drunk, but it is not a pleasant state of intoxication. In an attempt to solve this, she pours herself a drink. Then she reaches over and picks up a pad of paper and a pen in order to make a list.

Things to Get for Sublet

Better rug
Better sofa? (How long will I be here?)
Music contraption
Pictures of normal people
More wine
Husband

She sighs and throws the pad down again. So Jon didn't stay. She feels the dull reality of it, a cold ache. She pictures where her husband might be now. At a club, maybe, leaning into Denise on a velvet banquette. Or, worse, with Denise in Hannah and Jon's bed — a mattress selected according to her own finely tuned appraisals of width, springs, and plushness. No, her husband wouldn't do that. Would he? She doesn't know, actually. She's not sure anymore.

Maybe he called? She finds her purse. No missed calls. No messages. She tosses the phone on the sofa, wondering how this happened to her. Yet it didn't happen to her. *She* did this. Still—Denise? She's a PR consultant, for God's sake. A very pretty one, and smart, but…she's a twentysomething hippie.

She teaches a hula-hooping class in her spare time. Whereas Jon is a man—a nerd, really—who believes that Craig Newmark deserves the Nobel Peace Prize. Who never swears. Who subscribes to *Tin House* and *The Believer* and actually *reads* them cover to cover. His light-brown hair in the morning looks like hay; his favorite possession is his mother's quilt; he once threw a party to plan Britney Spears's mercy killing. He's dorky and hilarious and generous and perfect and she's really fucked up this time and has to do something about it.

Hannah finishes her vodka soda, tops it off with half of a sugar-free Red Bull left in the fridge by the previous renter, then downs a tumbler of water to stave off tomorrow's hangover. (A futile attempt, but each new day deserves a fresh chance.) She molts the dress, puts on Jon's favorite outfit—jeans, T-shirt, braless—and calls a cab.

Even after more than fifteen years, Hannah still has a mad crush on San Francisco. She loves the confectionary mansions, the thickets of crack dens, and the dense, surprising pockets of eucalyptus. The cultural compartmentalization warms her— Hannah can look at nearly any person she meets and almost instantly peg where they live. That girl in the Atari shirt and the green eye shadow? The Mission. The guy in the pink button-down and Dockers? Somewhere in between Cow Hollow and Pac Heights. The Indian guy in the jeans with a knife crease is Potrero. The woman with the sport top and the sunburned nose, either the Presidio or the Outer Richmond—somewhere with enough room for her surfboards.

The car slams on its brakes. A homeless man darts in front.

"Careful!" she shouts.

"The guy's on meth," the driver says. "What do you want?"

They stop at a light. Hannah turns back to look again, checking the man's height, hair, approximate age. Too short—not her father. She leans back into the seat, the man leaving as quickly as he came, replaced by what she will say to her husband. The words slip dangerously through her mind.

I didn't mean to. No. *I meant to, but I'm really sorry about it.* Try again. *I was stuck. I was depressed.* Too much "I." *You are everything to me.* God. *Without you I am a meaningless pile of nothing.* Maybe. *Please.* Maybe that?

The light turns green. The man retreats to the shadows, out of the limits of her sight.

Hannah sees her father about once a month. Not all at one time, of course. Not the whole person. And never when she's consciously looking. Last week, she saw his shoulders at a wine store. Then one of the buyers at Saks surprised her by having his hair: early-forties thickness, light brown with a little gray.

Her biology professor at Stanford had his nose. It was the first time she'd seen the nose on anyone other than her father—a rare find. Since then, she's spotted it only on the face of her hair stylist and one of the contestants on *Top Chef.* During the first class she had with the nose, she was mesmerized. It was a stupid class, and, as with many at Stanford, Hannah coasted through on autopilot. Still, after seeing the nose, Hannah found herself going to office hours twice a week and spending long, unnecessary tutoring sessions with its owner.

The rest of the man was nothing like Buzz. Short and dark, with bushy eyebrows and a smug, charmless voice, he immediately assumed Hannah had a crush on him. And who could blame him? She constantly made up excuses to see him, thought up inane questions about plant phyla and bird species and brought in flowers plucked from the quad. At first the Nose seemed to find her charming, but near the end of the term, he became exasperated.

"I have a wife, Hannah," he said, his caterpillar eyebrows straining to meet. "This is very flattering, really. Listen, you've got an A. An A plus, if there is such a thing. I promise. Just please, don't come back."

Hannah didn't bother to tell the professor her story, because doing so would be a self-indulgent action that would defeat the proverbial point of moving to California. For that reason very few people know that she has a father who went fishing at dusk when she was eleven and never returned. They don't know that Buzz Legare disappeared into thin air, leaving no note, body, or explanation.

The fact is, Hannah has a hard time getting those close to her to understand how she could be so preoccupied by someone who left more than twenty years ago. Under her mother's direction, she and her brother were discouraged from hanging on to things. Sentimental clutter in the form of, say, photo albums and bulletin boards are not encouraged in the Legare family. Daisy is nothing if not a responsible mother; after her husband's disappearance, Hannah and Palmer were dutifully sent to church and to see a family counselor, his office complete with painted inspirational posters bearing troubling slogans such as PUNISHMENT HALVED IS JOY DOUBLED! and YOUR YESTERDAYS ARE ONLY YOUR TOMORROWS, AGAIN.

Did the sadness subside? It did. And that's exactly when, with a groaning crack, the glacial divide in the Legare household began to form. For her brother, Palmer, the topic of her father was closed. Her mother, too, seemed over it, having remarried within a year, something Hannah has never quite been able to forgive her for.

So Hannah entered her twelfth year more than a little baffled. She still had — *has* — questions. For her, an empty boat floating on the harbor is not an obvious conclusion.

Hannah believes her father is alive. As in, still in existence and breathing the same air as she is, on this very Earth. It's not that she isn't tempted to believe otherwise; there are just too many unexplained factors. For instance, how does one fall off a boat on a calm spring evening? And why did no one see her father out in the harbor? And why was he fishing on a Monday at twilight? And if he drowned, why was no body ever found? And finally, why, *why* was the dog still there?

After six years of probing, Hannah succeeded only in estranging herself from her family. Palmer, Daisy, and her stepfather were tired of her questions, tired of what they saw as her relentless desire to cause upheaval in their lives. "What do you need?" Daisy once snapped in exasperation. "A shark-eaten carcass?" So when it came time for college, it became clear that Hannah's best option was just to leave. Since high school graduation, she's been back to Charleston only four times: a wedding, a Christmas, a funeral, and once with Jon — each visit an awkward jail sentence. It isn't that she doesn't appreciate the place. Who wouldn't adore the beaches and a local accent so complex it allows a woman to simultaneously seduce and reprimand in one single word? She probably loved it more than anyone, right up until that day in April when her father took off in his boat to find something better. A crappy thing for him to do, but as she's gotten older, she's come to admire her father for it. She's almost grateful, even.

Because certainly her father's departure gave her an unquestionable license to leave without looking back.

And she's thriving, isn't she? Stanford, a start-up, then Stanford again for business school, and now another start-up out of the ashes of the first. Three marathons, two biking centuries, a marriage (albeit slightly screwed) to a highly appropriate life partner.

Her father never would have dreamed of such a future for her. Often she wakes up in the middle of the night, wanting to tell him. I'm killing it, Dad, she'd say. How about you? She googles his name once a week. He left long before the Internet; still she sends e-mails to the kinds of addresses he might choose—buzz@ swampnet.com, blegare@charleston.net. But she receives only auto replies from strangers. *Action failed. Error. Your message did not go through.*

Taxis always have trouble finding Hannah and Jon's Upper Terrace apartment, and this one's no different. Not that she can blame the driver. On a map, the neighborhood looks like the inside of a brain. He refuses her help at first (pride, directions, men), and for a while, her inner Southerner politely lets him wander. After the second wrong turn, though, she becomes impatient and barks the directions. "Up Fell. Left on Masonic. Keep going. Keep going. Top of the hill. Around the bend. I know it's curvy, but I promise the street keeps going. Yes, this one. Thanks."

It was Hannah who found the apartment, a one-bedroom with good fixtures and spectacularly unfriendly neighbors. Not the best deal in the world; they paid $920,000 cash in a market that could only slither downward. Still, it's perched on one of the highest hills in San Francisco, meaning that from the living room, one can see the whole city — the coppery tops of the new de Young Museum, just now beginning to green, the washed-out Sunset District, the Crayola smear of the Golden Gate Bridge stretched out against miles of churning sea. The place is small, but that view, at least, Hannah reasoned at the time, had to be worth almost a million dollars. Jon was a bit reluctant, as there would be no room for pets or kids, but that fact, for reasons Hannah couldn't clearly explain, only made her want the place more.

The view has its consequences, of course. With nothing between the windows and the Pacific, the building is constantly under an onslaught of gale-force wind. Gusts rattle the windows, and sometimes, coming around the corner from the protection of the garage, Hannah finds her own private rainstorm opening up just above her head.

It's not raining tonight, but the wind is high. It whips at her hair and through her shirt. She looks up to the third floor. The lights are out. She'd use her key, but the locks have been changed. She knows this without even bothering to try them. It's a ritual she's gone through several times now: she screws up; her husband gets new locks. Then, after a large amount of seducing, cajoling, and gentle reasoning, he lets her back in and she pays the locksmith to make her another copy of the new key. Ringing the bell isn't an option either; he's most likely not home, and if he is, he won't answer.

Surveying the building, she thinks of the call she made to her brother a few weeks back. They rarely speak, but she had to do something that day to ward off the afternoon loneliness. Her brother's voice, still Southern, carried an unmistakable note of annoyance at the news of her separation.

"It's marriage," she explained. "I can't deal."

"How original," he said, sighing.

"I know. It's faith."

"Faith?"

"Being faithful," she said. And, after a pause, "It's a problem."

The first slipup — shortly after their wedding a year and a half
ago — was reasonably innocent. Jon was out of town and she'd
gone to a business dinner, after which she'd had too much Maker's
Mark; the next morning, she was naked in a hotel room. Hannah
hates secrets, so she told her husband immediately. He was angry
but forgave her with sad, unbearably tolerant eyes. Shortly after,
she slept with her yoga instructor. And then there was the thing
at her college reunion. But when the yoga mistake happened a
second time (different instructor), Jon finally took his mother's
heirloom ring back and kicked her out for good.

Hannah is not sure why she does this. It's as if the param-
eters of being a decent partner — boundaries once as obvious as
brilliant highway dividers — have been covered in snow. Before
she was married, she never had the inclination, because Jon was
obviously the person she was supposed to be with. This much
had become clear to her one certain day in her marketing class at
Stanford Business School.

She had already noticed him, of course. Everyone had. He was
so appealingly odd. A nice-looking person, with light-brown hair
and brown eyes; almost too nice, if not for a scar on his left cheek
that Hannah would later find out was from a drunken biking accident while he was at Oberlin. He always sat alone, and every day
he wore well-shined dress shoes and a gray suit. (A suit! To class!
In California!) He was distant, spending the time before class with
his nose in a book when others were chatting. Most importantly,

he paid no attention whatsoever to Hannah, which, naturally, put him squarely in the center of her radar screen.

Hannah's classmates called him the Suit Guy. They thought he was a douche bag. If you didn't come for beers at Nola's after class, you were a douche bag (male) or a snob (female). It was a way of categorizing people that even Hannah, who generally liked being surrounded by people who were certain to be somewhat successful, found tiresome. She was sleeping with a classmate named Skip at the time, a Korean engineer with flawless bone structure and a patent on some sort of hedge-fund-analysis software. Still, as the semester marched on, she found herself glancing longingly at Nola's threshold night after night, hoping the Suit Guy might, by some odd chance, darken its neoned door. So, yes, she was already interested. But it was the thing with Professor Ellsworth that did it.

"Knock-knock," Professor Ellsworth would pipe at least once a class. It was a truly pointless prerequisite, and the professor— clearly hired as a favor to some key donor—had an incurable penchant for jokes. When none of the students would answer, he'd say it again, a few decibels louder. "Knock-knooooooock!"

"Who's there?" someone would wearily reply.

"Justin!"

"Justin who?"

"Justin time to give me the statistics report on the success of online advertising targeting baby boomers! Ha!"

Then one day, Suit Guy raised his hand before Ellsworth could get his knock-knock out. Hannah turned, fascinated. The professor called on the Suit Guy, obviously annoyed that this young man was getting in the way of his antics.

"Yes?"

"Knock-knock," the Suit Guy said.

"Excuse me?" the professor asked.

"Knock. Knock."

The professor frowned, confused. That was *his* line. "Who's there?"

"The guy who thinks your class is a complete joke," Suit Guy said. "Look—I'm sorry, but I have a job. You know, a real one, to get myself through school. So can we please just get through this material?"

The other students stared, suspended in the thick gelatin of silence. It took the professor a week to fully recover and resume his joke assault.

Bingo, Hannah thought. That's my boyfriend.

It wasn't easy. When Hannah urged him to come to Nola's, he politely refused, saying he had to get to his job in the city. She invited him to parties, to dinner, even to the opera—no, no, no. Then one day, Hannah ran into him on the fringe of campus. Instead of his now trademark suit, he was wearing white shorts and a yellow T-shirt that read, KICK IT!

"What are you doing?" she blurted. Not the smoothest opener, but it was off-putting to accidentally come across her crush sporting striped kneesocks.

"I'm on a kickball team," he said, suddenly absorbed with his shoelaces. "Stanford has a league. Unofficially. You know—off-the-grid kind of thing."

"I *love* kickball," Hannah lied. "Can I play on your team?"

"We're full, actually. We're sort of the champions, so we've got a waiting list."

Hannah cocked her head. She had just asked to be on his kickball team. *A kickball team.* In other words, she had just offered to act like a fourth grader in order to facilitate sex. And this suit-wearing beanpole, this geek, had said *no?* Oh, it was on. She had to have this guy.

By the following week, through a certain amount of applied investigation and light flirting, she had finagled herself a spot on the opposing team. If Jon was surprised to see her on the diamond, he didn't show it; he simply returned her wave with a nod of what looked like annoyance. When it was her turn at the plate, she treated him to her biggest smile (freshly Crest Whitestripped), ran to the ball, and kicked it as hard as she could.

What followed was blinding pain and a view of the California sky. She had torn her hamstring, it would later turn out, and landed on her back. A crowd quickly gathered above her, and she spotted Jon's face bobbing on the edge of the cloud of heads.

"Look," she said, pointing to him. "I fell for you."

It was the first of their very own line of horrible jokes.

"I was flattered you followed me to kickball," he said on their first date (post–emergency room drinks). "Sort of. But to injure yourself? That takes dedication."

"It does," she said. "You must really be worth it."

And he was. He was worth a torn hamstring; worth switching from the Marina to the Mission; worth giving up the Korean's beautiful cheekbones. Because once one got past the feigned haughtiness, he was the warmest person in the world. Kind, tolerant, able to handle her post–Elbo Room drunken rants and her occasional midnight bouts of panic and tears. Hannah had found her person — someone she was perfectly happy to read next to on the couch without the thought that there might be something better out there. She was thirty, and she thought she was done.

The next four years were a happy, comfortable, adultery-free blur. They moved into a railroad apartment on 18th, across from the Bi-Rite and Dolores Park. Though they were both rather buttoned-up, preppy people, there was nothing to do now but become Mission hipsters. In a year they had both adopted the uniform of skinny jeans and T-shirts with ironic slogans. (CRAZY LIKE FOX NEWS; NUKE A GAY WHALE FOR JESUS!) Everything eventually became ironic: the fact that they hatched their business plan at the motorcycle bar, the way they ran a successful company out of the back of a record store. Once their shared specialty-goods company took off, Hannah and Jon were netting tens of thousands each month in a storage room they rented for $300. Oh, the irony.

Life had to change. Hannah and Jon couldn't be real hipsters anymore. They now had too much money to pull it off. They wouldn't admit to being yuppies, but they were something else in between. They started going to Tahoe to ski. Hannah hired the private yoga instructor. They threw open-bar parties and ordered takeout from slow-food restaurants. After the close of the third fiscal year, Jon announced they had more than a million dollars in the bank.

A million dollars, they marveled, toasting each other over a $115 pasta dinner from Delfina. What should we do with it all?

Buy an apartment. Get married.

It's not that, in the midst of all this youth and glory, Jon and Hannah didn't fight. Their arguments were flash storms that disappeared as quickly as they arrived, leaving the surfaces cleaner, cooler. These, Hannah knew, were what kept things interesting. They were not the cause of Hannah's postwedding crack-up. It was something else. Sometimes Hannah thinks it might actually be less about the marriage and more about the apartment. When they lived on 18th Street, there was nothing to see out of the windows. They were safe there, in their own little country, surrounded by craigslist furniture and stacks of Jon's emo records. But from Upper Terrace, she could literally see everything in the city out of her window. All the things she might be missing.

The first signs of her unraveling appeared as soon as they returned from their Cuban honeymoon. Usually, upon throwing down their bags after a trip, Hannah would be happy to be home, celebrating with a book on the couch or even, say, a quick screw. But something was wrong this time. The apartment, usually flooded with light, was so full of boxed wedding presents that the windows were blocked. There was no longer any *room*.

They pushed and rearranged the stacks, but it helped only slightly. Opening the gifts made it worse, because now there were all these things to store and mountains of empty boxes to recycle. Hannah began secretly throwing the boxes away without even opening them. Even that didn't make her feel better, so she started getting rid of things: clothes, appliances, the matching sets of polished chopsticks that had always inexplicably annoyed her.

"Where's the blender?" Jon asked, his hands full of smoothie-ready fruit. "Have you seen the microwave?"

Hannah claimed ignorance. She knew Jon wouldn't understand. Because while she wanted more personal space, he wanted less. Marriage was supposed to make them closer, he—rightly—reasoned. But whatever she conceded never seemed to be enough. Love wasn't enough; sex wasn't enough; sharing work problems wasn't enough; starting a business together, not enough; learning to backcountry ski (six weeks of avalanche training) and mountain bike (three Saturdays at Rock Hard Training School) just so they could have "new adventures together"—not enough. These things, her husband says, are necessary for a successful marriage.

But that's not all he's demanding. Often it seems to her that he wants the very inside of Hannah's brain.

"What are you thinking about?" he asks if, even for a moment, she drifts. It's such an unfair question. Because she is always simultaneously thinking *many* things. For example:

What Hannah Is Thinking Right Now

I'm hungry
Rusty ladder
Obama!
I need to shave my knees
Three stories, not so high
We have always been a family very close in spirit
I'm hungry

These are her thoughts. Hers! But Jon wants them—he wants *everything*—and at certain moments it makes her hate him. This is why, she believes, when she is put into tempting situations—drunk at Aqua, say, with an attractive associate, or engaged in the downward dog pose, being aggressively adjusted during a private ashtanga session—it's suddenly OK to ignore the fact that she has a husband.

She knows, objectively, that this is not OK. Being innately screwed up is not grounds for cheating. Yet in those moments, somehow, it has been.

She can hardly explain this to Jon, of course. It's not OK to cheat, but it's sort of even less OK, when your husband demands to know why you are unfaithful again and again (and again), to scream: *Because you are a human vortex of need, always there, always the same, and seriously I love you but oh, God, do I hate you, too.*

So she tells him she doesn't know. I don't know why I did that. I'm sorry. I'll never do it again. She lies because she needs him. She knows this, now that she may really have lost him. He is her person. He shields her from her mother, for one thing. And he holds her when she despairs over the thought of her father wandering through an empty landscape, lost.

She needs Jon. She cannot live without him. Which is why, though she has majorly screwed up these last few months, she will now climb up into her own window and humiliate herself. It's not the most brilliant plan. Professor Ellsworth certainly wouldn't approve of it. But it's also the only one she has.

Hannah hesitates. Getting up the fire escape itself will not be a complicated procedure; the only tricky part is climbing the neighbor's latticework. As she puts her foot up on the thin, flimsy wood, her sandal slips and she falls onto the pavement with a loud smack. She freezes and listens for stirrings inside the first-floor apartment. All remains quiet. Kicking off her shoes to get a better grip, she steps up again. The goal: to scale the lattice, hop up to the fire-escape ladder, and then quietly and quickly climb to her apartment, taking care not to wake the trustafarian couple on the first floor or the perky, permanently running-shoed couple on the second.

She hates heights, so she avoids looking down. One. Two. Do not look down. Three. Four. Why is she doing this? Oh, right. To beat out Denise. *(Climb.)* To find Jon and get him to forgive her and in general make things better. *(Climb.)* After all, he's allowed a Denise. *(Keep climbing.)* In fact, maybe it's better that he's with Denise now, because when he sees how superior she is—a wife passionate and loyal enough to climb through his window—she is completely certain that he will immediately expel that boob stick from his life and come back to her.

Creeping onto the fire-escape landing, she presses up on the window, then rocks perilously back in disbelief. It's locked. Since when does Jon lock his windows? She looks in and sees the bed is empty, then looks up at the roof. If she keeps climbing, taking care not to wake Mrs. Wong (the gold rush–era widow who bangs on the ceiling with a broom when they have sex), she can traverse the roof deck, scale down the emergency ladder that laces the front of the building, and drop onto the front terrace. That door will almost definitely be unlocked, as she broke the lock herself before leaving last time and never told Jon about it. It's all very easy, she tells herself. As long as I just keep looking up. She takes one last deep breath and resumes. Step, step. Keep climbing. Keep—

Suddenly, out of the depths behind Mrs. Wong's open window, a black, hairy being lunges at her with a demonic snarl.

It's the shock. It's the vodka. The wine. It's the loss of her husband. It's the Red Bull. It's the delicate combination of all these things, and with even one variation in these elements—one less drink, or, even better, one less Denise—she might be able to hang on. But all of these factors, along with Mrs. Wong's new Scottish terrier puppy, are now perfectly poised, no, stacked against her. So that Hannah Legare, as if at last facing an invisible wave of all her sins, is left to fall three long stories into the next unwanted chapter of her life.

3

The Night He Left

THERE WAS A rattling. It woke Hannah up.

She shut her eyes and tried to push herself back into sleep, but the sound persisted.

The sound of a car. Her mother on the phone. The front door opened and closed. Her mother was still talking. Hannah couldn't make out the words exactly, but she could hear the spikes of anger.

Time passed. Hannah waited for the rattling to stop. It did, only to start again, joined by a banging. She put her head under her pillow. When this didn't work, she sat up and got out of bed.

Bare feet on old wood. The sound was coming from the laundry room. It was the dryer. The door was shut, so she opened it and turned on the light. Someone was on the floor, under a pile of towels.

She stood for a while.

What are you doing? she finally asked.

My soccer clothes, her brother said. They're dirty.

What's banging?

My shoes.

She nudged the human-towel pile with her foot.

I like to sleep in here sometimes, he said. Under the towels.

But the shoes are banging.

Deal with it.

Dad come home yet?

No. I don't know. Probably.

I didn't hear him come home yet.

Just leave me alone, Hannah, OK? Leave.

She left for a while, then came back.

Can you take your shoes out, please?

No.

I'm telling Mom.

If you get out of here, I'll take out the shoes.

OK.

Don't tell Mom, narc.

OK.

She remembers her brother yanking the dryer door open. There was dirt under his fingernails. She can still see the scraped knuckles. He took the shoes out and threw them on the floor.

Hannah turned out the light and went back to her room. She got in bed. She'd promised not to tell her mother, but she could still tell her father. It seemed important. Something was happening to Palmer.

OK, OK. I'll tell Dad tomorrow. At breakfast, maybe. Or after, when we're alone again.

4

Palmer and Tom

WHEN TOM ANNOUNCES his desire to have a baby, it is
Friday. Palmer is annoyed. Friday is not the day to bring
up new relationship issues. Much better to deal with those on a
Tuesday or a Wednesday, when one is already problem solving
at the office. Friday is supposed to be a day of pleasure. It's the
day Palmer rotates his herb plants, has lunch with his mother,
and takes time off from the gym. It's the day before Saturday, set
aside for shopping or some sort of outdoor activity, which is the
day before Sunday, set aside for sex and laundry and reading the
imported *Sunday Times.* Unless Palmer happens to be on one of
his semiannual vacations (one out of the country, one in), he does
not stray from this routine. When people tease him about being
fastidious, he shrugs his shoulders and says, I'm gay.

The presentation itself: an amateurish effort at manipula-
tion. A cappuccino on the counter, the fleshy scent of homemade
crepes. Palmer frowns. Crepes are the sort of thing one has to

act thankful for but are more trouble than they are worth. He'd rather have plain yogurt and black coffee. He feels the same about morning sex, another of Tom's constant offerings. Disruptive, messy, but he partakes because the easy sweetness is there.

"Crepes," Palmer says, feigning enthusiasm. "Yum!" Tom slides the plate in front of him on the table; Palmer tucks into his paper. This is when, gullible as a retriever, he reaches out for the leaflets next to his plate.

ADOPT!; SURROGACY . . . FOR YOU?; GAY DADS, GAY MOMS: A BEAU-TIFUL PARTNERSHIP.

"What the hell are these?" Palmer asks.

His lover casts his eyes down and instantly retreats. "Never mind."

"Tom?"

"It's just an idea."

Palmer takes a breath. Tom's a tantra enthusiast and has been coaching him on meditation. It's all bullshit, but sometimes Palmer kind of likes it. He reaches inward to that calmer place.

"What idea?"

"I just think it would be good for us. You know, a baby. I think it maybe would be helpful for us to love something more than we love ourselves."

"I don't particularly love myself."

"*You* know what I mean. Experience a new emotion."

Palmer pushes his plate away. "I've had plenty of experience with emotions, Tom."

"Palmer." Tom's voice trembles, causing Palmer to wince. Friday is certainly not the day for fucking *tears*. "This is very important to me." He takes a breath. "This is something I want."

Palmer nods. Jesus. "OK, then. Let's talk tonight, why don't we?" he says, standing. "I'll make dinner."

The lowcountry fall air is thick and wet; the back door of his office sticks. Palmer uses his shoulder to push it open, already sensing the hum of activity within. He frowns at the smell. No matter how much steam cleaning or how many high-end home scents he pays for out of the petty cash, nothing rids the place of the sharp, sweet scent of urine (dog, cat, gerbil, the occasional reptile) that permeates the rooms. It will be a busy day at Palmer's veterinary clinic. The *Post and Courier* just ran an article about a rabid cat, and the waiting room is already jammed with anxious pet owners warily studying their animals for a possessed glint in the eye. He dives into work as soon as he gets in, studying the charts over black coffee.

At thirty-seven, Palmer Legare is a startlingly handsome man—tall, thin, and blond, almost Nordic. His looks give him certain advantages (note the reception area, filled with loyal female clients), such as being able to work without making idle conversation. There is something about a beautiful man silently handling an ill animal that affords respect, so clients rarely disturb him; today, Palmer uses the time to think over this new problem.

He will have to leave Tom now, of course. Palmer knew it would happen eventually. He's been waiting for the factor—could it be called a tipping point?—that would push the relationship into that dead place. He's surprised only that it hasn't happened sooner. It's been almost a year, the longest Palmer's ever gone. A shame, really. He likes Tom. He likes cohabiting with him—his architectural tastes, his sense of humor, the sex. He wouldn't say he loves him, really—he has never been able to say that about any man in his adult life. But he loves many things *about* him. He also sort of loves himself around Tom. He is nicer, somehow. More giving.

The giving is itself new relationship strategy for Palmer. He came across it quite by accident. It was one of those *aha!* moments he arrived upon when, one day, he picked up Tom's favorite moisturizer at Belk's just because he saw it, then brought it home and tossed it without ceremony on the counter next to the groceries; to his surprise, Tom embraced him and began wheeling him around in a sort of junior high school dance.

"Oh, sweetie!" Tom murmured into his shoulder. "You get it! You finally, finally *get* it."

And, awash in a warm bubble of personal epiphany, Palmer had to admit that yes—yes! He did! No wonder he'd had so many failed relationships before this . . . he'd never understood the needs-of-others part! The day of the moisturizer, he felt as if he'd been secretly allowed some oracular whisper. Ever since then, Palmer has made a concerted effort to meet Tom's needs, and the results have been overwhelmingly positive. When Tom told him he felt "emotionally neglected," Palmer bought him a juicer. When he wasn't "connecting," Palmer had a privacy fence built (male nude sunbathing being not especially popular in South Carolina yet). Palmer is happy because he is making Tom happy, and Tom is, well, happy to be happy. The thing is working, and while Palmer never expected to sustain it forever, it has been very good, moment to moment.

But a baby. This is much bigger than moisturizer. It's not that Palmer does not like children. A great many of them are smart and cute, and he'd like nothing more than to shop with Tom for T-shirts to send to, say, a nephew, godson, or other such nicely distanced baby. But one of the privileges of being gay, along with being forgiven for sex with strangers and the ability to sport a year-round tan without excuses, is that you can forgo reproducing without people telling you you're selfish. If you are a man, it seems to Palmer, you are either gay *or* a father. It's hardly necessary to be both.

So he will have to end it. The logistics of this will be so much harder than the others. Against his better judgment, he agreed to let Tom move in with him just a few months ago. Tom is an architect, and has ensconced himself in Palmer's life by making actual changes to his residence. The caulk around the plunge pool is still dewy; the paint on the walls of the home gym still fresh. Usually, when Palmer ends a relationship, he pulls a fade-out. In the best cases, the other person doesn't even realize it's happening until it's over. But this break will be tiring and dramatic. Tom will disintegrate.

In the afternoon, Palmer does a bit of research on the Internet. As he does, he becomes less concerned. Perhaps this is not a deal breaker. For it seems, according to the chat rooms and forums, that the chances of adopting as a gay parent in South Carolina are quite slim. They could always find a partner couple — two lesbians, say, who also want a baby and want dads in the picture and are willing to share the spawn. But here Palmer feels he is safe, because Tom, though lovable, is a bit of a snob toward lesbians. "I'm a Southern boy," Tom has said more than once, shrugging his shoulders faux apologetically. "I'm sorry, but I like my ladies to wear makeup and to like men."

Palmer switches off his computer and moves on to the next

patient, satisfied. He won't keep Tom forever; they've been lucky to have lasted this long. Still, he doesn't feel like breaking up today, and now he doesn't have to. He can wait it out, at least for a couple of months. And, more important, his child-free existence is safe.

Or is it? Because tonight, Tom arrives home breathless, bearing truly distressing news.

"I've found a surrogate!" he calls out, running in the door with yet more pamphlets. Rumpus — the Norwich terrier Palmer brought home two months ago when Tom caught him flirting with a construction worker — sambas at his heels.

"Oof!" the dog croaks. Rumpus is in remission from throat cancer and therefore has no voice box. Her owner fled at the sight of the bill, which is how the dog ended up in the adoption ward. Palmer thought Rumpus's inability to make noise would be a bonus, but the dog is desperate to vocalize, meaning Palmer and Tom's conversations are now punctuated with frantically whispered yodels.

"Ooooooooooooof."

"God," Tom says. "That *dog*."

Palmer fights to remain calm. He has been happily cooking and sipping the Riesling he selected to go with tonight's menu of salmon and vegetables en papillote. With a baby, would there even be Riesling? Or papillote?

"What surrogate? Who?"

Tom explains. He's found a woman who will have their baby: Naomi — a healthy twenty-two-year-old artist who needs money and wants to "help a couple out." Naomi works as a checkout girl at Earth Fare, which is where Tom happened upon her. She wants to have a baby, she says, but she doesn't want to *have* a baby. Tom

36

took her out for lunch, where she agreed to be his surrogate for $20,000 under the table, plus expenses.

"Now," Tom says, eyes shining, "all we have to do is find an egg."

Palmer feels his insides grow hotter. (And not just figuratively; Palmer has an intensely hot core temperature, a condition he treats with herbs, though with limited success.) In just one day, this badly sketched-out whim has become a blueprint with other people involved.

Shit, he thinks. Who but Tom could go to the grocery store and come back with a mother for our child?

Palmer instantly hates this Naomi, just as he does any person who wins Tom's easy affections. There always seems to be some new neighbor / life coach / raw-foods chef who will "change their life." And invariably, once Tom realizes that this person is, in fact, a freak, it's Palmer's job to get them out of it. Obviously, Naomi is a gold digger, a drug addict, or worse. Once one or all of those flaws become clear, Palmer will be tasked with extracting her from their lives. Not that Palmer can say any of this yet. Tom is too excited. There is just one piece of this ridiculous puzzle left. The egg. Palmer can still block the egg.

"Not a big deal," Tom says when Palmer gently questions him on this point. "Don't you see? We have a woman who will schlep the fetus. The *egg* is easy!"

"The egg is not easy, sweetheart. It's the *baby*. It accounts for who the baby will *be*."

"We can find one on the Internet. Hell, we can find an Oxford-educated supermodel that won the gold for curling at the Olympics. And I don't even know what the hell curling *is*. But imagine it! It's even better than having a regular baby with a wife, because there are always things you don't like about your wife, things you don't want in your baby. For instance, if you were a woman, I'd be, like — Well, I wish we could delete the huge forehead gene —"

"Thanks."

"Or, you know, the whole crazy-suicidal-dad thing. But we don't have to deal with that! We can pick what we want in our baby!"

"Look," Palmer says. "I made dinner."

"Oh, I'm too excited to eat."

Palmer plates the fish anyway, fanning the vegetables out on the china. I just want someone to eat fish with, he thinks. A bit of conversation, shared trips to Costco, a blow job every now and then, and nice quiet dinners of fish. Why can't I just have this? Why does everyone always want so much more?

"Tom," he says, "I think being a father would be" — Keep it in the conditional, he thinks — "a beautiful thing. But I want the egg to be someone we've at least met before."

Finally, there is the cadence of actual thought. Palmer can hear his partner processing the last point.

"You're an asshole," Tom says suddenly, pushing his plate away. "Do you ever think of anyone but yourself?"

"Tom..."

Just then, the landline rings. Upset by the noise, Rumpus emits a silent howl.

"Hello?"

"Palmer, it's your mother."

"Hi," Palmer says, actually relieved to receive the call. Bracing himself for this lesser evil, he watches Tom sip his wine with fury, a feat only his partner could pull off.

"We have a situation," she says.

Oh, Mother, you have no idea.

"What?" Hearing the dullness of his own tone, he is slightly sorry for it.

"We were having a *conversation*," Tom hisses from the table. Palmer makes a helpless face and points at the phone.

"It's your sister — she's out of control."

"And this is news?"

"Listen to me, Palmer." His mother sniffs. "This isn't funny. It's serious." Daisy goes on to tell Palmer the recently reported details, though none of it is anything he wants to hear: the infidelity (check), the drinking (disappointing), the three-story fall (fairly amusing and, to a brother, even a little bit impressive).

"There's a nail in her head," Daisy says. "It poked a hole in her skull."

"Brain damage?"

"Don't sound so hopeful."

Palmer snorts but stops laughing when it becomes clear that there will be responsibilities allotted.

"She's arriving tomorrow," Daisy says. "So, two choices: you can either pick her up at the airport or have her over for dinner in the next couple of days."

His temperature is rising again. Then, just as the sweat starts actually trickling down his forehead, Tom flips Palmer the bird and marches upstairs.

"We'll have her over for dinner."

"When?"

"I don't know, Mom. This week."

"I don't think you understand the magnitude of the situation, darling. Your sister is in trouble. She needs you."

"God, *enough*."

"Excuse me?"

"I get it!" He is shouting now, which both embarrasses him and pisses him off even more. "I get it, Mom, OK? Sorry. Call me when she gets in, all right?"

Palmer hangs up, sits down at the table, and eats his dinner, now cold. After a brief moment of consideration, he eats Tom's as well. He cleans up the kitchen and pours himself a whiskey. Palmer almost never drinks hard liquor unless they have guests, but already the night has careened from mildly unpleasant to slightly horrific. Whiskey seems highly appropriate, and Palmer is nothing if not that.

Tom has left one brochure on the table. GAY TODAY, LOVE TOMORROW: TEACHING YOUR CHILDREN TOLERANCE. Palmer crumples it up and shoots it in the trash. All right. He really will have to end it now. But when? The question vexes him; he slams his palm on the table, then reproaches himself. This feels dangerously close to the old anger he has been able to put aside for years. As a teenager, of course, he was a mess, but he long since beat that old, unruly self. Things are different now. He's a different person. He fields his mother's demands, weathers his stepfather's lewd remarks, caters to Tom's whims—all without so much as an inkling of his former unpleasantness. He has been able to rise above!

Still, there is one dark corner of his life that will not be neutralized, no matter how much he ignores it or breathes into it (Tom's suggestion) in order to be "present with his pain." It's a seldom-visited, bottle-green pocket where the subject of his father's disappearance lives, and where his sister, both by association and through her actions, also happens to stubbornly reside.

*　　*　　*

When Palmer thinks about being thirteen, he remembers the house on Atlantic Street as a place that was always moving. Previously reliable floors suddenly floated; the walls turned to Jell-O. He was surrounded by grown-ups who had no answers. It *could* have been suicide, Palmer heard the adults and police tell one another as they gathered in the living room for hushed cocktails. It might have been an accident. He may have been able to swim to shore. He would have come back, wouldn't he? He may have been cheating. He could have been depressed. Palmer waited, paralyzed, as they went on with their suppositions — theories so obviously empty, it made him sad just to hear them spoken.

And then, after a few weeks, the subtle shift in the form of a police letter. Palmer was in the first year of his teens, already radiating hormones, in and out of first love; yet nothing he had come across in his short life had touched him as deeply as that report. Finally, after weeks of fear and uncertainty as to what they would find, the grown-ups had agreed on a conclusion: It was sad but certain. Buzz Legare had drowned and was gone.

The facts presented were clear. And ever since, Palmer has been required to recount them to his bonehead of a sister at least once a year, when she calls with her disheartening theories. He remembers poring over the report the police presented — a slim sheaf containing a list of items and statements. The report did not contain theories. It contained the information everyone was actually certain of.

There was a boat. This boat, a sixteen-foot flat-bottomed aluminum craft, belonged to Palmer and Hannah's father. He bought the craft for fishing purposes on June 16, 1983, and registered it to his name. He had a slip for it at the Charleston Boat Club, which cost about $24 per month, in addition to his membership dues and sizable bar tabs.

On April 9, 1985, this boat was found four miles outside of Charleston Harbor. It was reported that morning by a shrimp-boat captain who had spotted it the night before, when it was still floating near some rocks that mark the mouth of the great water-way. When the coast guard recovered the vessel, it contained no people. The engine was in its lowest forward gear, long since run out of gas. On the boat were items almost identical to a list of things Hannah said they had taken on a trip three days before: water, Coke, beer, a net, a pole, sunscreen, unused life jackets, and one highly anxious, hungry dog.

Beyond this list of items, the Legares were forced to rely on the interpretations of others in order to piece together Buzz's last day. This was where things got frustratingly shady. Take, for example, the time at which Buzz's departure was witnessed. According to the Boat Club logbook, Buzz departed at 7:24 p.m. But after a pitifully small amount of questioning, the dock boy tearfully admitted that he was not certain about that. Turned out he'd spent the better part of the hours between six and eight o'clock in the buoy booth with a highly enthusiastic clubhouse waitress, and while the boy had taken mental note of the comings and goings he saw through the fogged-over window, his precision as to the time could only be called "compromised." So Dr. Legare, he admit-ted, might have left at 6:24 p.m. But maybe it was 7:45? All the boy really knew was that Buzz had departed during the most for-tunate part of the boy's shift, and that the sun was still up.

The Legares know some other things. They know, for instance, that Buzz had breakfast with them. They know he went to work. They know that Buzz liked to drink, but that didn't make him much different from any of them.

Whether because of or despite this jumble of facts and

observations—messy yet as telling as the contents of a woman's purse dumped onto a table—the police came to a conclusion: Buzz Legare was dead. The conditions were not survivable. There was no way a man could swim in from that far out.

Palmer saw the police report as a gift. It was terrible, knowing his father was dead. Even now it gives Palmer a bruised feeling to think of it. Still, it was better than the waiting, and at least now the Legares could get on with their lives.

But Hannah didn't want to. Indeed, this is precisely what caused the ever-widening rift between them. Rather than viewing the evidence as the key to a door out of the nightmare of their father's disappearance, Palmer's sister saw it as an excuse to remain trapped there.

She's been protesting the facts presented in the police report ever since its appearance on their kitchen table in 1985. "But there was no body," she said, looking at them steadily. God, that stare! At the time, Daisy and Palmer thought her ideas were merely part of a phase. But, to Palmer's mounting fury, even though he's tried to show her how much better it is simply to accept the truth, she still, more than twenty years later, won't let it go—she still picks at the scab. "He wasn't suicidal," she insists, as if *this* time she will surely persuade him. Or, "He knew perfectly well how to swim." And then, her favorite: "We have a *responsibility*."

It is this line that always infuriates Palmer the most. Responsibility? When did his sister become an authority on that subject? Every time she calls, she tells him something new that indicates yet again how completely irresponsible she is. She's having problems with Jon, she needs more money from their stepfather, she needs advice or just someone to listen to her talk on and on about her life. These time-consuming phone calls royally piss Palmer off. Does he call her just to burden her with his petty problems? His entire life is about being responsible, where she is anything but. He's the one who stayed in Charleston, choosing to open his animal clinic here. He is the one left to cater to his mother's whims. Palmer has built a home *here*, even though—as Tom is happy to point out with some frequency—there are any number of better places to live as a gay man that are more fun, accepting. What does Hannah do for the family? Nothing. Instead she just trots around in her fabulous life out in California. Calling home with her delusions, upsetting Daisy and Palmer both. Goddamn it, why can't she just keep it together? Why does she have to pull this bullshit now?

Palmer takes off his sweat-soaked shirt and lays it carefully over the back of his chair. He tosses the rest of the whiskey down the sink and climbs the stairs. When he enters the bedroom, Tom is watching *Top Chef* with the sound off.

"I like the guy with the spiky hair," Tom says without looking up, "but I can't stand to hear him talk."

"Listen, I'm sorry."

"I know," Tom says, eyes still on the TV.

Palmer stares at his small lover. When will I have to let you go? he thinks. In four weeks? Six?

"So your sister's visiting? Is that why you're so pissy?"

"Yes," Palmer answers. "She got drunk, I guess, and fell off a balcony."

"Hannah! Is she all right?"

"Some minor wounds. Her mouth, unfortunately, is completely intact."

"Well, when she comes over I'll hide the silver," Tom says.

"Come on, now," Palmer says, rubbing Tom's back. Switching

44

off the light and the television, Tom rolls away. Clearly he is still a little angry, but there are so many things in the bed between them already. Best to let it lie.

Let it lie. Something his father used to say.

Palmer is gifted at sleeping. Within a minute he is drifting with associative abandon toward dreams. He thinks of Hannah. His mother. Salmon. Tom's back. He thinks of the contestant on the show Tom was watching. Something familiar about him, his mind whispers just before giving out. Something in the eyes. Or, no. The nose.

5

Hannah, Home

THE DEWITT HOUSE — one of those places that actually deserves a proper name — stands with well-earned arrogance in the grandest section of Charleston, just off the cool, oyster-shell-paved square of White Point Gardens. The DeWitts are one of the oldest families in town, and their house reflects their long-standing social status in every detail, from its classic Georgian architecture to its historical scars. *Note* the exposed brick where carpetbaggers ripped the velvet from the dining room walls, the tour guides whisper when Hannah's stepfather allows visitors in for the semiannual house tour. *Look* at the cracks in the walls from the 1886 earthquake. This is an enviable, hulking pre–Civil War city mansion, a landmark by any standard. What person, she has often heard tourists say to one another in passing, wouldn't want to live here?

Hannah's stepfather, Will DeWitt, inherited the house over his two younger siblings, and it is his constant proclamation that he will never sell, despite the full-time maintenance staff required and property taxes that, were they a salary, would surely appease not a few of her Stanford classmates. Other families, Will nearly bellows at tonight's dinner, *other* families might be giving in and selling their South of Broad houses to outsiders and retired couples, but not the DeWitts.

There is but one word to describe Hannah's stepfather: "loud." Loud voice, loud golf shirts and pants, loud stories, loud boiled-crab skin. When he enters a room, Hannah cannot stop herself from picturing a Kool-Aid commercial circa 1986—the large, wobbling pitcher of pink liquid breaking walls and wreaking havoc.

"HannahBanana!" he bellowed upon seeing her this afternoon. "Lordy Lord, are you a sight! You actually make my eyes sore with that wound on your head. Hell!"

Will DeWitt eats like a Viking. He moves about the house like a drunken wildebeest. He could be worse, Hannah supposes. He never bothers her directly and gives her money when she asks for it. Still, Hannah has always had trouble comparing him to her own sleek otter of a father. It would be hard for anyone to fill Buzz Legare's shoes, but Will DeWitt stretches and soils them with his bunioned, swollen feet.

Not that, she has to admit, Will ever got an inkling of a fair shot at winning Hannah's favor, because he married her mother so soon after her father's disappearance. What kind of man does this? Daisy swears she'd never met Will DeWitt until after her husband's funeral. Yet Hannah has never been able to shake the suspicion that her mother is lying. Discovering your wife was having an affair with Will DeWitt would be enough to make a man leave, wouldn't it? Hannah's never been able to find proof, but she holds fast to the theory.

Her first night home: a dinner of chicken in a pool of butter (her mother's favorite secret ingredient) and a monologue about New Charleston. "It's the new people ruining everything," Will blusters at them over the banquet-sized dinner table. "Buying up the best houses, driving the prices up, and they don't even *live* here. They come for, what, maybe two weeks a year! Charlie's old house? Where he and his father grew up? You know who owns it? Some asshole from Palm Beach!"

"*You* could buy a house in Palm Beach if you wanted to," Hannah observes. "You've got enough money. Then you could be the asshole from Charleston."

Will ignores her. "These people are driving up taxes. And they've got no idea. None. We went to one of their parties—"

"They all want to be friends with us," her mother whispers.

"And these Yankees were serving Frogmore stew. Frogmore stew isn't for *parties*, for God's sake! It's what your wife cooks up when all you have is leftovers from the boat!"

"What a lucky wife," Hannah says, looking sadly at the table's lonely, used-up bottle of wine.

"Now," Daisy says. An authoritative, matron-of-the-house, we-must-stop-chitchatting-and-address-the-situation-at-hand sort of delivery. "Explain to me again how one gets a nail in the head."

"Mom, we went over this."

"Well. I just think if your life had a little more *structure,* you wouldn't be getting yourself into this trouble all of the time."

Hannah smiles wanly. Daisy DeWitt is all about structure. Hannah doesn't think her mother could even imagine a day of free, fluid time, let alone endure one. The woman lives by her ever-clutched lizard-skin planner. Lunch with a friend from the

48

Gibbes Museum board. A meeting with the tailor at two to have some pants taken in. (Yes!) Pilates at three. Tennis at five. Then dinner—dinner could be counted on for hours of time. The planning of, shopping for, preparation of, and consumption of the night's meal leaves no time in the evening for anything except a bit of guilty television watching or (better for the aging mind!) a chapter or two of a book.

"I do my best."

"For example, what are you doing tomorrow?"

"I..."

"What about a shopping trip? I'm not at all for this new style you've adopted."

"What do you mean?"

"It's just a bit...young for you."

"Jeans?"

"The *tight* jeans."

"They're not that tight."

"Painted on, Bo-bana," DeWitt pipes, heading to the sideboard for brandy.

"Pour me a splash?"

"No more liquor for you, Hannah," says Daisy. "Your head."

"Sorry, Cabana."

"I just think, darling, it's best to wear things that are a bit looser when...how do we say it? The bloom is..."

"Off the rose!" DeWitt chortles.

"All right," Hannah says, rising from the table. "I'm going to bed."

"Now don't get in a snit. I'm trying to help."

"Bed. Good night."

Hannah spends her first two days' worth of waking hours

wandering the mansion. The first-floor ceilings are eighteen feet high, and a grand helix of a staircase with a smooth, wide banister (excellent for sliding) spirals up four stories. Will studied period antiques for a few years in Europe and is therefore truly obsessed with keeping the house "authentic," while Daisy, if not as wealthy as Will, is as Old Charleston enough to have known not to refinish or overdecorate upon her arrival twenty-odd years ago. New curtains here, a velvet pillow there. That was it. Which, in the DeWitts' opinion, is what separates the new people from decent non-Frogmore-stew-serving locals like themselves. For this reason, the ballroom, though grand, is adorned with tarnished mirrors. The piano in the music room is a bit out of tune. Will and Daisy discuss these things endlessly — topics mind-numbingly dull to anyone who does not happen to own an antebellum mansion. Yes, let the mirrors tarnish! Keep the piano out of tune! As far as Hannah can tell, this house serves as fodder for almost all of their conversations.

There is, however, one corner of the house neither her mother nor her stepfather has discovered: the back of Hannah's closet. DeWitt, having the plans to the house, must at least vaguely know of the dimensions of the storage area. Still, Hannah doubts he's ever thought much about it, as the house is filled with any number of other, more interesting spaces — a room adjacent to the wine cellar accessible only by a secret panel door, an underground network of tunnels used by slaves in the eighteenth century.

Hannah herself forgot about it until she woke the second morning at home. She was hanging up some clothes, wondering if they were, in fact, too young for her, when the opening to her old fort winked at her from behind a bathrobe.

Nowhere. That's what she used to call it. A thirteen-year-old's joke.

50

Hannah, you've been missing for hours. Where have you been?
Nowhere.
Or:
Hey, where are you going now?
Nowhere.

Each time she said it, she got a little rush, a little twinge at the pleasure of fooling the mortals. It was a riddle she knew that her father, in particular, would appreciate. Now Hannah runs her fingers over an old dress, nearly undisturbed since her departure about a decade and a half ago.

Warren—

Warren Meyers. Even now, she bursts a little with the memory of her old boyfriend's hands, the pause before a terrified whisper. She wonders, for a moment, where he might be.

Warren, come up to Nowhere with me.

It looks like an ordinary closet, but it's not; someone, long ago, erected a false wall behind most of the clothes. In order to get to the hidden room, one must part the thick layer of skirts and dresses on the left side of the closet, then slip through a dark, narrow crevice. Nowhere is pitch-black, and to see anything Hannah always had to crouch down and switch on the kerosene lamp she stole from the camping gear her father left behind. But once that light was on—if her memory holds—the space was a teen paradise: the walls draped in old silk and velvet curtains; the floors littered with pillows stolen from her mother's less-frequented sofas and chairs. Stacks of books and magazines lined the walls, as well as photographs, torn out of *Vanity Fair* and *National Geographic*, of places she thought she might want to live someday, like Paris and Botswana. Anywhere, she used to tell whoever was listening. Anywhere but here.

There's a tapping in her chest as she parts the dresses and puts her arm through. An eruption of dust. It's darker than she remembers, and when she reaches around the wall for the lamp, something soft brushes her hand. She screams and shoots back to the center of the room, tripping on her robe and landing on the floor.

God. When did she become so afraid of everything? She puts her head on her knees and stares at the floor. She has too much time on her hands, she thinks. The day yawns ahead. Maybe she'll find a flashlight, a much-needed project. Something to pass the hours until she gets through this prescribed period of exile.

The last thing Hannah remembers about that horrible night is falling. She has no memory of hitting the ground, or of being discovered by the neighbors, collected by the paramedics, and shuttled to a hospital room. She woke up to a snapping fluorescent light. Someone down the hall groaned. Out of the corner of her eye, she saw a nurse enter.

"Oh, good, you're awake," the nurse said, devoid of tone. Unable to breathe correctly, Hannah refrained from immediate reply. There was a horrible ache in her side, and something was pressing on her forehead.

"What happened?"

"You broke a rib and fractured your skull slightly. You also came within two centimeters of dying."

"Really?"

"There was a nail in your head, though it didn't actually puncture anything other than your skull. Had it punctured the brain, you would have died within two minutes, tops."

"Is anyone here with me?"

"Your blood alcohol level was at .22 percent. Do you have any idea what that means?"

"That I was very, very drunk."

"Rehab wouldn't be the worst idea."

"I was drunk because I found out my husband is sleeping with someone else. That hardly warrants rehab."

Hannah looked out the window. She was not in a nice part of town. Down the street, a woman seemed to be performing a business exchange through a screened doorway.

"So, did Jon bring me here?"

"You were brought here in an ambulance and accompanied by a nice young couple."

" 'Nice' is not the word for what they are."

"They waited for a while for you to wake up and then went to get breakfast."

"Are you serious?" They were *brunching* while she bled?

"They said they'd be back."

An inner twist. A stab of pain.

"God!"

"Yes," the nurse said. "That would be your rib poking your lung. You still have a lot of alcohol in your system, but I'll give you a little something just so you don't faint from the pain."

"I love you."

The nurse smiled dryly, found a vein, and roughly pushed Hannah back into the padded chamber of drugged unconsciousness. When she opened her eyes again, the sun had changed positions and Jon was in the room.

"Hi," he said.

"Hi."

"Thanks for coming to see me," he said. "A valiant effort."

Hannah squinted at her husband. He was taller than she remembered from the dream she had just been having. Then again, in her dream they'd been chasing each other in a locked dollhouse.

"You know," he said, "I've always hidden a key beneath the ivy plant closest to the door. So you actually didn't have to break in and trespass on my property and privacy, or terrify the elderly upstairs neighbor, or upset her new Scottie puppy, or cause yourself major bodily harm. However, I'm going to take that key away now in case you come after me again with your lunatic ways. But I'm just saying, this could have been a hell of a lot easier."

"That was not a puppy. It was some wraith from the underworld."

Jon leaned over and pushed a button on a remote control next to Hannah's arm, causing the bed to incline. Pain ripped into her side.

"Jesus! Enough!" He inclined it one inch more and then dropped the controller.

"I'm calling the nurse," she said, gasping. "You're a sadist."

"I'd like to know what the hell you were thinking."

"I was coming to make you breakfast."

"How nice. Well, I wasn't there."

"I know. You were out screwing Denise."

Jon walked to the window, hands in his pockets. "Hell of a view you have here."

"Or maybe you weren't?"

"No, I was."

"Oh." Hannah was a bit crestfallen at this. "It doesn't matter. I don't care about her. I just wanted to talk to you."

"The neighbors called my cell phone. They said you were breaking in, and that you were in their moop heap, whatever the hell that is. They asked if I wanted to have you arrested. These people are Ecstasy dealers, Hannah, and they thought you were out of control enough to be arrested."

"Well, thanks for saying no. I guess."

"I should have you arrested, you insane woman." His voice cracked. He sat down on the vinyl visitor's chair, running his hands through his hair. He didn't look good. The scar on his cheek was particularly purple that day, something that happened when he wasn't in the sun enough. His green custom-made shirt had egg on it, and he needed a haircut. "I don't know what to do about you. You just…" He paused. "You are very, very bad for me. I cannot be around you anymore. But I'm so worried you're going to drive yourself into the ground, sweetheart. Like, six feet under."

"I won't."

He nodded and leaned back, crossing his legs.

"I called Daisy," he said after a moment.

Hannah shook her head.

"I had to."

"You didn't have to do anything."

"Hannah, wake *up!*" He was yelling now, the veins on his temples emerging like angry little rivers running down either side of his forehead. "You have lost everything. Get it? I can't be here for you anymore."

"What do you—"

"You're going home," he said. "It's either that or some kind of center. Daisy and I agreed."

"Daisy," Hannah repeated. "And you."

Hannah pictured her mother on the porch of the DeWitt House, white wine in hand, writing the next day's activity in her planner. It would be a warm, soft night on the peninsula. DeWitt would be in the house somewhere, listening to pop country music. She could hear the phone ringing, the soft tones of a pleasant greeting. Jon, how are you, honey? So good to hear your—

Hannah balled the sheets up in her hands.

"One month."

"Why did you call her?" she wailed. "Fuck you!"

"Yeah? Hell with you, too, for making me do it. You know I actually thought about having you committed?" Jon's voice cracked again, and suddenly he was next to her, his arms draped over her legs, his head in her lap. She put her hands in his hair. So soft, she thought. Such nice, soft hair.

"It's OK to say 'fuck,' you know," Hannah said. "It feels really good sometimes."

He shook his head. "I love you, Han. But I can't do this, you know? I married someone who's not right. In the head, I mean. You have any idea how much that sucks?"

So this was how Hannah's husband got her to go home again. He broke down, cried, and begged. It didn't take long for Hannah to relent. After all, she'd hit bottom. As she sat in the hospital, comforting her crying husband, this much was finally obvious. She'd fallen off her own balcony, and now no one was left to help her get back up.

Hannah gets up and dusts herself off. From far away, she can hear the door of the DeWitt House open and close.

"Hello?" someone shouts up.

She stands up, relieved. Mr. Mitchell, or Mitchell, as the DeWitt household and everyone else in town calls him, is actually one person in the DeWitt world Hannah sort of wants to see. She tightens her robe and ambles down the stairs.

"Hannah! I heard you were home." She makes a move to hug him, but he steps back politely and puts out his hand. Hannah blushes at her misstep. A seventy-year-old black handyman hugging the thirtysomething stepdaughter of his rich white employer? Not going to happen.

He looks at her robe. "Just getting up?"

"Still on Pacific time."

"Hmmm," he says. Hannah smiles. Mitchell has always been an unabashedly judgmental gentleman. "I was about to eat my sandwich. Why don't you sit with me on the porch?"

She nods and follows him outside. The DeWitt House porch is not your average outdoor sitting area but more of a grand colonnade, littered with black-cushioned wicker furniture and large, soft ferns. The sort of place suitable for sweeping hoopskirts. She sits in an overstuffed chair and looks out at White Point Gardens. Passersby peer curiously up from the street.

"So you back for a while?" Mitchell asks.

"No."

"Just a visit?"

She nods.

"Long time since you visited," Mitchell says.

"I haven't had a reason to come back."

"How's your husband? Mrs. DeWitt says you're married."

"He's fine."

"How come he's not with you?"

Hannah pauses, considering. Would Mitchell accept the

truth? Well, sir, because I screwed around on him so much that he finally wised up and began screwing someone else, too!

"He's working." She gets up. "Listen, I'm making coffee. You want any?"

"Sure."

Hannah goes into the kitchen and plunges the grounds to the bottom of the press. Forty hours down, hundreds (how many hours are in a month?) to go. She hears the front door open.

"Hello?"

Her mother's heels click on the marble. Hannah rises on her tiptoes and makes her way toward the back stairs off the kitchen.

"Hannah," her mother calls. "Stop. I can hear you."

Daisy appears, carrying a Goodwill shopping bag. While she now has more money than she ever dreamed of or currently acknowledges as possible, Hannah's mother grew up poor. Her father was from a respected family, but when she was a baby, he was discovered to have gambling debts. ("Respectable" doesn't always mean "smart," Daisy is wont to observe.) Consequently, she suffered through the experience of being from a "good" family in an unfortunate financial situation—a story that has graced many a Hallmark movie: the home-sewn clothes, the job in a dress shop after school while her friends hung out at the soda fountain, the soup flavored with tripe.

Happily, Daisy was—as she still is—indisputably beautiful. During her second year of college (on scholarship), Hannah's father met her on a porch, spilled a drink on her more or less on purpose, and promptly whisked her away to the solidly middle-class life of a doctor's wife. Still, Daisy was terrified of spending money. When Palmer and Hannah were children, she shopped for them at Sears and Kmart. They never went out to dinner. Birthday parties were homespun affairs of limp balloons and, once, a Banana Slide purchased on sale and stretched out on the grass with a hose. Groceries were bought in bulk, sandwiches packed on road trips so the family never had to stop at a restaurant.

Hannah had no complaints about her childhood. And thrift, she will tell anyone, is an increasingly precious virtue. Anyway, it was fun, aside from the occasional rock in the ass. Palmer and Hannah liked the Banana Slide. Esprit pants and Benetton sweaters were somehow more triumphant to wear when purchased at 70 percent off, even in sixth grade, when label-whoring was perhaps at its most rampant.

However, Daisy has been married to one of the richest people in the city for more than two decades now. In high school, alarmed by her mother's behavior (she was borrowing the housekeeper's S&H Green Stamps), Hannah once took Will aside and asked if he was having money troubles. Perhaps he was only land rich, she suggested, upon which his flushed face grew a frightening shade of purple and he started to laugh.

"Land rich? Sure, we're just land rich, other than the thirty million in the bank. Why, Check-o-slavana? You in trouble?"

"Czecho*slovakia*."

"Sure. I'll buy it for you. The whole place. Now scoot."

It seems, Hannah thinks as she appraises her mother's outfit, that Daisy still doesn't have a handle on her situation. She's always been a bargain hunter, spending weekend afternoons stalking sales like some famished lioness. But now it appears she's graduated down to the land of secondhand. This is a bold move in Hannah's eyes; it is her personal opinion that it's best to wear vintage when you yourself are not. But she has to hand it to her still-gorgeous mother: Daisy pulls off the looks of yesteryear with aplomb. Today she's fully committed to the seventies: fitted plaid polyester pants that come up high on her waist and a silky blouse with a large bow tied at the neck. She looks like a well-preserved Charlie's Angel.

"Some good finds?" Hannah says, nodding at her bag.

"Oh. Yes. Goodwill has such wonderful surprises. I got three shirts, a dress, and a slip for four dollars. And look what I found for you."

"What?"

"Trousers!" her mother says triumphantly, handing her a bag.

"What?"

"Slacks!"

"But—"

"That's what I realized you needed. I got you some nice slightly used linen things. You're still in your bathrobe?"

"I'm injured."

"It's been days, Hannah. Anyway, you've got to put some clothes on. Mitchell is here to see about the rotten sections of the roof."

"I know. We had lunch together on the porch."

"In your robe? Did anyone see you?"

"Yes, I flashed some boob and made out with him to give the neighbors something to gossip about."

"Lord, Hannah," her mother says. "When did you become so..."

"Troublesome?"

"'Stunted' was the word I was going to use."

"Ha."

"What are you doing today?"

"I don't know."

"You don't?"

"No."

"Well, why don't you play tennis with me?"

"Bad at tennis."

"Or get a massage."

"Too sore."

"Or walk."

"Nah."

"Well, Will needs some help with —"

"OK, I'll walk."

"And tonight?"

"Palmer asked me to dinner. Tom's cooking."

"Excellent." Her mother drums her fingers together in a manner that Hannah can only call Machiavellian.

"OK, then," Hannah says, abandoning Mitchell's promised coffee. "I'm going out."

"All right," Daisy says. "I'll be at tennis. Are you certain you don't want to come? We have a very nice beginner's ladder. You probably wouldn't lose too badly. It's mostly the heavier people. Oh, and poor Monica, with her missing toe."

"I'll think about it," Hannah says.

Nice, she thinks as she leaves the kitchen. It's only a month. I. Can. Be. Nice.

She jogs up the stairs, cringing at the pain in her side, then strips off her robe and pulls on jeans and a frayed old shirt. She pauses in front of the mirror. How could she have believed that she looked good just a week ago? Her eyes are bloodshot from the painkillers and lack of sleep; her forehead is marked with a slightly graying butterfly Band-Aid. She peels it off hopefully, but the puncture wound is too wince-worthy for public display, so she finds a new bandage and covers it back up again. She brushes her hair, glosses her lips, dusts her cheeks. At last, she's ready for morning. It's three in the afternoon.

6

The Last Time She Saw Him

THE MORNING BEFORE Palmer's soccer game. Monday. Hannah opened her eyes. Her father standing at her door, wearing a tuxedo.

"On a Monday?" the police officer asked later. He sat with her on the sofa, a notepad in his hand. "A tux? Sweetie, think hard. Are you sure?"

Hannah!
    Her father was wearing normal office clothes now.
    Dad!
    How many muscles in the body?
    About six hundred.
    Largest bone?
    The femur.

Smallest?

The stirrup of the inner ear.

Good girl. Very good girl.

✳

They all left at the same time that morning, flying in different directions. As if shot loose from a locked, pressured chamber. There was something about a soccer game. Tucker scratched his bleedy ears and then leapt up to follow her father. Fast—it was all so fast.

Have a good day, Doc, he said to her at the door.

She remembers running two steps after him. Nothing was ever certain. One had to nail him down on the specifics.

See you at the game, then?

What?

Palmer's game.

Yes. At the game.

✳

Hannah has thought about this morning thousands of times. She's not certain what she said back to her father. Did she just repeat his words? *At the game?*

She likes to think she said—Good-bye. I love you.

Or perhaps—I hope you have a perfect day.

It could be anything she wants, though, couldn't it? Memory is just a story, after all. With practice, one can adjust it. Shape the shadows to fill the empty space in your heart.

✳

"Hannah, 'at the game' doesn't mean . . ."

"He's coming back."

64

Her insides were boiling.

"Hannah, I think you need to accept—"

Her father looked back and waved. He was a handsome, happy young doctor going off to work.

I will see you again. He didn't say it. He waved it.

A wave can be a promise.

Can't it?

Dad?

7

Visits

CHARLESTON HAS GONE quiet on Hannah. The town where she grew up—a small, Easter-egg-colored city that baked in white afternoons—used to constantly buzz with voices. Walking by a friend's house, you could hear the clatter of silverware or Dan Rather on TV. But since she's been away, everyone seems to have outfitted their houses with double-paned glass windows shut tight and sealed. The only sound she can hear on this warm fall afternoon is the collective hum of ten thousand air conditioners.

Yet, standing on the sidewalk in front of the DeWitt House, Hannah is greeted with an oddly pleasant feeling of possibility. She can head west and lose herself for a few hours in the labyrinth of houses west of Legare Street; or she can turn north and head to the shops of King Street, where she might purchase some wine, maybe buy a new clingy shirt to aid her campaign to get her husband to think she's worth taking back. But instinct pushes her toward Charleston's grandest walk: a stroll along the harbor on

East Bay Street. Crossing White Point Gardens to the Battery, she then heads east, pausing to look at the Legares' old house on Atlantic Street.

Another family lives there now, a nice family from North Carolina, Hannah's heard. When she was in high school and living in the DeWitt House, she'd sometimes see the new inhabitants playing in the yard. They were just babies then, so Hannah thinks they are teenagers now. She squints at her old bedroom window, looking for the head of a girl, maybe — a nice girl in her senior year of high school with lots of boyfriends. But the room is dark.

She jams her hands into her pockets and moves on, up East Bay, then to Tradd Street. So far, her walk has gone quite well. No one recognizes her, and if they do, they don't stop to talk. Her hip and rib ache only moderately. It feels good to be out. She crosses Church Street, then Meeting. A few blocks down, she stops in front of the place she hasn't yet admitted she's going — a modest single house on Tradd with a classic Charleston side porch.

Hannah is fairly sure Virginia doesn't live here anymore. She hasn't asked her mother; she'd rather drink used battery acid than ask Daisy the whereabouts of Virginia or Warren Meyers. Anyway, according to DeWitt's diatribe, there's no way a high school music teacher could afford a three-bedroom house South of Broad these days. And yet! Look at that battered beast of a station wagon in the driveway, the one proudly wearing a MAKE MUSIC, NOT WAR bumper sticker. There are her ugly pottery wind chimes, clinking in the persistent fall breeze; those are her gaudily painted geranium pots; that is her bird feeder, almost empty and crusted with bluish-purple droppings. Hannah doesn't know why she's here. And yet, her finger seems to be on the bell.

In seconds, she's awash in the familiar: dogs barking, a screen door slamming, the heavy pounding of bare feet.

"*Hush*, puppies! For Christ's sake, be quiet."

The door flies open, revealing the mother of the boy Hannah used to love.

"Hannah!" Virginia exclaims and falls forward, enveloping Hannah in her purple hippie blouse and apricot-scented, long gray hair.

"Hi," Hannah says, extracting herself.

"Come inside!" Virginia holds the door open. The dogs—a disintegrating terrier and something brown and matted whose origins would lie somewhere in between rat and sheep—pool around her feet.

"Where are the retrievers?" Hannah asks.

"Dead. I finally got caught up in the breeders-are-bad thing. Just go to the pound now."

"They're nice." She pats one of their oily heads. "I can't believe the other dogs are dead."

"It happens. I haven't seen you in years. Not that I mind a surprise visitor. I love it, so long as it's someone as interesting as Hannah Legare." Virginia leads Hannah into the house and motions for her to sit in her old spot, an overstuffed green chair with down-filled seat cushions. "Hang on. Let me get you some lemonade."

Hannah looks around. Same white walls, same rough-hewn tables and chairs (Virginia spent some formative years in Santa Fe), same Jasper Johns prints Hannah could never make sense of. Nothing, it seems, has been moved. Virginia returns with two glasses of yellow-green liquid.

"Here, this should do."

"This house hasn't changed at all."

"Well, we put a new coat of paint on the outside. You know. If it isn't broken, don't pay people to fix it." Virginia sits back down. "How's your good old stepdad?"

"Boisterous."

"Ha! Love that man. And your mother, I s'pose, is fine."

"Yes."

"You're too skinny."

"I am not."

"And you've done something terrible to your head."

"I fell."

"You sure?"

"Yes, I'm sure, Virginia."

"Not that new husband, is it?"

"What?"

How could Virginia know about her latest disaster? Is she suddenly on speaking terms with Daisy again? They've hated each other ever since Hannah dated Warren—Daisy's loudly expressed opinion being that Warren was too "boring" for Hannah, and that it was a poor match.

"He didn't do that, did he?"

"Oh." Hannah can't help laughing at the thought of it. "No! He's as violent as a baby duck. I fell off a balcony."

Virginia looks at Hannah over her glasses. "You fell."

"Mmmm."

"Off a balcony."

"Well, I was trying to find him. My husband, I mean. . . . He's been seeing someone else."

"Ah." Virginia takes a sip of lemonade and makes a face.

Hannah pauses. "Yeah, but I was seeing someone else before that. More than one someone, actually."

69

Virginia looks thoughtful. "Sounds like my attempt at marriage."

"Was that too much information?"

"What I like about you, Hannah Legare," Virginia says, "is you always pretty much tell me what's on your mind." She smiles, showing her still-white teeth, and plays with a dangly turquoise earring. "Remember when you told me you had a crush on Warren?"

Hannah's face grows hot.

"I helped, remember? I invited you to dinner and told Warren to walk you home."

"Yes. I remember. You were very nice. Thank God you liked me."

"I liked you a lot."

"I can't even believe I did that. Maybe I could stand to hold a few things back."

"No. Absolutely not. That's the way boring people act. And we've got enough boring people in this town." Virginia wraps her arms around a pillow. "So? Want to know about Warren?"

Yes, please. Every detail.

"Not really."

"*Really* not really?" She pushes her glass away. "Just came over for the stellar refreshments?"

"I was walking by," Hannah says. "But yeah. I also sort of wanted to hear about Warren, I guess, in a masochistic kind of way."

"That's my girl. Well, he's married."

"Oh, I know." In an odd twist of too-small-town fate, Warren's wife happens to work for Hannah's brother as a vet tech. "Of course I know that. I sent them a set of red wineglasses."

"How polite. You really are Daisy's daughter."

"How was the wedding?"

"It was a wedding. A Charleston one. Big. At the Boat Club. Two hundred white people dancing to a black band."

"It doesn't sound like something Warren would like."

"It wasn't Warren's wedding. It was Jenny's wedding. Warren was just there."

"Well, it sounds nice."

"They're happy. They live on Colonial Lake in a house her parents bought them. And he's over at Grace."

"That's great," Hannah says, trying to sound genuine. "How long does divinity school take?"

"Three years. Then an internship."

"I never expected it."

"Think *I* did?" Virginia plays with the fringe on the pillow. "I gave the boy his first joint as a fifteenth-birthday present. But he loves it. And it's probably better than the writing."

"I actually read his book."

"How'd you find it?"

"I don't remember." This is an enormous lie. Warren's book, *The End of the End,* had a tiny run at a university press. As soon as she heard about it, she obtained the title, tracked down an editorial assistant at University Press of Mississippi, and bribed him into sending her three copies in the mail. Hannah even brought one home with her in her suitcase.

"Did you like it?"

"Yes."

"Really?"

"Well. I didn't like the part about the girl leaving the protagonist under a rock."

"Mmm–hmm."

"And she didn't have to look exactly like me. Or have my name. Or have to *die*, for God's sake."

Virginia throws her head back and laughs. It feels like warm, clean water.

"You left him, sweetheart. You completely dropped the kid. And he's a Southern hard-ass. Thinks he's James Dickey."

"James Dickey as a minister?"

"He had to get back at you somehow." She shifts in her chair. "Anyway. That was all a long time ago. I'm glad you're here to chat with me. I'm glad I'm alive and well here to chat with you. Jesus, I just turned sixty."

"Sixty is the new fifty."

"Enough," Virginia says. "I hate that talk. Can't people just get old anymore?" She draws her legs up under her. "Oh, Hannah. It's . . . hard seeing you. All this church. I have to be so good all the time. And Jenny's just . . . well, you're so much more . . ."

"She's prickly. Trust me. I know."

A flash of guilt crosses Virginia's face. "Oh, she's all right, though."

Come on, Virginia. Just be on my side.

"How are the kids?"

"Beautiful. Of course. But that's the thing about Jenny, isn't it? She's the prettiest girl in town. They've got two gorgeous daughters. Little blond, blue-eyed girls."

"Huh."

Hannah didn't think this would bother her. So few things do. It never bothered her when she stopped getting letters from Warren, or when he refused to see her on her visits home, or even when her mother told her Warren married the lint-brained pretty

72

girl from high school. None of that bothered Hannah except hearing about his children. Their existence, oddly, bothers her very much.

"He adores them. You should see him with them. He'd give his life."

"Virginia." This comes out more curtly than she intended. The silver-haired woman straightens. Hannah holds up her glass of murk.

"Do you have anything stronger than this?"

Virginia smiles and takes the glass to pour her guest a more fortifying drink.

Hannah thinks about them all—Virginia, Warren, and Jenny White—on and off for the rest of the day. It's irritating, how they continue to hijack her thoughts. In order to distract herself, she sits on her flowered, canopied bed (the very bed DeWitt's grandmother died in, as no stick of furniture could ever be bought new) and writes some halfhearted e-mails to her sales reps. The numbers are down in all of her territories, a fact she knows is largely her fault. It's been months since she's been able to show interest in what her staff is doing, and, left to their own devices, it appears that they've been spending a large amount of salaried time flirting with one another and deconstructing the latest episodes of *Gossip Girl*.

SweetJane, the company Hannah and Jon started together, is an overpriced line of luxury sex toys. ("Get it?" Jon likes to say to investors. "Sex is now a luxury!") The company was originally Jon's idea. The notion came to him after they'd been living together awhile. The sex, he said, was getting boring. In an effort to solve this—Jon is a solver—he decided to buy Hannah a vibrator. But his search was fruitless; he found his shopping experience so unsatisfying that he came away empty-handed, save for some upscale lubricant and a nicely illustrated copy of the Kama Sutra.

"I wanted to get you something nice," he said. "But then I was at Good Vibrations. All of these *hippies* worked there"—Jon is a staunch hippie hater—"and all they had was this crappy purple plastic." Hannah and Jon looked at each other, eyes wide, realizing instantly what he had done. For months, they'd been searching for a new business idea. Biodeisel stations, too messy. Oxygen bars, too stupid. And now he had found it. *There were no sex toys for rich people.* And hence, SweetJane (Jon's shout-out to Lou Reed) was born.

Creating the brand was surprisingly easy; Hannah basically just merged Southern taste with all-purpose raunch. The latter she approached like a true Stanford MBA, hiring call girls as consultants and paying them by the hour to participate in focus groups. Satin hand ties or silk? (Silk.) How tight should the handcuffs go? (Not very.) What are butt plugs, and are they something rich men would buy? (They buy them on the sly. Don't bother.) In the end, they came up with a full range of products: massage oils, candles, and blindfolds. The most popular item by far, though, is the signature platinum vibrator. Looking less like a penis than a cigar out of some space-age humidor, it sells for a cool $575, $625 engraved.

And the money. Money! SweetJane made Hannah and Jon lots of money. Of course, at the time it seemed impossible *not* to make money. They started the company in 2004. The post 9/11 dip was officially over, and there was money everywhere—the kids at Google and Facebook and Oracle didn't know what to do with it all. *San Francisco Magazine* ran an article on Hannah and Jon ("How the Bright Young Things Do It!"), and suddenly everyone wanted to invest in their dildos. They made a profit within a year, within two had paid their investors back and then some.

Unfortunately, because they've been in the black for so long, Hannah has stopped paying attention to the big picture of late, and due to her inability to put together a decent profit-and-loss statement, the company has been drifting dangerously in financial no-man's-land. She should plug the latest sales into the spreadsheets *now*, she really should, but the hour has arrived to go to Palmer's. I'll do it tomorrow, she resolves — as she does at the end of every recent workday — and shuts the laptop. At least Jon doesn't know (yet) that she's been fucking up in this particular area.

She showers, puts on a decent "look-I-am-not-crazy" skirt, and borrows Daisy's car to go to her brother's house. Palmer lives in downtown Charleston, near where he and Hannah grew up. Doing so, even for the moderately rich, is just barely affordable; her brother only manages it by clinging to the very top of the peninsula, the increasingly fashionable area high above Calhoun Street in a neighborhood near the Citadel. This neighborhood was strictly black when Hannah and Palmer were kids, but now ballooning prices have made it OK for whites and blacks to live together on the same block. If you're young, and you don't want to leave downtown, and you have a decent amount of money but haven't totally made it yet because you're sort of waiting on your stepfather to expire and leave you a fairly staggering inheritance, then a good-sized Craftsman off Hampton Park is just the ticket.

Though she'd never been here before, Hannah enters Palmer's

house without knocking. The house smells like warm bread, and Billie Holiday is crooning "Moonlight in Vermont" over the tastefully hidden speakers. They are of excellent quality; Hannah can actually hear the remnants of Billie's last cigarette.

She's always envious when she enters the houses of gay men. Perhaps it's the unbridled self-indulgence; the gleeful spending of tens of thousands on oversize Jacuzzi tubs, flat-screen televisions, teak decks fitted with wet bars. Or maybe it's the total lack of concern as to future developments. Gone is the half-decorated room held back from its full potential because it may—listen for the quiver of hope—"one day" be a nursery; absent is the basement-converted-to-in-law-apartment because a nanny or night nurse might have to move in. Nor does one tend to see taste clashes so often compromising shared heterosexual homes. No mountain bikes leaning on chintz Pottery Barn sofas, no framed photos of golf courses hanging above beds draped with floral sheets.

The theme in Palmer's house? Functional yet Fantastic and Fun. The walls of the living room are dove gray, and the sectional sofa is beige with nice clean lines, but then the room is saved from predictability by a cluster of orange silk-and-felt pillows, which match the very well-done painting of a rubber duck above the fireplace. The steel dining table is taunted by a vintage chandelier. The austere, requisite flat-screen television on the wall is framed by thin inset aquariums holding live saltwater fish.

Hannah ventures farther into the house.

"…can't you just talk to me about it? Instead of stewing in your famous fucking silence?"

A fight. Normally, she'd eavesdrop, but she's had it with battles for the moment.

"Hello?"

A small tan dog suddenly scuttles out of the kitchen to investigate her trespassing. It makes barking motions, but nothing comes out.

"Shit!" Tom runs out still wearing oven mitts and plants a kiss on both of her cheeks. Palmer's latest lover — has it been nine months? ten? — is truly the cutest boy-man she's ever known. About five seven, bright-blue eyes, yoga body, a sculpted little nose, all topped off by the most endearing mop of blond hair.

"You can't just barge in without ringing the bell! You've never been here before — you need a *tour!*"

"It's my brother's house," she says, poking at his perfect abs. "I'm supposed to barge in. What's wrong with your dog?"

"Rumpus has no voice box," Tom says. Upon hearing her name, Rumpus shakes with glee and rolls over, head cocked to the side. Tom takes his gloves off and fluffs his own hair. His right hand lingers on his temple as he looks Hannah over.

"Ew," he says. "Your head."

"I know. But I'm not talking about it without a drink."

Tom nods. He is the best kind of man: gossipy, kind, good at making cocktails. They got to know each other when the "boys" (DeWitt's label) visited San Francisco for the Folsom Street Fair. If he weren't always quoting from *The Power of Now,* he'd be real friend material.

"Come on."

She follows him into the slate-blue kitchen and glances around. Look at the huge blown-up photographs of vegetables arranged to look like sexual organs! And those little lights hanging from the ceiling that make everyone look as if they've just had a facial!

"Do you love the house?" Tom asks eagerly.

"Love it, love it, love it."

Her brother is seated at the kitchen island, with the newspaper in front of him and a glass of wine. Not for the first time, Hannah is struck by her brother's looks. It's eerie how much Palmer resembles Buzz. If she squints—

They greet. He folds the paper and puts it aside. Hugs, how are you, you look good, you, too. Palmer is the type to edit before he speaks, but his eyes are talking, and Hannah understands every word in a way possible only between siblings:

I'm tired. Tom is funny, isn't he? I'm worried about you. Should we let you drink? You look older. Are you going to bring up that same old shit about Dad tonight?

But perhaps she doesn't know what her brother is thinking at all. Who is she to presume she still knows what's in his head?

"So," he says, "are you going to bring up that same old shit about Dad tonight?"

"If you're lucky."

"Still the prodigal daughter. All it took was a nail in the head to get you home."

"Whatever."

"What was the story again?" He braces himself against the counter. "You got wasted and fell off your own house?"

"Oh, Palmer!" Tom says, handing Hannah a golden concoction in a martini glass. "Like you haven't had your own wild nights. Should I tell her what you did at Boys' Week in Kiawah?"

Hannah never caught on in high school that Palmer wasn't straight. Though in hindsight she realizes she simply wasn't paying attention. Palmer had girlfriends, lots of them, but no one he kept for longer than a week. Hannah remembers them lurking around the house, limbs magnificent in their short cut-off jeans. The specifics of his doings were never made clear to

Hannah — Palmer didn't interact socially with his sister — but according to the gossip, he was having sex, plenty of it. There was a story in the Charleston Prep halls about two couples going at it at once in her father's old Volvo — the seats tipped back and the girls rising above, glorious as fooled angels.

When Palmer announced, at perhaps the most awkward DeWitt-Legare dinner to date, that he was a homosexual, it made her brother more human somehow. For no matter how loudly Daisy and DeWitt might voice their support of Palmer, proclaiming over and over and over — to Palmer, to the other DeWitts, to friends at the Boat Club and at dinner parties — that there is *nothing wrong with it,* Palmer's being gay finally brought him down to Hannah's own flawed level.

"How's work?" Hannah asks. "How's Jenny Meyers? I still can't believe you hired my ex's wife."

"Get over it. She's an excellent technician."

"She cries all the time," Tom says. "Palmer can't ask her to do anything without her starting to sob."

"What's the problem?"

"I think it's her hormones," Tom says. "The pill or something. She wants to double-date, but no way I'm going to dinner with that estrogen faucet."

"Ha." Hannah takes a sip of her cocktail. "Ginger?"

"Ginger, lemongrass, and vodka."

"Should you be drinking?" Palmer says. "I thought the point of this trip was to clean up."

"It's all organic," Tom says helpfully. "Very clean. Practically no alcohol at all. Do you love it?"

"*Love* it." This is how Hannah and her brother's lover communicate. Easy, oft-proclaimed adoration. "Love it, love it, love it."

Beaming, Tom turns to the oven. Palmer may not be into women, Hannah muses, but he definitely found Charleston's best wife.

Dinner is low carb and succulent, served on glazed rectangular plates. ("So you can serve at an angle, Hannah!") Tom fills her in on the latest gossip while they eat. Daisy's still running every charity board in Charleston and plays tennis every day. DeWitt is growing even more good old boy, in an endearing way. He's talking about getting Palmer into a fund he likes.

"Are you going to do it?"

"We're considering it," Tom says. "Twelve percent a year can't hurt. But we'll have to wait on the real money. It doesn't look like he'll be dying anytime soon."

"Would you please not talk about my stepfather that way?" Palmer says, carving another slice of pepper-encrusted skirt steak. He does it the same way their father used to do it, brows furrowed with concentration, as if in lifesaving surgery.

"It's OK, Tom," Hannah says. "I'm wondering how much the death package will be, too."

"God, Hannah. You're so bitter," Palmer says. "What did DeWitt ever do to you except move you into a mansion and then pay for your college and business degrees?"

"Well, he made the moves on our mother at our father's funeral," Hannah says, "but other than that, I guess he's got a clean slate."

"Can y'all not do this?" Tom's voice suddenly cracks. "I've made a peach crumble."

"Sorry." He's right, she thinks. Why can't I just be nice?

"Seriously, he's done a lot for us," Palmer goes on. "He's old school, I know, and obnoxious. But he's family."

"I'm not going to talk about DeWitt anymore. Tom has a crumble."

"Fine." Palmer pushes his chair back and crosses his arms. Hannah does the same.

"So what about Jon? Mom says you're officially separated?"

"Yes," she says. There is a sad pause. "I'm hoping it's just for a little while."

"Bet it's nothing a week of blow jobs can't fix," Tom offers, getting up to don his oven mitts again.

"Stop it!" Palmer snaps, slapping his hand on the table. "That's just — disgusting."

Hannah decides not to press the issue. She doesn't want to make her brother angry. She knows they have their differences, but she loves him. She also loves that, after being so surly for so long, he's managed to create this perfect life for himself. The designer house. The loving partner. The organic garden. We came from the same place, Hannah marvels, and yet somehow he's found everything he's been looking for.

"We can't all be as perfect as you, Palmer," she says. "Christ, you even have a dog that can't bark."

"And there's even one more thing he might get to have," Tom says, beaming.

"A houseboy from Laos?"

"A baby!"

"What?"

"Tom," Palmer says, using the same tone as when Rumpus strayed too near the door, "*not* now."

"Why the hell not? She's your sister."

"We have not decided on this."

"Please stop fighting," Hannah says, leaning into Tom. "Tell me what you're talking about."

"We want to have a baby," Tom says.

Hannah looks at Palmer. He says nothing, but Hannah can see everything: Tom wants to have a baby; Palmer most definitely does not.

"Huh," Hannah says.

"But we're finding that we're challenged."

"Beyond the obvious lack of uterus in the house?"

Tom rolls his eyes. "All we need now is an egg," he says. "We *have* the surrogate."

"Well, that's a start."

Tom goes on. Adoption won't work; they don't want another woman directly involved in the parenting process. Hannah nods and groans in the right places. She commiserates about how hard it must be. She crinkles the corners of her eyes with feigned understanding.

"I'm so sorry," she says finally. "I wish there was something I could do."

Which, of course, is when Tom slides a plate of crumble in front of her and asks if he can harvest her ovaries.

"What?" Palmer cries.

"What?" Hannah echoes.

"Look, I've been thinking all about it. Palmer, I'm sorry I haven't told you. But, honestly? I just wanted to put it out there before you could shoot it down. Just think about it—we want a baby together. And using Hannah is going to be as close to having a baby together as we can get."

"Using Hannah?"

"OK, sorry. I'm not exactly a wordsmith."

"But I don't *want* a baby," Hannah says.

"Right, but you won't have one," Tom says patiently. "*We* will. You won't even have to be pregnant. The procedure's totally easy. And, of course, we'd pay for everything."

Hannah turns to her brother, who looks as if he's just been diagnosed with testicular cancer.

"You think this is crazy, right?" she says.

"Crazy?" Palmer says, wincing at the distaste of it all. He looks at Tom. "Sick is what it is."

"It's not sick!" The pitch of Tom's voice now lurches danger-ously toward hysteria. "Open your mind a little."

"You want to sperminate my sister's egg," Palmer says. "You're insane."

Tom throws his knife into his crumble. It clatters off the edge of the table and onto the perfect bamboo floor. Hannah sinks down into her chair. She has never handled conflict well and will do almost anything to avoid a fight. She tells jokes, she makes inappropriate comments. Once she set fire to a napkin.

"I'm sorry," Tom says. "I'm getting a little flustered here."

"It's OK," Hannah says.

"I'm going for a walk." Tom yanks the leash off a hook on the wall. "Rumpus, *come!*"

In a show of self-preservation that Hannah can only respect, Rumpus scuttles over to Palmer's feet.

"*Rumpus.*" Hannah takes hold of the dog's collar and regret-fully offers her up. Tom clips on the leash and yanks Rumpus out of the house, but not before the dog can give both Hannah and Palmer a parting look of disgust.

"Wow," Hannah says. "He seems to be . . . acting out."

"Yes."

"You're not really going to—"

"Of course not," Palmer says. "I'm no father."

Hannah chooses not to answer.

"You want kids?" he asks.

"No."

"Really?" Palmer says, pouring more wine. "That kind of surprises me. Is that true?"

True. Hannah once had a therapist who said something very wise about truth. She's had five therapists. One woman, four men. This was the woman, an attractive fortysomething. She always wore all black and was the best one by far. She was so good that Hannah had to get out of the relationship, eventually breaking up with her by text. In the session before Hannah freed herself, they talked about truth.

"I am not a natural liar," Hannah told her. "But it seems like much of my life is fiction."

The therapist suggested she say something true, and then add the word "because."

"You'll be surprised how that changes things," she said.

"I thought the whole point of truth was that it can't be changed. Otherwise you've just started out with a lie."

"Oh, there are all sorts of varying degrees of truth. Come on—give it a whirl."

"This sounds extremely dangerous."

"Exactly," the therapist said, leaning forward.

"OK," Hannah said. "You want truth? Fine. I screwed around, OK? I cheated on Jon."

"You cheated on Jon," the therapist said, *"because..."*

"I cheated on Jon because I wanted to."

"Not good enough."

"I cheated on Jon because I drank too much."

"No."

The therapist knew Hannah was copping out. They didn't get much farther that day, but afterward Hannah went home and sat on her balcony to meditate on it. *I cheated on Jon because. I cheated on Jon because.* The therapist was right. Other truths came bubbling to the surface. Hannah cheated on Jon because he was getting too close to her. She cheated on Jon because he knew her too well. She cheated on Jon because she wanted to screw up the relationship before it screwed her. The good doctor was too right about it all, really, which is exactly why Hannah bailed on her and then proceeded to cheat on Jon again.

So, her brother's question. Does Hannah want a baby? No. She does not want a baby. Because? She does not want a baby because babies are loud and expensive. She does not want a baby because she is a disaster and will surely drop said baby, or accidentally leave the baby in a suitcase, or put the baby down in Starbucks on a chair and forget it's there and leave the baby and then end up in jail. So, really, Hannah does not want a baby because she does not deserve a baby. Because she cheats on her husband and then climbs up balconies to get him back and then falls off buildings. The one bad thing she doesn't do is smoke cigarettes, and that's only because she respects her teeth.

"Not right now," she says. "So how's it going with Tom, anyway?"

"It was pretty good, until this baby crap."

"Living together," Hannah says. "Big step for you."

"Probably too big."

He pours them both a glass of wine and begins clearing the table.

"Well, commitment's always been a problem for the men in our family."

"Meaning?"

"Meaning Dad took off."

Palmer pauses at the sink, then sets the dishes in with a clatter.

"Dad drowned."

"Maybe he left. People leave. Maybe he wanted a new life and felt this was the best way to go."

"So, what, our father rigged a fake death? Tied a bag to his ankle, swam to shore?"

"If I was going to leave," Hannah says, "that's exactly how I'd do it."

She would. She's thought about it often, that if she were her father, she'd leave the same way. At this point, Hannah has extricated herself from many relationships, and she knows that unless a person disappears completely (e.g., a move to a new city or a military enlistment), there is no such thing as a clean break. Inevitably, you see the person around. You have feelings. You decide to have a "talk" or go for a "walk." Your walk ends up on the sofa or the kitchen table, clothes littering the garden. You really *look* at each other, right down to the inky cells of the pupils. That nose . . . you forgot he had such a perfect nose. Dear God, you'd die for the whorl of that ear. Isn't there some way we can —

No. The best thing to do is vanish. Move to Greenland. Take your fishing boat and fake a drowning.

"You know," Palmer says, leaning against the counter with his hand on his hip, "this is the center of it all."

"What do you mean?"

"This is why you're so...why everything is unraveling. Because you've never been able to just let this go."

Hannah climbs up on a bar stool and looks at her brother intently.

"It screws with your head. Because there's no proof whatsoever that you're right."

"So?"

Palmer throws up his hands. "You're impossible."

"Why are you so worked up about it?" she asks. "Why can't you just let me think what I think?"

"Fuck it." Palmer grabs his jacket from the wall. "Let's leave this mess. I've got to go to the office."

"The office?" Tom says, entering with Rumpus through the kitchen door. "Now?"

"Paperwork."

"But the dishes—"

"Don't touch them. I'll do them in the morning."

"Are you sure?" Hannah follows him to the door. She doesn't want Palmer to go. She doesn't want them to leave things like this. "Please don't. I'm sorry I said that about Dad. Really. Stay. We could play cards or something."

"Let it lie, Hannah," Palmer says, glancing at her briefly, his eyes so dead they make her stomach turn.

How can you disappear so completely? Where did you go?

"Good night." The door shuts behind him.

Let it lie. Let it lie. The words reverberate in Hannah's mind. Familiar. Infuriating.

"Oof," the dog whispers. "Oof."

8

The Thing Palmer Did on the Porch

ANNAH WAS UPSTAIRS on the porch—eleven—sitting by
herself on the joggling board. The funeral crowd pulsing
in the house below. She rocked back and forth, watching her feet
dangle. Those frilly anklet socks.

There was a rattling of the screen door. She hunched down. It
was her brother.

Stole cigarettes from Dad's closet, he said. Want one?

OK.

Don't, though. You shouldn't.

OK.

They could see the water. Hannah squinted. No boats.

We should have taken pictures, Hannah said.

Of what?

Funeral.

Why?

For when Dad gets back.

Stop it, Hannah.

Why?

He's not coming.

He might.

He's gone.

How do you know?

I know, OK?

How?

I just know.

What happened to your hand? she asked. Your knuckles are all—

Palmer suddenly flipped his arm upward. Without looking over, he brought the lit cigarette down on his white wrist. There was a sickening hiss. The smell was worse.

Stop!

I can feel that, her brother said.

Palmer!

I can *feel* it. I can't always. You know?

What do you mean? Please, *stop stop stop* . . .

For the first time that day, Hannah cried. She remembers licking the salty tears off her lips. Palmer stayed for a few minutes, not talking. After a while he pocketed the cigarette and slipped back through the curtains, leaving her alone.

9

What Palmer Won't Ever Tell

THEY GREW UP on the same street. Palmer's house was number two, Shawn's was eight. Over the gardens, through the dense foliage of a live oak tree, they could just see each other's bedroom window. Every night, they signaled by flipping their lights on and off.

They played soccer. Secretly, Palmer hated the game. He hated the way the uniforms itched, the dull obligation of practice, the tedium of passing the slick ball from shin to shin. He especially detested when Charleston Prep faced off against better, tougher teams from across the Ashley and Cooper rivers—their stronger legs, their country sneers. The thing was, he was really good at it. While the other kids toiled over passing skills and footwork, Palmer would spend six months never touching a soccer ball, only to show up and outplay everyone without breaking a sweat.

Shawn was quick on the field, but Palmer was, hands down, the stronger player. Together they were pretty invincible. Shawn would get the ball up to the front of the field, and then, just when he was surrounded, Palmer would catch up to reinforce. It was the only reason he kept at the sport. He was able to save Shawn daily.

The first time Palmer saw Shawn Cohen, the boy was on his hands and knees in the dirt in front of his house. Palmer had heard about the new kid in the neighborhood — the Cohens were Jews, which no one on the all-Episcopalian street was thrilled about at the time. Curious, Palmer rode over to him on his bike.

"What are you doing?" he asked.

Shawn, a floppy, licorice strip of a person, looked up.

"Planting."

"Planting what?"

Shawn sat back on his heels. "My mom thinks they're flowers, but this kid back home gave me some pot seeds. I figure no one will think to look right in front of the house."

Palmer was fascinated. Drugs! Next door!

"Wanna help?"

"Awesome," Palmer said, throwing his bike on the ground. When the pot plants failed to materialize (the seeds turned out to be ragweed), Shawn and Palmer conducted other narcotic experiments. (A batch of wine made from apples culminating in a foul, chunky explosion in Shawn's closet; an afternoon sniffing Elmer's glue followed by four-hour, achy naps.) Soon the two were inseparable — sitting under tables playing war, thinking up long strings of swearwords. Shawn, it turned out, was truly talented at swearing. His combinations of words and images would ghost Palmer's head for days.

"Greasy elephant fucker!"

They were behind the field house after a game, sharing a ciga-rette. Shawn was two years older than Palmer but in the same grade, as he'd been held back a year and Daisy had started Palmer early. "That forward was a shit-eating, greasy elephant fucker. Wasn't he?"

"He was," Palmer agreed.

"That was a great play. You're a tiger-fucking good player."

"Thanks."

"That asshole. He should crawl into an old zebra ball sac and die."

"Zebra ball sac?"

"Spooge-encrusted." Shawn fell back into the early-spring grass. When he stretched out his arms and feet, it was a miracle of limbs.

Because Shawn was older than anyone, he soon ruled all of the middle school without contenders. When he wore a rugby shirt, all the boys had their mothers buy them. If he hated the seventh-grade science teacher because she was an "itchy-loose-rat-butt-tonguer," down she fell. He could sway the opinions of his peers in a way that caused many of the teachers to predict a future in politics. This made him valuable as a best friend. Middle school, after all, was a minefield; one day you were doing fine, the next you were exiled for a poorly timed fart. But as a friend of Shawn, Palmer was untouchable.

"Palmer's coming," Shawn would say to the other kids before they went anywhere. And if there happened to be a car involved: "Scoot over for my man Legare."

Palmer was thankful for this popularity, if wary of its nego-tiability. He was not witty—a little oafish, even. His status was

entirely due to Shawn, and he was aware of its potential imperma-
nence. Every night, he felt the same jolt of anxiety as he worked
the light switch with his fingers, two ups and a final down. Sometimes there would be no reply, and Palmer would climb into the
cool, slightly gritty sheets of his bed feeling wilted. Two nights out
of three, though, the light flickered back, and Palmer turned joy-
fully into the pillow, acknowledging to God himself how lucky he
was to have a best friend. With a best friend, especially one whose
lamplight he could make out through the leaves, he would never
be alone in the world. Shawn and Palmer. Palmer and Shawn. He
had an other.

Then, the summer before eighth grade, things unraveled.

Shawn went away to camp in North Carolina with Roy and
Ben, two other kids from Charleston Prep. Palmer chose to
stay home and take sailing lessons. No one ever told him about
camp—the bonding that would happen over cheap, watery meat,
the loyalty born out of "color wars." After five weeks together,
Ben, Roy, and Shawn returned home inseparable, cheeks pink
with mountain air, nails black with honest dirt. They spent hours
reliving moments in the dining hall and at the lake; they sang
angry songs about "Choctaws"; they collapsed into giggles over
inscrutable private jokes.

Palmer was patient. He knew this had to be a phase, because
he had observed brief changes in Shawn after he'd come home
from other trips. There was the cowboy-hat week following a trip
out to a dude ranch in Wyoming; the chatter of going away to
ski school after spring break in Aspen. Yet the camp glue stubbornly persisted, even after school started, even into the fall and

through the late winter, when practice for soccer season began. Roy, Ben, and Shawn did everything together, and while Palmer was always invited—he was still Shawn's best friend, after all, and it had been decided that he *had to* join them for the session at Camp Halowakee next year—he couldn't help feeling like an afterthought, an extra duffel dragging behind the singing green camp bus.

The change was miserable. He and Shawn were hardly ever alone, and the configuration was all messed up. Now they roamed the streets as a foursome; nothing—not grades, not the latest profanity, not so much as a Cheeto break—was privately shared.

"Nintendo?" Palmer would ask.

"Cool. Roy and Ben can come," Shawn would say. "Doubles." Or:

"Want to go to the Seven-Eleven to score some beer?"

"Sure. Call Roy. His brother's got an ID."

But then, one Friday, a ray of hope. Shawn had just inherited a long-coveted digital Battleship board from his brother, complete with model ships, colored pegs, a green purring electronic screen, and sound effects that mimicked the whine of falling bombs and the roar of explosions. He asked Palmer three times to sleep over to play the game, and when at lunch Roy asked what they were doing that night, Shawn, to Palmer's disbelief, turned and said, "Nothing."

"Don't tell Roy what we're doing, OK?" Shawn whispered a few moments later. He squinted conspiratorially. "Only two people can play Battleship. It's ear-fucking boring with three."

Palmer struggled to breathe normally. *(Ear-fucking!)* It had been so long—months—since Shawn had wanted him alone for anything. He felt his entire body sing, especially when, outside, the rain began to fall and a plan came to him. Under different circumstances, he would never suggest skipping practice. He knew better. But going today would be dangerous. Roy and Ben would be there, and seeing them might prompt Shawn to invite them over after all, for Battleship doubles (was there such a thing?), or worse, to tell Palmer to stay home and invite one of the campers over in his place. This was just not something he could risk, which is why, with a shaking hand, he slid a slip of paper onto Shawn's desk:

Practice in rain is for tiger ass lickers lets skip play battleship i am ready to kick your sorry war ass!!!!

He watched, holding his breath, as Shawn unfolded the note, read it, then shrugged and nodded. "Cool," he mouthed before turning back to the teacher. Palmer clenched his fists under his desk and closed his eyes. The first step on the road back. Shawn was his, his, *his,* for the whole night, and now the entire afternoon as well.

It was not lost on Palmer that he was becoming overly attached to Shawn.

The recurring dream he had was simple: his friend's dry fingers, reaching. Palmer would wake up, confused and throbbing, to the familiar, sticky wetness that was beginning to lace his mornings.

He wasn't alarmed that the cause had been a boy. He liked boys. This was something he had realized long before. Girls, at the time, repelled him — their lotion-tinged smells, the way they

95

floated past in squealing herds. Perhaps this would change. For his mother's sake, Palmer hoped so.

Yet the thoughts plagued him. He couldn't help staring at older boys. Soccer coaches, sailing instructors. Their strong, muscled legs made Palmer so *curious*. Sometimes, unable to stop himself, he had to run to the bathroom to get himself off. Not that this in itself was a problem. Since seventh grade, it had become accepted procedure to get off in the stall next to a friend doing the same. They were supposed to, Shawn, Roy, Ben, and Palmer agreed; they were teenagers. The difference was, everyone else was getting off while thinking of the training bras of the girls who daily spurned them. All Palmer had to do was think about whoever was right in the very next stall.

But Shawn. His thoughts about Shawn were a problem, as they carried the potential end to his most precious friendship. It wasn't just that he wanted to get off with Shawn; he almost wanted to *be* Shawn. Or at least to be with him all of the time.

As a member of a middle-school soccer team, Palmer was often put in precarious, confusing positions. For example, the locker room. He had developed a strict practice for such situations: he kept his underwear on for as long as possible, stepped quickly from one outfit to the next, spoke little, and maintained a blank, even slightly unfriendly expression. Still, he was petrified of giving himself away. One afternoon, Palmer and Shawn, kept after to talk to Coach— *You boys best stop hoggin' that ball*—were the last to dress. Palmer had just zipped his jeans and was stuffing various articles of clothing into his backpack when Shawn said:

"I'm getting bigger."

Palmer froze momentarily, then silently continued to gather his belongings.

"Dude, you hear me?" Shawn whispered. "Seriously. It's growing. Look."

Concentrating very, very hard on the crucial neutrality of his expression, Palmer glanced over. Shawn was standing approximately ten feet away—a safe-enough distance—his legs braced beneath him. His green, puppy-patterned boxers were pulled down slightly, and he was holding himself with both hands.

"Huh."

"I used to be able to put only one hand around it," Shawn said. "Now I can put two."

"Wow."

"Can you put two hands around yours?"

He averted his eyes to his backpack. "I don't know," he said. This was a lie. As a thirteen-year-old with a tape measure stored under his bed, Palmer knew exactly how much of his hands fit around it. He knew its exact length (four and a half inches), its approximate diameter (one inch, four centimeters), its ability to harden (tireless), and how it stood in comparison with the eye-balled size of other boys' (average). But what he understood that day in the locker room was that he was in the highest danger zone. One slip of the tongue or eye would alert his slightly-more-well-endowed-than-one-would-think-for-his-size friend of his desire to measure and test the body part in question in ways that would damn them both forever.

"Let's go," Palmer said.

Shawn gave a brief giggle, then zipped back up. Together they ran out to the idling station wagon that was waiting to take them to a pizza party—a warm, innocent house smelling of baking crust.

The whole week after, he felt unsettled. Had his best friend been trying to trick him? Some of Shawn's favorite targets were "faggots," or, as he referred to them on more than one occasion, "antelope-asshole lickers." Did Shawn know that Palmer was a faggot? Was he trying to get him to admit it so he could tell Roy and Ben and whomever else? Shawn was his best friend, but he didn't trust him, really. Palmer was left to guess that showing one's privates to a friend was normal. Perhaps at camp everyone stood, boxers down, comparing penises before bed — a thought that excited Palmer wildly, given that his mother had already sent the check in to Camp Halowakee for next year.

And now, here he was, lying on his stomach on the deep-pile carpet smelling faintly of urine, blissfully aware that, just a few blocks away, his soccer teammates were trudging through a wet, mind-numbing practice. The gray afternoon dripped into evening, but Shawn didn't seem to notice, too absorbed in the miniature war zone of Battleship.

"G four!" he cried, throwing forth a maniacal laugh when rewarded with that tinny explosion. They played all the way up to dinner, breaking briefly for a set of hastily ingested burgers provided by Shawn's mother, who then left for a party at the Meyerses' house. By ten o'clock, Palmer's eyes burned from staring at the screen; his fingers hurt from pressing down on the missile button; his mind was numb from boredom.

"Seriously, Shawn," Palmer said, "last game."

"Fine," Shawn said, heaving out a loud sigh. "This can be the last game, but then it has to be the Championship of the World. Five-dollar bet."

"Fine." With the end in sight, Palmer showed no mercy. He beat Shawn quickly and sat up. "Done. Cough up the fiver and let's watch TV."

Shawn's face reddened.

"Or not," Palmer said, tired. "I don't even need five dollars. Let's just go."

"One more game," Shawn said.

"Shawn, come on." A wave of uncontrollable irritation washed over Palmer. He'd do anything for him, but he was being such a . . . *zebra fucking ball sac.* "We've been playing for seven hours."

"One more."

Palmer flipped over and rubbed his eyes until he saw green-and-red spots. He was so tired of Battleship. He was so tired of the stinky carpet. If they hurried, they could still catch the end of *T. J. Hooker,* maybe the *A-Team,* maybe sneak some more of Mrs. Cohen's wine like they did last—

The world stopped. His eyes snapped open. His friend's hands were on him, moving.

"What—"

"Shut up. OK? Just shut up, Palmer. *Shut up shut up shut up shut up.*"

The answer to months of wondering. The long reach of damning dreams.

What are the faculties of a thirteen-year-old lover?

Enthusiasm, mostly, fueled by the fear of being caught. Quiet, quiet. The feel of flesh quivering oddly in the mouth—long, firm. The terrified seconds before the fascinating, sour burst.

Theirs was not love, though. At least not the type Palmer had seen in the John Hughes movies. As in school, Shawn was the unquestioned, almost tyrannical authority figure. It made sense. He had just turned fifteen. And the imagination he drew upon in creating swearwords proved consistent in this new area; Palmer often felt molded into a new shape.

At school, nothing really changed. If anything, Shawn grew more distant in public. Palmer was still allowed to ride bikes and cruise with Ben and the others, but there were no private jokes or talks, not even a stray game of Battleship. The friendship shifted; Palmer was demoted. Still, he could count on that flickering in his window, which now meant something entirely new.

Looking back, Palmer is not certain how many times it happened. Mostly he remembers the taste of terror. A teacher had been fired for being gay just the year before. Then there was the story of the woman on Church Street who found her husband in bed with another man: she sued him for all of his money, his ancestral home, and the children, all of which he relinquished shortly before putting a shotgun in his own mouth and firing. The boys knew that being gay was a crime. It had been proven. Getting caught would ruin them.

Shawn would take out his fear on Palmer, sometimes verbally, sometimes not. "You've turned me into a cat-fucking faggot."

"I'm sorry. I didn't mean to."

Often he would cry, his thin shoulders shaking. "Oh, God. We're so fucked, Palmer. Just go home, OK?"

"But it's three in the morning."

"Just, *please*."

In this way, many nights ended with a tiptoed sidle out the back door. Palmer spent at least three endless dawns shivering out in the Cohens' shed, waiting until it was late enough to sneak into his own house.

It was Buzz, of all people, who noticed the change. This was surprising to Palmer; he'd never thought of his father as noticing much. He seemed to live on his own happy plane. And yet—

"Palmer," he said one night after dinner.

"Yeah."

They'd come across each other in the front hallway. Neither expecting to see the other there. They jumped back a little, exchanging guilty glances at the coatrack.

"Where are you off to?"

"Shawn's."

"I'm going to the office," Buzz said to the question Palmer didn't ask.

"Oh."

"Christ, you look awful. What's that scrape on your elbow?"

"Soccer."

His father regarded him for a moment. "You all right?"

"Yeah."

"All right. I'll let it lie. Gotta go. Patients."

On a spring Monday shortly after, Charleston Prep's opponent was a public school for the gifted from the north of the peninsula. The players were mostly black, a fact that made the Charleston Prep parents wary. This was South Carolina in the mideighties, a time when racism still coursed through the grown-ups in Palmer's world like a river running strong but barely audible beneath the ground. The line of parents on the bleachers visibly stiffened as the players trotted onto the field. Shawn's mother took his father's hand.

Palmer's mother was there, but his father wasn't. This only slightly annoyed him. He had promised to be there, sure, but he promised lots of things. And in some ways, it was easier not to have him standing on the sidelines. Sometimes he was a quiet, slightly distracted spectator. Other times, he could be loud, yelling out plays he didn't even understand or, worse, shouting at Palmer nonsensically to KICK! Palmer always wanted to stop the game when he did that, just so he could walk up to his father and say, *Of course* I'm going to kick. The whole *point* is to kick. But of course he never did.

Jogging out to the middle of the field to facilitate the kickoff, Palmer could sense Shawn behind him. The boys on the other team fought as hard as undersized gladiators. Shawn missed pass after pass. When he feebly tried to kick the ball in Palmer's direction so that he could execute the move that had become his specialty—a graceful receive, followed by a quick, aggressive dribble right up past enemy lines—Palmer deliberately stepped away from the pass. He couldn't say why he did it. He just did.

The locker room, after. Palmer had told his mother to go home without him. The other boys had left. It was early evening by now, almost dark, the edge of the sky a pleasant stretch of conchshell pink. Palmer waited for Shawn for what seemed to be hours. When his thin figure entered the doorway, Palmer braced himself.

"You warthog-vagina-puke-sucking-dick-cheese-licker."

"I'm really sorry, Shawn."

"You missed it on *purpose*," Shawn said, voice cracking. "Why?"

"I don't know."

He really didn't. He didn't know anything. He was thirteen.

Shawn gave a small whimper. Palmer remembers it striking

him as pathetic. Then he drew his hand back and slapped Palmer's face.

Palmer was stronger than Shawn. The boys had been ignoring this fact for a while now, but that evening, he showed it. Shawn's face was a question. Palmer answered with a strike. Shawn looked at him, surprised, and Palmer hit him again. Something in Shawn's face bent. The nose? There was blood. They rolled over and their limbs tangled. Shawn, looking as if he were going to spit in Palmer's face, hesitated and quickly pressed his lips on him instead. The taste was metallic.

Could this be, *could* this—

"Oh, my God," Shawn suddenly cried, wriggling away. "Fuck, fuck, fuck. Oh, Jesus."

"Sorry, I—"

"Someone was in the window."

"What?"

"Someone's watching in the window."

"Who?"

"I don't know, I don't know. I looked up and he went away."

"Is he still there?"

"Shit shit shit shit shit—"

"Did he *see* us?"

"Oh shit oh shit oh shit." Shawn gathered his things.

"Come on, dude. Seriously, did you see who it was?"

But Shawn just left. Palmer waited a few minutes, then slowly ventured outside. He didn't see anyone. The only thing to do, it seemed, was run. Palmer didn't know how long it took him to get home, or what time it was, or even the day. That became clear only later.

It was Monday, April 8, 1985.

Palmer snuck in the back door and put his clothes in a bag. They were smeared with mud and a bit of blood. He would wash them after everyone went to bed. When he came downstairs, his mother was reading the paper, her tan legs crossed.

"Palmer! I was worried you'd been abducted, but I figured they'd smell your sweaty clothes and bring you back." She looked up at him. "What happened?"

"Nothing." Palmer looked around. Something was off. "Where's Dad?"

"He's not with you?" she asked, confused. Even as she spoke, everything fell away. "When it got dark, I left a message with his service for him to go get you. I'm surprised you missed him, actually. He's probably over there looking for you right now."

After dinner, Palmer went to his room. He waited for a moment, then flipped the light switch. Two ups and a down. But there wasn't an answer. There would never be an answer.

So this is it. The thing Palmer knows, the thing he won't tell. It had to have been his father's face in the window. Buzz must have witnessed the desires of his thirteen-year-old son and—disgusted? shocked?—left. Palmer often pictures the scene. His father jogging away from the field house, in his Volvo speeding away, turning right on Broad Street toward the Boat Club, most likely failing to signal. Perhaps there was a screech. The only thing he can't imagine is the face of the driver. No expression, no details. Those features, forever lost.

10

What Hannah Finds

THE MORNING AFTER dinner at Palmer's, Hannah wakes to the loud knocking of DeWitt's voice from somewhere downstairs, followed by the light buzzing of her mother's reply. The morning sun streams determinedly through the opening in the curtains. She turns and puts the pillow over her head. A few minutes of unsuccessful dozing later, she lets her hand wander between her thighs.

She pictures Jon. How he loves, as he calls it, "the morning connection," reaching for Hannah while they're still half asleep. Those are her favorite mornings, when she finds she's having sex with her husband before even waking up. Those are the safe mornings, no room for the dark moments between nightmare and consciousness, or the keen sense of loneliness she is experiencing at present, even though she is trying, trying, oh, *please*, trying to distract herself by rocking her hand back and forth—oh, this is working, she can almost feel the pressure start to build, please, come on—isn't it?

No. Because instead of Jon's hand on her hip, what she finds herself imagining is another hip thirty states away. It's Denise's legs he draws around his back, up over his shoulders even, as he circles his pelvis forward and backward and forward again. And as close as Hannah is—hell, she could probably get herself off to the image of Denise and Jon rolling around in her own five-hundred-count Egyptian cotton sheets—pride won't let her finish. She takes her hand away and sits up.

"Screw you, Denise," she says to the wall. "Get the hell out of my bed."

"Oh! You must be on the phone." Her mother pushes the door open.

"I—"

"Can I come in?" Daisy asks, looking around.

"You *are* in."

"Thought I'd bring you some coffee." She perches on the end of the bed, holding a paper cup.

"Already back from conquering the town?"

"Well, I've been to the gym and the gardening store. That was my second trip to the Starbucks. It's a splurge, but I can't help it. Here, just for you."

"Thanks." Hannah takes it and draws away slightly.

"How'd you sleep?"

"OK. I miss my own house."

"I bet." She pats Hannah's leg. "I bet you do. So? What's on the agenda for today?"

"I don't know. I could work a little. Make some calls."

"Or I thought we could go to Goodwill."

"Maybe."

"I'd love to find you and Jon something antique for your house."

"Well, I don't *live* in Jon's house anymore, and since I've been relegated to my mother's house three thousand miles away, there's a very good chance I'm missing any opportunity I have to move back in."

"Hannah," her mother says, "a little break is always good, no matter what the problem. Give him a chance to miss you."

"We're throwing away any chance that we might reconcile."

"Let him *miss* you." She scoots closer, leaning against the headboard. "By the way," she says conspiratorially, "I know what you two are selling."

"Oh?" Hannah pulls the covers tighter. She has never told Daisy the exact nature of their business. "Have you talked to Jon?"

"No. I looked it up on the World Wide Web." Hannah can't help but smile. Her mother still treats the Internet as if it is a magical force only wizards might master.

"World Wide? I take this to mean you haven't graduated to e-mail."

"I don't trust it. I still won't put any of my personal information anywhere near it. But Will turned his computer on for me. It's quite easy, actually, this Net thing. I just typed your name into the little box, and then Jon's, and then 'company,' and it came up. SweetJane. Nice name, too. Very catchy."

"Thanks."

"I think it's very bold, what you are doing. Very . . . today."

"Well, it's mostly Jon's idea."

"God knows it can get boring after years of marriage. Will and I—"

"Noooooooo no no no no! Can't do it, Mom. No."

"All right. Though it *is* the way you're making money, so I thought you'd be comfortable. But fine. Anyway, I thought perhaps I could help. With sales or something."

Oh, God, Hannah thinks. Here it is.

"We could have a party here—you know, like a Tupperware party. Charleston's gotten very modern, actually. Did you hear Eliza Walters is a lesbian now?"

"Shopping," Hannah croaks, putting her coffee down and rubbing her brow. "Let's stick to shopping."

"I just wanted to—"

"Let me think about it. I really don't want to see anyone, to be honest. Plus, it's not really a Tupperware-party kind of thing. We sell units in big quantities…to department stores. A little party wouldn't be worth the trouble."

"Well, Lord—some of the things on your World Wide Web site cost over five hundred dollars! If you sell ten of them—"

"OK. All right. I'll think about it." Instantly, she feels guilty. "And thank you for wanting to help. It's really very nice." She climbs out of bed and begins straightening the sheets.

"You're more than welcome," Daisy says, looking pleased. "So? Shopping?"

"No, gotta work. Maybe later."

"Fine." Her mother sighs. "Stay in your lazy little cesspool if you like."

"Sorry—I don't mean—"

"Just watch out for bedsores," she says crisply over her shoulder.

Hannah throws off her nightgown and pulls on her jeans. A sex-toy party? This visit just officially crossed over to the bizarre. She looks at her forehead in the mirror. Still disgusting. What to do today? She still can't quite face those P&L spreadsheets.

"Hannah-Tropicana!" DeWitt bellows from the doorway. He elephants in and settles at her suddenly rather vulnerable-looking vanity table. Hannah tries to hide her displeasure. It would be easier on everyone if she would just like her stepfather. But whenever he's around, she feels uncontrollably irritable.

DeWitt nods and crosses his mutton arms. "So, you bein' a good girl?"

"In what sense?"

"Don't want to go shopping with your mother?"

"Not really."

"Busy?"

"Errands to do."

He nods, snorts, and taps his knuckles on the table.

"Need anything? The car or something?"

"No thanks. I'll bike."

More knuckle tapping.

"So things are going all right for you here?"

"They've definitely been better."

"Right." He picks up an old bottle of perfume, smells it, and makes a face. A moment of awkward silence settles. Hannah flinches at the attempt at fathering.

"Did I ever tell you my theory of the keys to a good marriage?"

"You know, I was just going to shower. Do you think maybe we can talk later?"

"Good sex, good money, good talks."

"Brilliant."

"You gotta have at least two out of three. Don't have those, throw in the towel."

"OK, well, I have to—"

"Your mother and I have all three most of the time."

"That's lovely."

"Even down to one, though, you're in trouble. Only money, forget it. Only sex? That'll last you a good six months."

"Right."

"Your mom and dad only had one. Maybe. They—"

"I am *not* talking about my father with you."

It comes out more sharply than she intended. Or perhaps it's exactly what she meant. A dart aimed squarely at his chest. DeWitt is unfazed.

"You want to come birding with me while you're here? A lot of women like it. Might help get your mind off things."

Despite herself, Hannah is somewhat touched by this. Not enough, however, to crawl around in the mud searching for ducks.

"Probably not. Thanks, though."

"You need money?"

"Maybe." She doesn't, really, but better not to draw on Jon's and her joint bank accounts if she doesn't have to. Besides, she might as well let her stepfather believe he's accomplished something.

"All right. OK, then." DeWitt slaps his knee, jumps up, and disappears. Hannah listens as he trots down the stairs and fumbles through a drawer; he returns a few moments later, a huge smile on his face, checkbook in hand. "Two thousand? Three?"

They have a long-standing tradition of this. False father-daughter moments smoothed over by offers of cash.

"Sure. Thanks."

He writes out a check and leaves it on the dresser. "All right, then," he says happily. "Good luck with those errands."

He really isn't that bad, Hannah thinks as she lights a large candle. I'm home for a month. Maybe I'll work on our relationship. Do that inner-self crap Tom kept going on about when he and Palmer visited San Francisco.

Taking hold of the lit candle, she approaches her closet. Hannah was not a neat teenager. Dresses are mixed indiscriminately with sweaters, belts, and scarves looped thoughtlessly on the throats of wire hangers. All of it colorless; it looks as if she convinced her mother to buy the Gap's entire 1990 line of sweaters, shirts, and dresses all in dove gray. Warren once said she dressed like she didn't want to be noticed. He was right.

The thought of Warren reminds her of a dream she had recently. She stops, remembering. She and Warren were standing in a church, with people watching. Were they getting married? His hands on her waist. His body leaning into hers. *This is—*

She shakes her head, brushing the memory away. Dreams are lies. A waste of precious thoughts.

Parting the clothes, she thrusts her head into Nowhere, holding the candle in front of her. It's still too dark, so she steps back out, grabs a handful of clothes, and throws them on the ground, letting light from the bedroom fall in. The rug, which she remembers as thick and luxurious, is just a dirty old shag, while the cheap, frayed, gilded cloth that served as her "tent" is nailed unevenly to the walls and ceiling, hanging at jagged angles to reveal in places the naked wood that she never bothered to reach. Books and magazines are heaped in careless stacks. Photos litter one pillow-strewn corner. The Coleman lamp is not by the door where she remembers it but back in the far corner. To her delight, it still works, so she pulls the clothes back over the opening to recapture the old feeling.

Like so many things in life, the room improves greatly with less light. Hannah leans back into the cushions. She used to love looking up into this gold fabric; once, she would imagine it was a circus tent. She had gone to see a small carnival with Warren in the grim, brown outskirts of the city and had been instantly fascinated by the spangled trapeze artists. She dreamed of swinging through the air, joining them in their dented trailers, being taken by an 18-wheeler to the next place, and the next and the next.

"I could be a carny," Hannah told him one afternoon. They were lying together on this floor. "I could run away."

"You're not going anywhere." His mouth on her ear.

Where is he now? Did Virginia tell him I'm here?

Two gorgeous daughters, Virginia said yesterday. *He'd give his life.*

Hannah flips over to look at the boxes on the floor. In high school, Hannah went through all of the pictures in DeWitt's basement. Already her mother's things were mingling with Will's, but Hannah was determined to keep her own father's snapshots separate. One hot, sad afternoon, she sifted through them and took the ones she guessed were Buzz's to her room and put them in these boxes; they've been up here for years now, unopened.

She hesitates, then opens a box and begins excavating. The ones she likes to look at are mostly of the family. Hannah, Dad, and Palmer on the johnboat. Hannah holding up a fish. It hurts, how happy she looks. Daisy and Buzz at different social gatherings, with friends, at beach houses, at parties. Daisy in the kitchen, laughing in a tennis outfit, her legs long and tan. Hannah's mother has fantastic legs, and it's clear from these photographs that she knows it. In almost every photo her legs are visible from some angle, stretched out lean and taut from beneath a tennis skirt or peeping out from the side slit of a dress.

Hannah draws the candle closer, studying each picture carefully. There is a large series she always liked from a beach party out on Sullivan's Island. Hannah was eleven years old, the very age she was when her father left. She knows this because the party took place the week just after her eleventh birthday. It was a successful birthday in terms of presents: Hannah was given a Barbie Dream House, complete with the blond, smiling plastic dream girl herself, bedecked in a red off-the-shoulder dress and a checked apron. Palmer, too, got a gift—Atari paddle controllers—even though his birthday wasn't for months. This was shortly before her brother turned into an asshole, and Hannah fondly remembers her and Palmer bonding over their sudden luck. All this awesome stuff! they whispered to each other. Their parents had gotten so totally cool!

The next day it all turned out to have been a trick, when their parents announced that they were going away for the weekend. For three nights, the children were to stay at their grandmother's condo—a cold, grim place that reeked of broccoli and bleach. Palmer and Hannah protested, only to be given the unassailable response that "You just got a present any kid would dream of having. Are you really in a position to complain?"

They weren't, and they knew it, so they dragged the enormous box containing their new toys up the stairs of their grandmother's house while Daisy assured her mother that they would be good. It was a "no kids" weekend, Daisy told her apologetically. And they'd keep themselves busy. See? They have these great new toys! And so she kissed them good-bye and got into the car to drive to this much-photographed party on Sullivan's Island. As soon as the car was gone, Palmer and Hannah took the Dream House out back, where, for the next two days, Barbie and Ken would perform every sexual act imaginable to an eleven- and thirteen-year-old. (Which was, surprisingly, quite a lot.)

The Dream House and her denizens are gone now. (Faint

memories involving a Bic lighter and a lynching by dental floss.) But the pictures from the adult side of that long-ago weekend whisper stories of what went on in the large, old beach house with its lovely wraparound porch. Hannah later went to this house for a party thrown by her classmate Tommy Nelson, but this celebration held by his parents looks like the kind she'd rather have attended. The group has the carefree air of an early J.Crew photo spread, only most of the subjects are carelessly holding cigarettes, lungs be damned. Buzz and Daisy are glowing and beautiful from a day in the sun. The other people in the house, too, are tan and laughing, gathered around the grill or sitting at a picnic table covered in liquor bottles. The Nelsons are there, as is Virginia, decked out in tie-dye, her then blond hair spread around her in glorious ringlets. Hannah flips through the photos, smiling at her father, his blue eyes glazed above his filterless cigarette. She's about to move on to the next pile when one particular picture causes her to stop short.

It's a shot that, were you selecting from a group of negatives, you'd surely toss. A group photo taken several moments too late, with everyone tired of posing or half dispersed. Most people's eyes are closed or squinting. Buzz stands behind Daisy, his hand on her shoulder, his pleasant face turned toward a group of men to the left. Virginia's teeth are bared in violent laughter, as a joint is being brought out from behind her back. There is no particular story to the picture, no solution as to what might have caused her father to leave them. But a clue is at least slightly discernible, in this blur of motion. For there he is, her stepfather, a little thinner in his plaid Bermudas, lurking in the background. Will DeWitt—the man her mother claims she never met until after Hannah's father was gone.

11

Parties, Recalled

Singing from the dining room. Beach music. Palmer and Hannah, curled up together in the guest room on top of the coats.

Every weekend, a different house. Virginia's, the Nelsons', the Legares'. Month after month of Saturday nights. The same couples drinking in different rooms.

In the earliest hours of the morning, their father would retrieve them, smelling sweet and sharp. Hannah now knows this was bourbon. He would swing his children over his shoulders as if they were rice sacks. She remembers waking up and watching the stars from his back.

Hannah can picture this party in the photo; she and Jon go to the same sort of parties in California. Her mother and father would have climbed the stairs, hurrying a bit at the last two steps when they heard voices through the door, jonesing for a smoke, maybe. Who's here? Are we late? In the kitchen, a group of newly freed parents gathered around a tray of artichoke dip, taking in the burned-rubber smell of an overworked blender.

Is that how it would be? Her mother, leaning on the counter. Her father, pouring a drink.

She concentrates, trying, trying to remember any telling detail. Did she ever see plaid shorts? Hear her stepfather's booming laugh? Please, can't there be some kind of remembered clue?

Wait. There is something. She remembers, she remembers... it was the Legares' turn. A party in their living room. Bacon-wrapped scallops speared by greasy toothpicks.

Hannah wandered out, looking for Palmer. Grown-ups talking, so boring. She got on her hands and knees to lie next to Tucker on the floor.

Really?

Voices above, half whispered. Far, too far to hear.

Wait, when did they—oh, shhhh, tell me later, Buzz's here.

A forest of legs. Cigarette smoke. Poppy lip prints on a highball glass.

12

Hannah Goes to Church

S O HANNAH CALLS her husband, who, as expected, doesn't pick up his phone.

"A photo!" she says on the voice mail. She's been screened so many times during the last few days, she's memorized every pause and intonation of his outgoing message. "A photo. An old one, before my father left. But my stepfather is in it, meaning he was around *before*. Do you see what I'm saying? Please, I need to talk to you."

She hangs up and sits on the floor a few moments, chin on her knees. "I've got to get out of this house," she says to the furniture — a habit she's developed as of late. Then, without so much as peering in the mirror for what would only be a confirmation of the ugly truth, she propels herself downstairs to the bicycle room.

Back in San Francisco, Jon and Hannah both have bicycles. Biking was something Jon insisted they do together, and so the couple invested in both mountain and road bikes, costing upward of a thousand dollars apiece, complete with titanium frames, special hydraulics, and reinforced shocks. Later, after the sport lost its sheen, they moved on as they always did; keeping company with the bikes in the Upper Terrace garage were downhill and backcountry skis, snow shoes, rock-climbing gear, surfboards, and his-and-hers golf clubs. She pictures the gear with an acute wave of nausea. What, she wonders, could drive a woman—a supposedly smart woman with good business sense, a desirable husband, a bike with a *titanium frame*—to go and screw it up beyond repair?

There are no fancy bikes awaiting her in the DeWitt basement today. Instead, she'll be riding the hot-pink Earth Cruiser she received for Christmas in seventh grade, complete with soda holder and flower-pocked basket. Despite the decrepit state of the other bikes, the Cruiser's tires are mysteriously inflated, and the chains reasonably greased, as if someone knew she'd be needing it.

She wheels the bike out into the street with no destination in particular. Still, it feels good to be out, moving those fat pedals up and down. She finds herself cruising around the Battery, which by this time of day is crowded with fit, tan women pushing off-road-adventure Baby Joggers. Then, turning away from the water, she rides up Meeting past the Four Corners of Law and up through the Business District. Out of the corner of her eye, Hannah notes the glances of a few people on the street and in their cars. She thinks she may recognize a couple of neighbors and old schoolmates, but rather than making actual eye contact or stopping, she pumps faster, climbing higher and higher uptown, past Wentworth, past Calhoun. She finds her brother's street easily enough, but no one's there. Even Rumpus is gone.

Weaving through traffic, Hannah heads back downtown. The

air smells of fresh water—imminent rain. She coasts away from the park, back down Meeting, then takes a right on Wentworth toward the big white steeple whose bells are just now chiming the hour. She dodges a honking oncoming car, hops the curb, then rides straight into the parking lot of Grace Episcopal Church.

It's been many years since Hannah has been to a church. This is in no way accidental. The last time anyone even suggested it was on a big trip with Jon. She'd managed to avoid all ecclesiastical buildings, steering Jon instead to art museums and palaces—any place of interest that didn't involve God or Jesus. "I don't like the architecture," she said when he questioned her demand that they go see Italy's largest cannelloni over a tour of the Vatican. "The buildings are too *big*. Too—I don't know . . . pretentious."

"Of course they're pretentious," Jon said. "The chief pretense being God is actually watching. That's the point."

"Well, it bothers me."

"It's not like God really *is* watching, you know," he said. "Besides, we're just going to look at the art."

"It's *bad* art. Depressing. How many thousands of times can we see the same image of a bleeding man on a cross?"

"Um, sweetheart? The Sistine Chapel? The whole God reaching for Man thing?"

"Right—depressing. They reach and reach and never get there."

"The whole *thing* is that they're reaching. If they touch, there's nowhere to go, is there? It's brilliant."

"I get it, OK? Tantalus, the river, that other guy rolling the rock up the hill. Blah, blah, blah. Whatever." She then took off her shirt, opened the guidebook, and put it on his stomach. "But an eighteen-foot-long cannelloni?" She pointed to the listing. "How could we miss out on that?"

"You're such a pain."

"Maybe. But I'm very generous with the sexual favors." It's the kind of statement one is required to prove, annoyingly. So she did: that day, and the next, and the next, until Jon stopped mentioning cathedrals, instead packing their itinerary with royal architecture, weird art exhibits, and must-visit restaurants.

One of her less-astute therapists told Hannah it was her memories of her father's funeral that gave her this aversion to churches.

"It's a good theory," she responded at the time. "I see where you could get that. But as you know, I fully believe my father's funeral was a sham."

"Huh. Well. Tell me more about that."

"Stan, I *have* told you about that. Several times."

"Hmm, well. Maybe that's what you believed at the time, that the funeral was a sham...but your father's death—or, OK, his disappearance—was very painful for you. Which leads me to wonder whether you don't associate churches with that painful time in your life."

"Isn't that a little too simple?"

"Sometimes the answers *are* simple."

"Right. And I'm giving you a simple answer. I think church is bullshit; hence I don't like the buildings. Especially old ones. They're cold and they're dark."

"But is it church you think is bullshit? Or God?"

Sometimes Hannah's anger has a taste. Bitter, metallic. Like bad gin. The fact that he could be so wrong and was insisting on wasting her precious time made her want to pick up the cracked *Chicago* paperweight on his desk and throw it at his head.

"You're probably right," she said, lowering her eyes, at which she was rewarded with such a pleased look from this poor, dandruff-ridden man touting his tired Freudian theories that she felt as if she'd given him a prize. It's a talent Hannah has, knowing how to make men happy. It's why she almost always insists that her therapists be male.

Really, she doesn't know why she detests church so much, beyond the general boredom and the gloom. Though there is one thing that happened—something she's never told Jon, or her therapists, or anyone.

It happened in Paris, long before Hannah met Jon. She was in college on a DeWitt-sponsored semester abroad. It was winter, and she was on an architectural walking tour with some other students. The guide was speaking in French, telling them about the legend of Quasimodo, the Hunchback of Notre Dame. Already familiar with the story, Hannah drifted away from the group and stared at the crowds.

There were hundreds of people in Notre Dame that day, shuffling through, pointing at the soaring ceiling, the buttresses, and the snarling gargoyles. Hannah stared at them for a while, eyes glazing over, which was when the people's faces faded to a blur. Hannah blinked several times, trying to bring their features back into focus, and then, right in front of her, their clothes fell away, until this line of tourists who just a moment ago were wearing backpacks and visors became a herd of bodies moving through this ghastly church, blank and powerless as toys on a conveyor belt. Hannah wanted to ask them what happened, but her voice wouldn't work, and a blue-black cloud pressed down from above and she heard a ringing in her ears and that was the end of what she remembers of that moment.

Was this just a sophomoric attempt at understanding, this bizarre vision that took over her mind? Or was it the sort of thing that happens only to crazy people? Hannah certainly doesn't want to be crazy, nor does she want people to believe that she is. Which is why, when she woke up on the floor of Notre Dame, surrounded by the other students from *Bonjour, Stanford!* looking earnestly worried, she just told them she had a blood-sugar issue.

"Sorry," she said, smiling at the guide reassuringly. "*Excusez-moi.* This happens all the time."

Yet here she is, at a big, gray Episcopal church. And not just any church. Warren's. She stands outside for a few moments but doesn't want to be seen skulking by the doorway, looking guilty. It's not so much that she cares about what people might think—she's just been spotted by half the town on a hot-pink Earth Cruiser, after all. But this is Warren. When they see each other for the first time after more than a decade and a half, she doesn't want to be standing in a doorway. It just shouldn't work that way. In fact, this whole situation is wrong. Yet Grace Episcopal Church is what she has to work with, so Hannah puts her head down and pushes the door open.

Adjusting her eyes to the dim light, she sees it's pretty nice, for a church. The walls are mostly plain, stone and brick. There are some stained-glass windows depicting holy scenes in Froot Loop colors, and the floors are pleasant black-and-white tile. It's all very classy, like a good Vermeer painting. She looks around. Will Warren be wearing a robe? Will he be standing behind a pulpit, practicing a sermon? She can't even picture it. He was always such a quiet person. Shouldn't he be just the way she remembers him, in a stained flannel shirt, reading a book in a corner?

Could he really be a minister? Warren?

"May I help you?"

Hannah jerks her head toward the voice. Someone has

dropped an effervescent tablet into her chest cavity. There's a figure near the altar, but it isn't Warren. It's an older man holding a broom and dressed in the basic Charleston uniform — chinos and a light-blue button-down shirt.

"Are you a reverend?"

"No." The man shakes his head. "I'm the choirmaster. You here about services?"

"Oh, *no*." Her voice is a little too emphatic on this point, and the man shoots her a less than friendly look.

"Sorry. I'm looking for my friend. His name's Warren."

"Warren Meyers? He's back in his office. I'll take you." The man puts his broom down and walks past her, indicating she should follow.

Hannah hasn't moved yet. It shouldn't be this easy, she thinks. I can still run.

The man pauses beneath an archway. "Coming?"

"Yeah," she says. "Sorry." She hurries after him, following him down one hall, then another, then up some stairs to a gray, carpeted corridor. Again, it doesn't make sense to her. Warren doesn't belong in a church. He doesn't belong in a building of any kind. He should be chasing yak in the Gobi Desert. Or on some sort of large iron rig, bobbing about in the middle of the ocean.

But Warren Meyers is not in any of those places. As they pause in front of the open doorway, it seems that he is, in fact, here, slumped in front of an outdated computer, living his days in the greenish glow of a fluorescent overhead.

"Someone here to see you, Warren," the choirmaster says. Hannah's escort looks at her, his eyes free of even the smallest glint of curiosity. "Oh, I'm sorry, honey. I never got your name."

13

What Happened Before
She Left

S HE NEVER TOLD him good-bye.

    She could have. She thought about it. But it just seemed better to do it the other way—to leave three days earlier than he thought she was.

"DeWitt's throwing a party the night before I go," she told him. "Friday night. He's going to let us have beer."

"I don't want beer," Warren said. They were naked in Nowhere. They were teenagers and naked as much as possible. "I'll be too sad."

Hannah stared at the tapestries bellying down from the ceiling. It was a mercilessly humid summer afternoon. They'd spent the day at the beach and then, when the sun got too strong, driven back and slipped into the DeWitt House, where they kicked off their sandy bathing suits.

They were quiet for a long time. This didn't mean something

was wrong; Warren and Hannah were often quiet together. It was what they did.

Things with Warren and Hannah began in tenth grade. It was a very distinct shift in her life. She'd accepted a dinner invitation, and then, at his mother's prompting, Warren walked Hannah home. After that, they were together. It was that simple.

How to explain the young Warren Meyers? Hannah's best answer, looking back, is that he was an endless puzzle. She had known him when they were children, of course—her father was friends with his mother. But she didn't really *see* him until high school. When she finally did, it was as if he were from some other dimension. He was a quandary.

Hannah was always comfortable around boys. She liked them. And they, in their ninth-grade, hormone-addled way, liked her back. She knew what to say to them, knew that just by being direct and smart she could get them to do what she wanted. She wasn't pretty, but she was one of the first girls with breasts, which kept their attention. Nor had she ever been a prude, so she was game to satisfy their curiosity under the bleachers at lunch or behind the gym after school. She still remembers them all: Tommy Nelson was the first to feel her chest, while Dave Logan, who later served as Charleston Prep's fatal-drunk-driving cautionary tale, stuck his tongue so far down her mouth she gagged. Hannah felt the occasional penis, she let them yank at her zipper and explore the territory in her underwear. She knew the girls called her a slut, but Hannah didn't care about girls; what she cared about was the boys wanting her, which, for certain things, they did.

Hannah knows this is all totally textbook. The missing father, the desire for male attention. Her actions might have been idiotic, but she was always a smart and inquisitive person. Even back then she'd read *Madame Bovary, The Bell Jar, The Catcher in the Rye;* she understood characters and motivation, the wound, the consequent actions. But that's the thing the therapists don't really like to talk about, isn't it? Just because you finally realize *why* you're acting unhealthy doesn't mean you're not going to screw up again.

Warren, though. He was the one boy to throw off the pattern. Even though she was fooling around with what seemed like half the class, Hannah found Warren unapproachable. It was as if he were surrounded by an invisible force field. And so all during ninth grade, she let trembling football players paw her. When, really, Hannah was just watching Warren Meyers.

It was an interesting study. Warren loped on the edge of a group of boys that were hard to define; some were athletes, some pot smokers, but they had formed a loose sort of band, and Warren existed on its fringe. The other girls, as far as Hannah could tell, didn't notice the depths of Warren Meyers. This wasn't surprising. Although he had a square jaw and steady eyes, his right cheek had erupted in a case of volcanic acne. (The left side of his face stayed oddly clear, affording a glimpse of what he might look like if only the Clearasil fully kicked in.) He wasn't popular or cool or funny, but by second semester, Hannah figured out that he was the smartest out of anyone—a stealth nerd who silently made excellent grades. He never raised his hand, but on those occasions when called on, he would respond, however reluctantly, with succinct answers on ancient Greece or Shakespeare or the Constitution that were so thought-out and articulate, the rest of the class would inevitably turn and look over with surprise.

None of that would have even mattered, though. There were lots of smart boys, lots of loners to bond with. It was the way he stared that brought Hannah down. Warren was always staring absently out the window or at the wall. He did so with a constancy that's really only acceptable when you're a teenager; an adult acting the same would be written off as either a stoner or mentally challenged. And such an intense stare. This wasn't your ordinary boy space-out in contemplation of breasts or what Alyssa Milano might look like naked. No. Warren Meyers was fully *away*.

Hannah had not spoken to Warren other than to borrow a pen or to ask about a writing assignment. And when she did risk those questions, palms sweating, heart beating high in her throat, the answers she received were monosyllabic:

"Here."

"You want a blue one?"

" 'History of the Ages,' pages thirty-three to forty-nine."

As she continued to observe, Hannah became more and more desperate to know him. Warren Meyers, Warren Meyers, Warren Meyers. He was a Rubik's Cube with a block missing. Something to solve.

It took a while to understand how to get to him. He didn't fall for the easy tricks other boys did: stretching in class while wearing a tight sweater, or bending over to pick up a pencil she'd "dropped." He didn't stiffen when she brushed up against him. Hannah even stooped to hooking up with boys with whom he seemed friendly—Alex Winters, the boy who talked only about sailing, and a chunky, quiet kid with rainbow braces named George. This didn't work any better. And when she ever so casually asked about Warren, they didn't know anything about him that she didn't. Hannah thought they might at least talk about her among themselves in titillating, graphic terms (she'd eavesdropped enough on Palmer and his friends to know it was a distinct possibility), but if they did, Warren Meyers seemed not to be listening. He didn't even so much as glance at her.

In tenth grade, Hannah decided on a different tactic: she signed up for Virginia Meyers's Music Appreciation class. Hannah already appreciated music plenty, but she thought perhaps by observing Ms. Meyers, a notorious pothead, she might collect at least a few little crumbs about Warren's life. As it happened, Virginia was delighted to have Buzz Legare's daughter in her class. She was the sort of teacher who got in trouble for having favorites, and that semester Hannah was her favorite by far. Virginia took her to lunch and gave her free concert tickets. After school, they would sit and talk in the classroom.

"It's one of the things in my life I am gladdest about," Virginia said on one of these afternoons, tipping back in her chair. "Waterskiing by the light of the moon. Your father's idea, completely. We all piled into this boat and—"

"What do you mean?" Hannah asked. "Where were you?"

"Oh, we were at some party. There was always a party." Virginia and Buzz had briefly dated in high school. It was a period that Daisy never wanted to talk about, but one Hannah was endlessly fascinated by.

"But where was the party? What party?"

Virginia then did that maddening thing adults do to teenagers when they don't want to talk anymore: she simply pulled rank. "You know, I've been meaning to talk to you about something," she said in an entirely different tone.

"My dad?"

"Your behavior."

"What about it?"

"You're too easy."

"What?"

"Well, for example, look at you now. Your shirt is inside out."

"Oh." Hannah's face turned scarlet. Joel Firth in the parking lot.

"Hannah," Virginia said, "I'm not your mother. God knows that! But I'm close enough, I think, to tell you that you've got to stop slutting around."

"What?"

"You've got no girlfriends, sugar."

"I don't need friends. I don't even really like girls."

"What about a nice boyfriend? One nice boy?"

Hannah paused. She knew this was an important, important moment.

"I would date Warren," she said carefully. "He's a nice boy."

A long, cruel minute of silence passed before Virginia finally sighed and laughed. "I thought so." Her laughter died, and she paused again. "Poor Warren. He's never had a girlfriend."

It killed her, but still, Hannah said nothing.

"All right, sugar," Virginia said. "Come to dinner. Sunday night."

And that's all it took. Virginia's approval. Once Hannah realized this, she was shocked she hadn't figured it out sooner. Warren adored his mother, and after a magical supper where wine was served to the minors, it was clear that Virginia was endorsing Hannah. So he turned that stare, the one she'd been observing for more than a year, on *her*. She felt it in every hair follicle, every cell.

After dinner, they walked home together, and Hannah could almost hear in her head the quiet, reassuring sound of a latch falling perfectly into place.

"Should I pick you up for school tomorrow?" Warren asked.
She nodded.

Click.

"I'll be there at seven forty," he said.

In the morning, Warren Meyers's Honda Civic was waiting out in front of the DeWitt House. It was there the next day, and the next. After the first week, Hannah couldn't remember what school had been like without him. He defected from his group of friends. It was all still perfectly civil, but Warren was with Hannah now. He sat with her on the lawn at lunch; he found her at break; he came home and hung out at the house during those delicious afternoon hours while their parents were out. Hannah still received grins from the under-the-bleachers boys, but learned to let her gaze slide idly over their bewildered faces, so that soon the message was clear that if Hannah Legare used to be an easy feel, she was with Warren Meyers now— *Yeah, Meyers, palming that ass. Dude, he must be getting some serious action, nice.*

It took two weeks for Warren and Hannah to have sex. They were both virgins—Hannah never having let the feelers go all the way. The first few bouts were a joke: multiple tries with the condom, fits of uneasy hysterics. And then, again: *click.* They did it at least once a day, and usually two to three times, as if storing up for a long drought. They went deep and long. Searching. This is when Hannah learned about the athleticism of sex, the closeness, the orgasm, which she mastered after a few busy weeks. Hey, she thought—she was riding the wave—look, I'm good at this, too.

But there was more to the sex than this. When Hannah was there, she knew she was close to the place in him that remained undefined. She could hear it. It was there, in a moan, in the glint of an eye. Visiting the shady borders of Warren Meyers's subconscious was completely addictive to Hannah. It was the first place in a very long time where she felt she was supposed to be.

They were close enough to elicit lectures by her mother, intense enough to cause the other kids to whisper about them when they passed. They weren't invited to parties, and their teachers disapproved of them. Still, at the top of their class (she first, he second) and with almost perfect SATs, they were untouchable. Indeed, other than the vigorous sex, which was tacitly tolerated, they were pretty much models of good behavior.

Although Warren was indisputably a good kid—among the smartest in school—Daisy was, from the start, adamantly against the relationship. "I just think you should see more than one boy," she lectured.

"I don't like other boys," Hannah said. "Besides, that sounds kind of schizo. Why look for someone else when you're with someone you like?"

"Interesting theory."

"Don't you like Warren?" Hannah asked.

"He's fine. Not the most sparkling boy, but fine."

"Then what's the problem?"

"Mediocrity, Hannah, is my problem. He's just not all *there*. Lord, what if you get pregnant? And you'd have to marry him? And then—"

"Mom, this is crazy. Besides, you're the one who got me on the pill." Daisy, ever the cerebral organizer, sent Hannah to the gynecologist as soon as Warren began picking her up for school. "It's a boyfriend, Mom. People in high school have them."

"Well"—her mother sighed—"I suppose college will solve the problem."

But, as the application period grew near, it turned out that

Daisy was wrong; college would solve no problem, because Warren and Hannah applied for school together. It was easy. Warren wrote their essays. (This was how they did all of their homework—she did the math; he did the writing assignments.) They applied to all the same schools, save Warren's safety, Chapel Hill. Hannah didn't bother with safety schools; her grades were good, and there could be few better college-essay topics than a father who goes missing when one is eleven years old. Hannah and Warren were both accepted almost everywhere. Warren didn't get into Stanford; Hannah was wait-listed at Brown. Yet when both were accepted at Harvard, the choice seemed pretty obvious.

It has often struck Hannah that important days, the ones that change things forever, feel like any other good day. You've just found $20 in your pocket, and then a bus hits your car; you're eating blackberry ice cream in the sun, and a piano falls on your head. The third Sunday in February was such a day. Hannah went to Warren's for dinner. Virginia always welcomed Hannah with a slight air of triumph. She didn't appreciate Daisy's objections to her son, and so she always loved that Hannah would rather be at her house than at her own. When Hannah came in, Virginia was poring over the newspaper, her fingers wrapped around a large glass of white wine.

"Chicken for dinner." Virginia didn't look up. "Couple of hours."

"Thanks," Hannah said. She climbed the steps two at a time up to Warren's room—a spare, white chamber haphazardly decorated with covers of old Beatles albums and pictures of the marsh. He was reading *Crime and Punishment*. She kissed him and sat down on his bed to start their calculus problems.

"These are tricky," Hannah said. "Remind me to show you the parabola stuff before the test."

A few minutes of silent working passed. Warren was jiggling his foot, which he did only when something was bothering him. Is Dostoyevsky that bad? she remembers thinking. Finally, without looking up, he said, "Hannah, I'm going to Chapel Hill."

At first, she didn't understand.

"It's about money," he continued. "I got a Morehead Scholarship. I can't turn it down."

She shook her head, refusing to believe him. She thought about how a snake's body still moves back and forth long after its head is cut off.

"But you're going to Harvard," she said. "With me."

"I'm not. I'm not going."

"But you can't go to North Carolina."

"Chapel Hill's a good school."

"It's not Harvard."

"They have plenty of good professors there."

They have plenty of good professors there. That was it, the thing that made it start to sink in. He was reasoning it out for her. Warren wasn't the type of person to waste breath on excuses. He had made his decision. He was going to North Carolina, and Hannah was going up to Cambridge alone.

It would be all right. That was what they told each other over and over in the next hour, facing cross-legged on the bed. They wouldn't date other people. They'd visit all the time—there were direct flights between Raleigh and Boston—and their parents wouldn't even have to know. They decided not to talk on the phone; they never really connected unless they were in person. Warren said he had heard of some new way of sending letters on the computer, so they'd figure out how to do that and write every day.

By the time Virginia called them down to dinner, everything felt settled. Hopeful, even. They ate and talked about the news.

"So he told you, huh, sweetie?"

"Mmm-hmm." Hannah was trying to be brave, but her voice wavered.

"Don't worry, Hannah. It'll be OK."

Hannah hates lies. It's why she can't stand politics; empty words instantly depress her. But this. She really, really wanted to believe it. So badly that she chose to ignore the fact that, for the first time in her experience, Virginia's voice hit the zone of the superficial, her tone as delicate as a bubble of dish soap—thin, shiny, ready to pop.

And then, April, a month Hannah has always hated. To any other teenager, April meant the long-awaited arrival of warm weather and kissing outside. But to Hannah, the month of her father's disappearance six years before meant thirty days of waiting for something horrible to strike. This April, though, things were looking bright, and hadn't she already endured an entire month's worth of disaster back in February, when Warren announced he was becoming a Tar Heel? In fact, so far, this April—sleepy and naked—had been just fine. Great, even.

Then the last very good day: the thirtieth of April, the Tuesday before the senior prom, which had always been Senior Cut Day at Charleston Prep. This was an unofficial holiday when, instead of driving to the cigarette-littered school parking lot, the seniors turned their cars east and headed out to Sullivan's Island, a three-mile strip of sand buffering Charleston from the ocean. It was a tradition started by the Class of 1962. Buzz Legare's class, as a matter of fact. According to Virginia, the whole thing had been his idea.

The Class of 1991 was particularly lucky, in that Tommy Nelson's parents happened to be in Bermuda for the week, rendering the Nelsons' old, rambling beach house available for the day's festivities. A little after eight, the Nelsons' neighbors were just ambling out onto their porches, clutching cups of coffee; upon seeing eighty-six girls and boys disembarking with kegs of beer, they retreated into their houses, shutting their windows and doors for the day.

A perfect day, April 30, 1991. The sun was high, though it was still chilly for the thin-blooded teenagers who'd grown up in 102-degree summers. Instead of going to the beach, they chose to gather on the Nelsons' large deck. They shed their wraps and shirts, baring just-shy-of-twenty skin. It's something to celebrate, being that young. It's the kind of thing that gives one a reason to drink before nine in the morning.

It wasn't long before the bounds of long-established social divisions began to loosen. Melvin Bovine, the class nerd, shared a cigar with the quarterback. Warren, usually a reticent loner outside of his relationship with Hannah, sat talking with Jenny White, the airheaded homecoming queen. By noon, everything had escalated: Ella McCarthy, the drama nerd headed for Wesleyan, was making out with Joe Coleman, a notorious redneck whose truck was decorated on both sides with huge Confederate flag decals. A beer funnel was rigged up off the deck, manned by a group of bikini-clad girls. They fed warm Bud Light through the hose to a line of boys at the bottom, their faces shining up, eager as hungry chicks.

A few couples had claimed rooms upstairs in the Nelsons' house for the afternoon, but for once Warren and Hannah abstained from sex, choosing instead to stay outside and talk to classmates they'd mostly ignored for the last two years. The Boone's Farm wine was causing Hannah to feel true love for these people she had overlooked for so long—even Joe Coleman, even shit-for-brains Jenny White, even Tommy Nelson. It made her wonder, as her skin turned browner and the shoulder straps of her bathing suit grew looser, why she had been so determined to cut these nice people out of her life.

Toward the end of the day, over a second Apple Blossom bottle, Hannah fell particularly deep in conversation with Charlotte, a druggie girl she'd always kind of liked.

"I thought you were a bitch," Charlotte said. "Or a slut. You used to be sort of slutty."

"It's not a crime."

"No! No way. It's just that you seemed so...unfriendly, you know? But it turns out you're just fucked up like the rest of us."

"Thank you."

"Is it because of your dad?"

"Probably."

"You should work on that," she said. She was pretty high. "You know? That shit'll screw you for life."

"Yeah," Hannah replied. And then the conversation turned idly to gossip—who was going where for school, who was screwing whom. Eventually their talk petered out, but Hannah felt good about it. It was the closest she had come to a female connection in years.

The day ended in a sleepy, happy haze. At four she and Warren fell into a wine-, beer-, and marijuana-induced slumber in a plastic chaise longue. An hour and a half later, they woke up, shivering in the increasingly cool dusk air, and were genially shooed out by Tommy Nelson, who tearfully told Warren how much he loved him and, while Hannah stared, kissed her boyfriend on the lips. Warren wasn't bothered by it. Even as a teenager, he had an easy way with people. He just pulled gently away. *It's OK, man.*

After the party Warren drove Hannah back to town, windows open, cool spring air roaring sweet and heavy into the car. Before dropping her off, he took Hannah around the Battery so slowly it felt like they were idling. She stared out the window happily. She loved this boy beside her. She wanted to turn into smoke and drift into Warren Meyers's pores.

The next day, the Class of 1991 filed back into the cinder-block halls of Charleston Prep—tan, nervous, slightly sheepish. The administration was annoyed, but it was no different than the problem they faced every year. There was no way to suspend eighty-six students. Just in case, Hannah had DeWitt write a note. From the start of the marriage, she'd learned to go to DeWitt when she needed things like money and notes to get out of class. At 10:43 in the morning, she had seven precious minutes left in her midmorning break, just enough time to deliver the note to the principal's office and find Warren to say hi before AP History.

The office was down a long hallway, but she saw immediately that Warren was standing in the breezeway just outside. He had to be the only person she could recognize at that distance: the thin, slouching silhouette, the olive smudge of a flannel shirt.

Even after two years of dating, the sight of Warren at the end of the breezeway caused Hannah to hurry. She threw her books into her locker and walked down the hall, slowing when she got close. He was talking to a girl. Hannah saw blond hair, a pink polo shirt tucked into a khaki skirt. Jenny White.

Jenny was not a particularly nice girl in high school. She had a reputation for being kind of dumb, although Hannah had long suspected she was smarter than people gave her credit for—her pearls of ignorance just a bit too perfectly timed, her clueless stare a tad too adorable. She was also inarguably the most beautiful girl in the Class of 1991, and while Hannah had never doubted her own ability to wear jeans well enough to disarm any boy who might walk behind her, Jenny's obvious beauty, paired with her bitchy friends and her snobbish attitude (*"Ew,"* Hannah once heard Jenny whisper to Bitsy Ravenel when Hannah walked by wearing one of her father's old shirts), made her impossible to like.

As Hannah got closer, she remembered Charlotte mentioning just yesterday that Jenny was headed to North Carolina for college, too. It wasn't that she had the grades, Charlotte had said. Duh. Shit for brains. But that's what being a legacy will do for you.

Now Jenny was laughing, and Warren was laughing, and, as Hannah watched, Warren Meyers, *her* Warren Meyers, reached out and put his hand on Jenny's slender arm.

Hannah was too close to run. So she just said, "Hi."

Warren snatched his hand away.

"Hey," Jenny said, giving her a pleasant look as irritatingly empty as a golden retriever's. "Oh, my God—my trig homework! I totally spaced. OK, we'll talk later, Warren." Jenny gave a maddening little wave and glided away.

Hannah looked at Warren, setting her face in a pleasant expression. Though what she wanted to do was scream. Because Hannah knew Warren Meyers better than anyone in the world. She knew him better than she knew her mother or brother. She knew his habits, his likes and dislikes. When his eyes twitched, it meant he was sleepy. He was always on time, sometimes annoyingly so. He got grouchy when he was hungry, without even knowing he needed food. (Hannah stored candy bars in her backpack to ward off those sugar lows.) In his pockets he kept notes written on tiny scraps of paper to remind him of things he needed to do. And when he thought another girl was pretty, he slouched slightly and looked at the ground, studiously avoiding Hannah's face until the moment had passed.

The thing was, Hannah didn't care very much about Warren flirting with Jenny White. Sure, it hurt, but it was OK for him to find other girls pretty. She knew that it came with the territory of being a boy. Besides, Hannah did the same thing. Warren was hardly the best-looking boy in school. He'd gotten better-looking, sure; his arms and shoulders had filled out a bit, and his acne had all but faded. Still, there were other boys around — cuter boys — and Hannah thought about them, sometimes even pausing to watch them at soccer or football practice as they swarmed by in spectacular herds.

So it was all right for Warren to think Jenny White was pretty, and even to wonder what she looked like under those perfectly coordinated ensembles from Banana Republic. Hannah wasn't the hysterical type. And she certainly didn't want to be like one of those cheerleaders who flew into a rage at a party when she saw her boyfriend grabbing a beer for another girl. Intelligence, one hoped, could override jealousy. If you weren't the prettiest, it paid to be the smartest, because you could train your mind to understand these things.

What was not all right today was that, aside from slouching and looking at the ground, Warren now began to talk.

"Yesterday's party was so fun, wasn't it? Even though Tommy was being weird. Are you hung over? God, I am. I still feel like shit. I went to bed at eight. Crazy."

It wasn't completely off, what he was saying. It wasn't offensive. It was just that the Warren she knew always chose silence over chatter. And so, as he went on, barely allowing her to answer, Hannah began to feel physically ill. Because what this meant, of course, was that, on top of thinking lusty thoughts about Jenny, Warren was ashamed. Shame was different than lust. It meant that while he might not already have done so, he would, at some point, betray her.

"She's really pretty, isn't she?" Hannah interrupted.

"Who?"

"Jenny White."

"What? Oh — no. Not really. Why?"

It was the lie that tipped it. Of course Jenny White was pretty. His saying otherwise was like suggesting that Strom Thurmond would be voted out in the next election.

It was still early enough, so she called Harvard and told them thank you, but no, she wouldn't be coming to Cambridge in the fall. Then she called Stanford and told them she'd be thrilled to accept a place in the Class of 1995. She didn't tell anyone except her mother that she'd done these things. Throughout the summer, when she spoke of school, Warren would have assumed Hannah meant Harvard. She never actually lied about it; she'd just say, "When I go off to school."

Eventually, she did lie, though. At the end of the summer, Hannah told Warren her plane was leaving on a Saturday, when in fact her flight was on a Wednesday morning at 8:06. Even on that last Tuesday night, the seconds of which she knew to treasure as the end of her time with Warren Meyers, Hannah kept to herself the fact that she'd be gone in twelve short hours.

Hannah's mother didn't entirely understand Hannah's reasons

for secrecy, but she was overjoyed that Hannah was finally getting rid of Warren. And now there was college! The possibilities! The men! An undeniable look of pleasure crossed her face when Hannah told her she and Warren wouldn't be seeing each other anymore.

"Very wise," Daisy said. "I'm sorry to say so, but it's true. Why waste college on a high school boyfriend? Very smart, Hannah. Exactly what I would have done if I'd been lucky enough to go to a school like Stanford."

When Daisy told Hannah over the phone about how Warren came to the house to look for her the next day, she wouldn't let herself listen. And when she got letters from Warren (Palmer, unable to stand the inquisition, gave him the address), Hannah threw them away without opening them. When he tracked down her number and left messages on the answering machine, she told her roommate to erase them. After a couple of weeks, he gave up trying. Clearly he hadn't cared *that* much. Not enough to fly out to see her. Not enough to take out school loans and go to Harvard. Not enough not to date Jenny White as soon as he got to UNC. By Christmas, Warren was a Zeta, Jenny was a Delta, and they were together. He married her two years after college. Shit-for-brains Jenny White.

When Hannah heard about the wedding, she was happy, in a way. It proved that her actions had been right. She had followed her instincts, and they had protected her. They still do. She feels almost lucky that she had a father who disappeared when she was eleven, because now, she can always sense when someone is going to take off. This has been an invaluable skill. After all, Hannah often theorizes, life is basically just designed to kick your ass, isn't it? Give a friend five minutes, and they'll tell you about how lonely they are. Talk to a stranger on a plane, and they'll tell you how someone broke their heart. Hannah doesn't have to face this, because of a promise she made to herself in 1985. She was eleven years old, sitting in a church, humiliated because everyone was wondering why she wasn't crying; it was then she decided she would never, ever let anyone else leave her, whatever the circumstances or what she had to do. Warren Meyers was the beginning, but there have been others, and evidently there will be more. No matter what happens, Hannah makes certain she's always the one to leave first.

It's a tragic thing, that a person's body has to change.

She is standing next to the choirmaster, looking at Warren's back. There's extra flesh above the belt. His backside has widened. It looks like he's gained thirty pounds. Which is not so surprising, she supposes. Most men in Charleston gain weight with age. There's too much salt in the food, and beer is served at just about every meal after eleven in the morning. "Charleston puffiness," Tom calls it. You can avoid it with diet and exercise, of course, but it takes diligence, and Warren has obviously fallen prey.

There are other changes. The back of his neck, once tan and smooth, now appears surprisingly hairy. So are his wrists. He wears a blue oxford identical to the choirmaster's, something he would never have worn when Hannah knew him. In fact, it would be rather easy to convince herself that this isn't Warren Meyers at all, if not for the inimitable slouch of his back and the jiggling of his right foot. Even now she can tell it means he has a problem he's trying to work out. Once upon a time, it would have been a transition in his history essay. Now she supposes it's something about the congregation. Or God?

Yet she is happy to note that she feels absolutely nothing. No excitement, no nerves—just the slightly sad satisfaction of curiosity, observing what happens to a person after the passage of a certain number of years.

"I'm Hannah Legare," she tells the choirmaster.

Warren looks up from his computer and turns around slowly, his hands on the arms of his ergonomic chair.

"Hi," she says.

His face registers no surprise or emotion. He appears to be as removed as Hannah, only now her blissful objectivity is falling away. Because his face is exactly the same. Lined around the edges, sure, but the same. The crooked nose, the distant eyes. No, Hannah doesn't feel that removed at all anymore. Every nerve is crackling, and her chest will not, *will not* be quiet.

"Hannah," Warren says. He stands up and puts out his hand. She gives her best business-school shake. "Mom told me you were in town."

"Ministers have computers?" A stupid thing to say, but she's feeling pretty stupid right now. Her palms have sprouted rivers.

"Sure," he says with a polite smile. "We've got to work somewhere." He motions to the chair next to his desk. "Sit down if you have time."

It's as if she is a client. Or a potential hire.

"You look great!" she practically shouts.

"You, too." Again, his tone is maddeningly hard to read. She knows he couldn't really mean it; she has a big wound on her head, and her T-shirt and jeans are dirty from crawling in the closet, and she's sweaty from riding up here on the Earth Cruiser.

"What can I do for you?" he asks.

Hannah's not quite sure where to start. I love you? Sorry I ditched you? I've got to get ahold of myself, she thinks. It's not like he's special. He's just a regular guy now, with none of the otherworldliness she remembers. It makes her a little angry, in fact. How could such a special person turn into someone so ordinary? How could he let himself devolve into an oxford shirt with Charleston puffiness? How could he be married to shit-for-brains Jenny White?

"I guess I don't really know what I'm doing here."

"Well," Warren says patiently, "take a moment."

She stares at him. Still nothing. No connection in the eyes, not even the slightest turn of a smile. Are you *in* there?

"How's your family?" he finally asks.

"Everyone's good."

"And how's... San Francisco? That's where you live, right?"

Is she detecting a trace of bitterness? Could he be cracking the door open ever so slightly?

"Listen, I'm really sorry about... you know, back in high school. The way I left and everything."

Warren shrugs and waves his hand, as if brushing away a fly. "Water under the bridge."

"It was a crappy thing to do. I know you must have been upset."

"Oh, it was years ago. Who cares now? We were kids."

"Still, I'm sorry."

He looks at her evenly. "Apology accepted." The computer gives off a little e-mail *ding!* Warren glances at the screen, then looks back at her with a pleasant, dim smile. He must have picked up dullness from Jenny, she thinks. How cute.

"So do you have porn on there?"

She knows she's being obnoxious. But right now she'd do anything to garner a rise out of him.

"What?"

144

"Porn. That's what all men keep on their hard drives. Even ministers, I imagine. So? What do you have on there?"

He pushes his chair back a little.

"You *do!* You'd answer if you didn't."

Warren pauses for a moment, then grabs a frame on his desk and flips it around so she can see it.

"This is my family."

Hannah leans forward to look. Virginia was right about the girls. They're perfect.

"Jenny White." He tells her about how they started dating in college. How Jenny was the girl right after her.

"You've got a beautiful family," Hannah says.

"Thank you."

"Congratulations."

"Again, thank you." He picks up the photo and looks at it for a moment, then puts it down on his desk. "And you?"

"I'm married."

"Great." He nods. Once, twice. Again, a flicker of something she thinks she recognizes, but she has to work pretty hard at it. It's like trying to find CNN in rural Slovakia.

"Hey," she says. "I need your help, actually."

"Sure." He looks relieved at the concrete nature of this request. Hannah leans over, digs the photo out of her bag, then slides it across the desk.

Warren picks it up and looks at it. He frowns, then squints and brings the picture closer to his face, trying to make sense of the image.

"Hey, that's Mom," he says, smiling. He looks at it again. "Oh, and your parents."

"Yup."

He squints at it again and brings it closer to his face. He flips it over to see if there's anything written on the back, then turns the photograph right side up again and stares at it quietly. A minute passes. Then another.

Hannah knows not to say anything right now. And she's glad for this silence, because what it means is that, despite the church and the wife and the two gorgeous daughters and the softened body, her Warren Meyers is still in there somewhere.

"What is this?" he finally asks.

"It's a picture, Warren. Of our parents."

"Where did you get it?"

"I found it in my closet. You remember, that room behind—"

"I know."

He won't look at her.

"It's still there."

"Huh." His face is no longer so pleasantly impartial. Another minute passes. Then, without looking at her, Warren tosses her photo in the trash.

"What are you doing?" She dives to grab the bin.

"Leave it," he barks.

"Sorry," she mumbles, reddening when she finds herself on her knees under his desk.

"Leave it, Hannah," he repeats.

"Fine," she says, climbing back in her chair again. "Why?"

"Because that picture can't help you."

"I didn't say it could."

"Listen. *You* got yourself to where you are now," Warren says. "Your dad died, but now you've moved on; you're married and happy and independent. You've been blessed, Hannah. Obviously God—"

"Screw God, Warren! God has got nothing to do with me."

"If you feel that way—"

"I'm *not* happy. You want to know where I am now, really? I'm separated from my husband because I can't stop screwing up my own life."

"Well, I'm sorry. I'm sorry to hear that." He does seem sorry, and pauses for a moment. "The best I can do is try to guide you toward a more spiritual path."

"Come off it, Warren."

"I'm a minister, Hannah, OK? But I *can* say it won't do you any good to revisit the past. Do you understand?"

"But there are questions. You saw the photo—"

"Your father is dead."

"We don't know that."

"We do know it, Hannah. That is the information we have."

"You never used to think that."

Warren pauses carefully. "Your father's gone," he says. "So your mother moved on. Digging this sort of thing up doesn't help anyone."

"I think it might help me."

"You're lying to yourself."

They glare at each other a moment. She is so frustrated she has to keep herself from yelling out.

"Think about coming to services," he says, serving up the dim smile again.

"OK. Yeah. Thanks."

"You're more than welcome."

Their tones are merely civil now. Strangers in church. He stands up and extends his hand again, but Hannah can't deal with it a second time and hurries out. The rain that threatened

147

before is here now, coming down in torrents. It's warm, at least. She hops on the bike and pedals for a block, riding through the puddles on purpose and kicking up huge sprays of mud and water before remembering she's left her picture in Warren's trash.

"Shit!" she screams, ignoring the group of tourists gawking from a horse-drawn carriage in the street. She wheels around, rides back to the church, and, throwing her bike against the gate, runs up the stairs.

Hannah is soaking. Water drips from her hair and clothes to the floor. She didn't bother to wear a bra under her shirt this morning; this is a decision she now regrets.

When she gets to the doorway, she stops, surprised. Warren's head is in his hands. He's fished the picture out of the trash and laid it on his desk.

"Warren."

He jumps slightly.

"I just came back for my picture."

He nods. His right finger plays with a curl on his head.

"You're wet."

"It's raining."

He holds out the photo in front of him.

"Come to services."

"I hate church, Warren."

She takes the picture, her old lover's hand still hovering in the air.

"Just come," he says. "I'll bring someone who can help."

14

Palmer Gets a Call

A s soon as he opens his eyes, Palmer knows today is not going to be a good day. Tom has risen already without bothering to wake him. He hears the rain on the roof and remembers he never covered the hot tub, he still has a kitchen he promised to clean, and Rumpus, no doubt, will not have been walked. He'll have to take the dog with him to the office, where the other animals will nip at her, causing Rumpus to urinate both on the floor of the office and, later, at home, on an expensive rug of her choice. Still, Palmer deals. He dresses, showers, grooms, cleans, puts away, collects Rumpus, and heads to his own personal world, the office.

When someone asks Palmer why he chose to be a veterinarian—and people do, all the time, the same way they ask firemen and writers, though never bankers or computer programmers—his answer is always the same. *Control.* At the office, Dr. Palmer Legare controls air-conditioning levels, happiness, morphine, and the satellite-radio-station music piped into the waiting room. The day is never dull. Never the same routine twice. He wields death, prolongs life, and helps the world while doing it. It's a good job, he says. He's lucky.

As with all things, this is only part of the answer, but the full reply to the question is too revealing for Palmer to say comfortably. What people like Tom and Hannah know is that Palmer became a vet because of Tucker, the dog his father left behind.

When Buzz disappeared, Tucker became Palmer's dog. It was not a smooth transition; Tucker was highly distraught by the loss of his owner, and a year of horrible behavior followed, resulting in the destruction of upward of twenty-five shoes. After losing a pair of hand-me-down Ferragamos, Daisy even threatened to put the dog down, but seeing the expression on Palmer's face, she silenced herself on the subject. Palmer patiently trained Tucker, taking him everywhere he could, including to football games and school. (Dogs were not allowed on campus, but in light of Palmer's "circumstance," a special exception was made for Tucker.) By the end of two years, even Daisy agreed that Tucker was so well behaved he had almost human qualities. He fetched his own leash and got the paper. Neighborhood legend was that the dog could sometimes be seen walking himself around the block.

In high school, Palmer developed a typical fondness for marijuana. On chilly winter afternoons, he would sit in his large bedroom at the DeWitt House, taking deep hits on his bong and communing with Tucker. The more Palmer smoked on those stark, bright days, the more certain he became that Tucker could understand him more deeply than anyone else. At those times, Palmer would try to glean information. This animal, after all, was the only being to have any idea what really happened to his father. He *had* to be able to communicate something.

"Did he fall out, Tuck?" Palmer asked, looking deep into the dog's brown eyes—so *soulful*. "Was it a wave? Another boat?"

When, inevitably, he received no answer beyond a wet-nosed nudge or an accelerated thump of the tail, Palmer would make sure his door was all the way shut and practice confessions:

"I'm gay, Tuck. Do you understand?"

"I like dick, puppy. Got it?"

Tucker never judged. Afterward Palmer would lie on the floor and indulge himself in an athletic fit of stoned giggles. *This is insane.* Still, he secretly believed that, in some way, his statements were being processed. It didn't make sense, but he knew it, the same way he knew that if you made a wish at 11:11 it would surely come true, or that if he ever did meet River Phoenix, things would work out between them, screw his girlfriends—it was destiny.

Why must a dog's allotted time on Earth be out of step with those who love him? By the time Palmer was in his third year at the Citadel, the dog's snout was white and his eyes clouded over. He hobbled after Palmer at the beach and around the house with pitiful determination. Palmer tried to ignore the growing limp and the arthritic gait. Then one day, in an ill-advised attempt to leap into Palmer's car, Tucker broke his hip.

"It's up to you," Daisy said. "Will can pay for it. We can fix it if you want." (Never an animal lover, Daisy refused to assign pets feminine or masculine pronouns.) Palmer was tempted. He counted on Tuck's heavy head resting on his chest in the morning, on his breath chugging a foot behind. But looking at the dog's eyes, tired and dazed from drugs, Palmer knew the correct answer. After a day of deliberation, he gathered the animal—now little more than a nest of bone and loose skin, smelling of an old mushroom—lifted him gently, and drove him to the vet's office.

Even losing his father was easier than this. No one there but Palmer. No throngs of mourners, no somber receptions with ham biscuits and whiskey. Just Palmer and Tucker waiting in a cold room for the vet to end the dog's life.

The vet's name was Dr. Greene—young, tall, and lanky, with a surfer's haircut. He had permanently flushed cheeks and an easy grin. Something about him even seemed a little bit holy. Dr. Greene put a gentle hand on Tucker's head and left it there as he injected the twitching animal, didn't move it until Tucker was fully still and gone. His demeanor left no room for doubt that, as a team, he and Palmer were doing the right thing. And at that moment—sobbing by the body of his lifeless dog—Palmer understood that while vets help animals, really they save people. So on that lamentable day, two things happened. He fell silently in love with Dr. Greene, and, more constructively, he chose a fulfilling, attainable profession.

When Palmer walks into his office, his assistant, Jenny, is chatting with the receptionist in the lab over coffee. He looks at the day's lineup: almost all dogs. Not surprising; Charleston is a dog town. There are dogs in cars, dogs tied up outside bars, dogs leashed to the legs of strollers. Dogs pace in the backs of trucks, dogs surf the bows of boats, dogs roam the beaches, their college-student owners too distracted by beer and skin to notice their animals knocking over small children. No apologies necessary when this happens. In a dog town, the dogs win. There are some cats, too, of course. Snakes, rabbits, gerbils, a few ferrets. But mostly Palmer's patients are canine: big, shaggy, and forgiving—even when receiving their thermometer in the rectum or a final dose of barbiturates into the inside of their ailing paw.

Joining his employees for a moment, Palmer peeks out into the waiting room. "Good morning," he says.

"Morning," Jenny replies.

It's clear that he has interrupted their gossip, so Palmer retreats into his office and sits at his desk. Within a minute, Jenny appears in the doorway. Palmer looks approvingly at her sunny breasts, somehow perceptible through the loose blue scrubs. If Palmer were going to have straight sex again, it would be with Jenny, who is blond and soft and feminine in a way he vaguely misses. He never would, though. It would be like ordering an ice-cream sundae as a side to prime rib. Besides, straight affairs are more complicated than gay ones, particularly at work. A gay fling would most likely be a onetime thing that would quickly evolve into some slight office discomfort and a few catty remarks before being forgotten altogether. Sex with Jenny would require tears and long talks. Not to mention that she happens to be the wife of his sister's ex-boyfriend. Still, he can appreciate Jenny's skin — soft, tan, bearing the inexplicable scent of cooked butter.

She smiles at him wanly. Palmer thinks he might have heard her voice quiver. He braces himself. Jenny is a crier. She cries on birthdays, when she can't find her keys, when it's too cold out. It would be worth firing her over, but fortunately the one thing she doesn't cry over is animal euthanasia. When it comes to pet killing, she's a battle-ax.

"Warren like his birthday present?" he thinks to ask. Earlier in the week, Palmer went with Jenny to Croghan's to select some cuff links for her husband.

"He did." She pauses, sniffs, and takes an ever-present packet of Kleenex out of her pocket. "At least I think he did."

"Maybe we should have gone for the band saw?"

"No, he liked the cuff links. I don't know. With Warren, it's just hard to tell."

"Mmm." Palmer does not particularly like Warren. He didn't like him when he dated his sister in high school, and he doesn't like him as Jenny's husband. Warren is bland, unfeeling, and, frankly, boring. Sure, he has great eyes, but that doesn't excuse his lack of enthusiasm over a birthday present his wife clearly spent hours picking out for him. Still, who is he to say? He's not going to get involved.

She dabs at her face. "How's Tom?"

"Fine, thanks," Palmer says.

"It would be such fun if we all went out. Have you asked him?"

"I keep meaning to!" he lies. "But my sister's in town now. Had her over to dinner."

He is immediately sorry he mentioned it. Jenny's face instantly ages at least eight years. Moisturizer would help, Palmer thinks. Would Tom be pissed if I bought some of that stuff he likes for Jenny, too?

"Oh." Jenny looks down at her pile of charts. "All right, then. Well, we've got three patients already in the waiting room."

"Should we get started?" Palmer asks.

Nodding, Jenny returns to reception and calls the first patient in: a cat with lumps. The owner, a woman in her sixties, hair dyed an aggressive shade of red, clutches her pet to her chest.

"Miss Matthews."

"Palmer."

As is the case with many of Palmer's clients, Palmer has known Hattie Matthews since he was a boy.

"Palmer, I thought you got all of this last time. But now Tinkerbell's got the lumps again."

"Well, that's the thing about cancer, Miss Matthews," Palmer says gently. "It'll tend to grow back."

"I'm very disappointed, Palmer."

Palmer doesn't answer. He could say that he's sorry, but he's not; by looking at the cat's teeth, he can see that Tinkerbell is at least fourteen. She peers at him and hisses.

"Hang on, Bell."

"*Tinker*bell. Palmer Legare, do you even know who this cat is?"

"Of course I do. Sorry, Tinkerbell. I'm just a little distracted because I'm very busy right now."

"I was the first one in!"

"I know — just, I've got a big day ahead."

She narrows her eyes.

"Well, I just hope I've made the right choice, bringing Tinkerbell to you."

"You have indeed, Miss Matthews."

"I don't know what I'd do without her," she continues, her voice beginning to shake.

"I'm sure you have nothing to worry about. Tinkerbell's not going anywhere just yet."

"But you haven't even felt her *lumps*."

Palmer nods. He does have a tendency to put a positive spin on things before fully investigating. "Well, let's just have a look." He puts his hands on the cat and tries not to recoil at the cottage-cheese consistency that gives under his fingers. No question about it; the cat's a goner.

"Well?"

"Ummm..."

"Oh, no." Miss Matthews's eyes well with tears. "Is it bad?"

Most days, Palmer is quite honest with his patients, yet he is unable to break the news to Hattie Matthews today.

"I really don't know, Miss Matthews. Let's keep her here for some tests."

The cat looks at him, exhausted.

"But—"

"I'll be right back." He hurries down the hall. A dog howls.

"Jenny!"

"Yes?"

"I need you to set up Tinkerbell for some tests."

Jenny stares at him. "Are you serious?"

The receptionist cranes her neck to hear.

"Of course."

Jenny looks around and lowers her voice. "I checked that cat on the way in. Its organs are sawdust."

A trickle of sweat. Core temperature rising.

"Jenny, bag the cat."

"Palmer, what is your problem?"

"Just—"

"Fine. Mrs. Murphy and her dog are in Room Two."

Palmer spends the next hour petting, prodding, diagnosing. He knows why he is being so short with Jenny. He has to break it off with Tom. Today. He thought he'd have a little more time, but the episode with Hannah proves it. He needs to shut this thing down.

By ten thirty the waiting room is packed. Between a blind golden retriever and a spaniel with a tail burned from a shot-

156

gun barrel, he takes a break and, assuming the demeanor of an executioner, calls his lover. "You didn't wake me this morning."

"I had to get to the office. We're completely behind on the Gibbes Street project."

"We need to talk," Palmer says.

"I know — good idea."

"Dinner?"

"All right," Tom says. "I can take you to La Fourchette if you want."

"That's very . . . perfect."

"Look, I know I'm crazy about this baby stuff, and I'm *really* sorry, OK?"

"No, really . . ."

"No, I know I've been kind of unreasonable. So let's just shelve it."

"Tom, I don't think it's a good idea for you to give up what you want for me."

"Let's just forget it."

"No, see, what I *need* to tell you tonight is that . . . this isn't working."

There is a silence on the other end.

"Tom?"

"What do you mean?"

"I'm just not really feeling it."

"Feeling it?"

Palmer rolls up his sleeves. How to best put this? What did he say the last time? "I hate to do this over the phone . . ."

"Do what?"

He lets the silence answer for him.

"Palmer, are you serious?"

"Look, I—"

"You're *dumping* me?"

"I was going to wait until tonight, but—"

Palmer winces at the sound of a sob over the line. He pictures Tom slumped in his sleek, all-white office, crying. He knows he should feel sad at this imagined scene, and yet . . . nothing.

"Tom, I'm really sorry. Really."

"You're such a fucking coward, Palmer."

"Tom?"

But the line is dead.

Well, that was easier than Palmer thought it would be. He blinks, waiting a moment in case he's about to be hit by some sort of unexpected emotion. Once he is certain of the familiar void, he returns to the front of the office.

More patients are waiting; still oddly numb, he neuters a poodle, stitches up a pug.

Finally, it's time for lunch. It is customary for Palmer Legare's Office of Veterinary Medicine to close for lunch from twelve to one. This is a sacred hour; sometimes, depending on the number of patients, it begins before noon, but the hour never ends early. And often by the time the staff returns there is a line of pets and their owners standing patiently by the door. Today Palmer decides on his time-alone ritual: a deli sandwich and an iced tea on a bench down at the Boat Club dock. He gathers his things and prepares to head out the door quietly (so as not to alert Jenny), when his phone rings. Probably Tom calling back. He looks at it and frowns. Hannah.

"Hi," he says with as much spirit as he can muster.

"You think Mom was having an affair with DeWitt?"

He hears someone in the room; it's Rumpus, who has awakened from the nap she was taking under the table. The dog eyes him, turns around three times, then lies down with a great sigh of annoyance.

"Palmer?"

"I'm sorry. *What* about DeWitt, now?"

"I found a photo — you know, an old one. Of Mom, Dad, DeWitt. They're all at this party."

"So?"

"So I thought Mom had never met DeWitt."

He picks up his pen to doodle.

Dad, he writes. *DeWitt.*

"I'm not sure I even understand what you're talking about."

Hannah's hysteria on the other end of the line is building. "Remember that weekend when we made the Barbies have sex and then burned and lynched them?" she says, voice rising. "When Mom and Dad went to a party on Sullivan's Island? DeWitt was *there*. At the party."

"Hannah, I'm sorry. You're just not making any sense."

"No one will fucking listen to me!" her voice explodes over the phone. "Jon won't call me back. And when I showed the picture to Warren, he said —"

"You saw Warren Meyers?"

"Well ..."

"You mean, the minister Warren Meyers? The one married to my assistant?"

Silence.

"Why the hell did you do that?"

More silence.

"Hannah?"

"I was at church," she says defensively.

"Oh, Christ." Palmer pulls at his hair.

"It's not like it sounds," she says.

"You're here to clean *up*, remember?" Palmer yells. "To meditate, you know? Do a cleanse with Tom. Or, I don't know — yoga or something." He takes a sip of water, trying to get ahold of himself. He will *not* let his sister ruin his day.

"Screw yoga. Something here is very weird."

"Hannah, you're being crazy. Get a grip."

"I *have* a grip!"

"Hannah. Calm down. What are you so mad at?"

"Life," she says, and hangs up.

Palmer stares at the phone for a moment and then throws it at his desk. He still has a bit of time to get his sandwich, so he picks up his keys and heads out the door. He tries to remain calm as he drives, but already his temperature is up. He opens the window and rolls back the sunroof. Mad at *life?* What right does she have? She's smart. Her businesses have done well. She has a husband who adores her — or did, anyway, before she went and screwed around on him. She has all of her limbs. She lives in one of the best cities in the world. What could possibly be wrong with her "life"?

He parks in front of the Old Ashley Ice Cream Shoppe, a deli his father used to take them to sometimes after school. Downtown Charleston has at least a hundred places to get lunch, but Palmer still likes to patronize this place, tucked away within an old shopping center. It's shabby and unpretentious and still has posters on the walls from the '70s featuring black, white, and Asian kids having ice cream together, the kind of images Palmer remembers from his middle school math books. He orders a turkey sandwich.

Mind still polluted with exasperated thoughts of his sister and Tom, Palmer gazes out the window. There's Tom's blue Saab pulling into the parking lot. The door opens and Tom himself emerges, resplendent in a crisp white shirt.

Palmer is surprised to feel his heart lurch. Maybe Tom is lunching here, too? Not likely. Usually Tom prefers lunch places offering organic butternut squash soup and salads topped with tuna still fleshy in the center; the Old Ashley still serves sandwiches on toasted white bread and second-rate ice cream, the kind with ice crystals on the less-visited surface areas.

But as he watches, he sees that Tom is on the phone, headed to the natural foods store. Of course. He's either shopping for some sort of body product or going to speak with that Naomi woman about God knows what.

"Your sandwich is ready," the girl behind the counter calls to Palmer. He pays for it and hovers by the door. He is being ridiculous. He's done with Tom now anyway. He needs to let it lie. But it strikes him that he could just as easily go the other way with this. The sight of Tom just now has left him literally breathless — is that not love? Maybe this one time he should try to make it work. Why not just go into Earth Fare and retrieve him? I love you, he could say. OK, let's *try* this baby thing, as ridiculous as it sounds.

He's still standing in the deli, holding his bag, even as Tom leaves the grocery store, even when he looks pointedly at Palmer's car. It's hard to miss Palmer's 1971 BMW, with its bright-blue paint job and crooked bumper. Tom has been begging him to upgrade to a Prius for months, but Palmer loves the car, despite its lack of air-conditioning and the fact that he has to take it to the shop so often he is on a first-name, gift-exchange-at-Christmas, gee-you-got-a-haircut-since-last-week basis with his mechanic.

This would be the perfect time to just walk out there and fix the whole thing. Perhaps this unfamiliar thrill—caused by, of all things, a *person*—is worth sticking it out for. Maybe he'll even tell this to Tom when he opens the door. Yes, he will! He will do it. Fuck the baby. He will save them.

But he can't. Physically, he's paralyzed. So, as Palmer watches, Tom gets into his car, stares at the wheel for a moment, and, without looking over again, starts the car and drives away.

When Palmer finally emerges from the deli, squinting in the sunlight, he feels a wave of nausea, and it occurs to him that under these new circumstances, his stomach is not going to accept a turkey sandwich. He goes back in and orders a ginger ale. The girl takes his money, raising her eyebrows when he throws the still-warm, freshly wrapped sandwich into the bin. Instantly, Palmer feels guilty; someone else could have eaten it. He considers apologizing but thinks better of it. He can't help it. He's mad at life.

15

Sunday Services

WHEN HANNAH COMES downstairs dressed for church, DeWitt looks up from his paper with curiosity.

"Mexicana! All these days of pajamas, I was startin' to think you didn't have clothes."

"I'm going to church," Hannah says with a proper amount of superiority.

"Ah! I like it. All the sinners gotta crawl back at some point."

"I'm actually going for research purposes."

"Got it. Checkin' up on the old boyfriend. Keepin' tabs."

Hannah looks at DeWitt with surprise. How does he even remember whom she dated in high school? She goes into the kitchen, carrying a bag of organic coffee from Jon's favorite roaster in San Francisco; she puts the kettle on and grinds the beans. Her mother comes in to watch, leaning against the marble counter.

"Well, a nice Grande Macchiato is tasty enough for me," she says. "Mmmm. Though I can see how that would seem bourgeois to *Hannah* after living in a city like San Francisco. Now *Hannah* has sophisticated San Francisco tastes!"

"Why are you speaking about me in the third person, Mom? I'm right here."

Her mother shrugs. It's a sharp movement. A physical exclamation point.

"Anyway, I don't have sophisticated tastes. Look. This is as simple as coffee gets."

"Well. May I please try this magically simple yet delicious coffee?"

"I only made enough for—" But she stops herself. "Sure." She pours her mother a cup and ponders her next question. She hasn't brought up DeWitt's picture yet; in fact, she's mostly been avoiding both her mother and Will all week. "So, Mom. I have a question."

"Which is?"

"Are you certain you never met DeWitt before Dad left?"

Daisy picks up her cup, smells the coffee delicately, takes a sip, and scowls.

"Lord, that is strong! How do you drink this?"

"Mom?"

"Hannah, we've been over this. First of all, darling, your father is dead. He didn't leave; he drowned. So don't be all loony about it. Second, no, I did not meet Will. Never spoke to the man before the funeral." Daisy shakes her head and goes to the refrigerator for some milk. "So why are you dressed up? Do you have a lunch?"

"I'm actually going to church," Hannah says, resisting the urge to pull out the photo in question.

"You've found religion, I suppose."

"Mom." Hannah pauses to strategize. Her smartest thera-pist—the one she fired—once gave her advice on speaking with someone who is being difficult. Talk about your feelings, she told Hannah, rather than voicing a criticism of the person herself.

"You know, I'm feeling like you're really taking the offensive right now, Mom. Your words make me feel caged in, and I feel that I deserve more respect than your tone allows."

"Well, your *feelings* certainly are busy this morning."

Hannah sighs and picks up her mother's discarded cup.

"Are you drinking my coffee? That's very rude. So what church are you going to?"

"Grace."

Daisy crosses her arms. "He's married," she says. "He married Jenny White."

"I'm aware of that, Mother. And guess what? *I'm* married, too!"

"Well, what are you doing, then?"

"I just ran into him, that's all. I'm curious. He's a minister. Wouldn't *you* be?"

"I've never thought there was anything to be curious about concerning the subject of Warren Meyers. He was about the dullest boy in your class."

"Well, why don't you come with me?" Hannah asks. But as soon as the words drift from her mouth, empty as little balloons, she's sorry. There is no way Daisy, with her relentless curiosity, will be able to let her daughter go to Warren's church alone and unobserved.

"I certainly don't want to go to *Grace*," Daisy says initially, with feigned haughtiness. Daisy and DeWitt are members of St. Michael's, Charleston's oldest and most conservative Episcopal church. They rarely go, but pay enough tithes to make sure they have a pew permanently reserved in their name.

"OK, well, I'm about ready to leave." Hannah gathers the coffee items and puts them in the sink. Out of the corner of her eye, she can see her mother is picking imaginary lint from her sleeve.

One.

Two.

"You know, I have so much to do in the garden . . ."

Three.

Four.

"And that dinner party to plan . . ."

Five.

"But I suppose I *am* a little curious as to what they've done with that parish building. I'd be very surprised if things were up to code."

"I'm leaving in five minutes."

"All right," Daisy says, getting up. "I'll drive you. Just let me find something appropriate to wear."

Although Grace Episcopal Church is just a pleasant walk from the DeWitt House, they drive together in Daisy's Ford Taurus. As Charleston's tiny streets were originally designed to comfortably fit one horse-pulled carriage and perhaps a hoopskirt or two, the city's ice-cream-colored walls are just inches from Hannah's window. Daisy drives with a girlish carelessness that explains why her car is pocked with so many candy-hued dings.

In just under three minutes, they are in Grace's parking lot, not far from a starched and ribboned throng at the church door. Daisy gets out of the car and scans the crowd.

"Are you coming?"

"You know, I've just got to call Jon back first."

"He called you? When?"

"Last night."

This is a lie. Since she has arrived, Jon has not called, e-mailed, or so much as answered the phone during any of Hannah's countless attempts to reach him.

"Well, tell him I say hello!" her mother says with a smile, then whirls around and throws her hand up to greet friends she sees in the distance.

Hannah presses the silent phone to her ear as she watches her mother through the window. Daisy speaks to her friends animatedly, waving her hands and laughing. There are a couple of people in the crowd even Hannah recognizes from high school, toting small children. And, by the time her eyes land on the shining tresses of Jenny White-Meyers, it occurs to her, not for the first time, just how bad of an idea this second visit to Grace may have been.

Hannah flips the phone closed, suddenly shamed by the pretense of speaking to the husband she's only pretending to have. She gets out of the car and walks over to her mother.

"Here she is!" Daisy chirps. She's speaking to a group of Charleston ladies, mothers of her classmates. They are all so much older now. But then, she thinks, so am I.

"Hello, Hannah," one of them says. "We hear from your mother that you're doing very well out in San Francisco!"

No, not really, Hannah is tempted to say. I'm a total sniveling mess.

"Yes. Thank you."

"And she says you have a new company?"

"Yes, that's right." She glances at her mother — how far should she go with this?

"And what sort of business is it? Is it some sort of shop?"

"It's sex toys," Daisy says flatly. "My daughter is selling sex toys. Apparently it's the newest thing."

"Really?" Tommy Nelson's mother asks. She leans forward.

"Yes. We're going to have a party to sell them. Like those housewives do with the Tupperware."

Hannah feels a tap on her shoulder and looks up to see a tall, severely pretty woman. "I'm Georgia," she whispers with a grin. "Be sure to put me on the list."

The group disperses to go inside.

"Mom? What are you doing?"

"Just helping your business," she says. "All right. I have no idea how they work the pews here. Looks like mass chaos, which doesn't surprise me. Let's go find ourselves a couple of seats."

The service is like every other Episcopalian service Hannah can remember: dull, belabored, with incessant standing and kneeling. Warren's sermon, though well-written, is slightly academic and thoroughly boring. Before he speaks, the choirmaster is called on to turn up his mike. The congregation fidgets. Someone's cell phone goes off, but no one bothers to silence it. A child screams and throws a hymnal in the aisle.

Hannah spends the first half of the service much as she always did when coerced into going to church: she thinks about sex. Most of the imaginary sex is with her own husband in her own bed, but some of it is with Warren, who now stands 150 feet in front of her in his ecclesiastical robe. What would it be like to touch him now? Different? Somehow she perversely thought taking Communion from Warren might be a turn-on — kneeling in front of her old boyfriend, having him place a piece of bread on her tongue. But the reality is a soggy wafer jammed in her face with no eye contact. She shuffles back to her pew. More overwrought hymns and indecipherable lessons. Finally, the service ends, and Warren joylessly leads the procession to the doors of the church.

"Thanks be to God," he calls out.

The crash of the organ.

"Well," Daisy says, "that was a nice nap."

"Mom, I'm just going to quickly say hi, OK?"

Hannah drifts through the crowd, which is loud with chatter, heavy with failing deodorant and perfume. There is a line to talk to the ministry. She watches Warren greet an old man—no one she knows, but he seems to be in distress. He speaks to Warren, his spotted, bald head bobbing, his vein-scarred right hand jerking back and forth. Warren puts his hand on the man's shoulder, which immediately calms him. Hannah wonders what the man is saying. Warren just listens and nods, mostly, barely talking at all.

She stands at a distance, considering whether or not to join the line. It seems wrong, somehow, getting in line to speak to the person she lost her virginity to, no matter how long ago it was. A different century, even.

"Hi, Hannah." The voice. So Southern, yet so nasal. So sweet, yet so completely disingenuous.

"Jenny. How are you?"

"Oh, so great! Just—fantastic."

Jenny White. A woman with all the depth of a wading pool. How could he have picked her? Do perfect bone structure and breasts (and they are, especially up close) really make up for a lifetime of dim conversation?

"I'm just loving working with your brother, I have to say."

169

"Great, I'm glad to hear it."

"He really is such a gem."

Hannah smiles politely, choosing not to tell Jenny that the gem is currently being an asshole.

"Have you told Warren you're in town?"

"I think he saw me."

"Oh," Jenny says. Then, after a moment: "These are my girls."

Of course, Hannah is already aware of the tiny beings flanking the wife of Warren Meyers. She is aware of them the same way she always notices children: small, bright figures that remain out of her range of immediate sight. Angling her gaze downward, she is met by four eyes—two brown like Jenny's, and two the color of worn pencil lead.

Many women speak of the desire to have children. Hannah doesn't have a bevy of female friends, but several of her acquaintances from business school spoke often of ticking clocks, of the problems in balancing work and family. Hannah has always seen herself as distinct from these women. She does not want children's voices bouncing off the kitchen floor, their small feet pattering on the tile, their little fingerprints on her windows and walls.

So it is a surprise, these kids. They cause Hannah to feel something strange—it's the maternal instinct, she supposes. That thing that happens when you look at a child and think, Oh, right. She could be *mine*. "Hello, girls."

They're gaping at her; she realizes it must be because she's wearing a different style of clothing from the other women: a fitted nylon skirt with zippers and a cashmere shirt. It hadn't even crossed her mind before; it takes the eyes of children to make her see just how much she stands out here.

"Well, I guess I'll get in line," Hannah says. "You know, talk to the 'man.'"

Jenny gives her a small smile. There. That's how she's changed since high school, Hannah notes. Her smile is smaller.

"You in town long?"

"Not if I can help it."

"Oh, it's a nice town." The words are eerily familiar.

"You sound like Emily Webb."

"Who?"

"You know. From *Our Town*."

"Oh." Another blank stare.

"Thornton Wilder? It used to be one of Warren's favorites. Remember? He rips it off, like, eight times in his book."

"What?" Just then, one of the girls tugs Jenny's hand. "Not now, honey. I'm sorry, *whose* book?"

"Warren's." Something is not lining up here. "*The End of the End*. You know . . . right?"

Her face says she doesn't.

"Oh, well. It was a little thing. Something he wrote a long time ago. I think."

"How long?"

"Um . . . I'm not sure."

"But you've read it?"

"A long time ago," Hannah repeats. She doesn't get it. Warren wrote the book in college. Maybe a little after. But Jenny was *there*. She was with him. Could she really have not known?

Jenny gives a hollow laugh. "I guess I'll have to ask him about it."

"It was just a little thing."

"He never told me."

Hannah bows out of this conversation. Obviously Warren has lied to Jenny, and other people's lies make her tired. She steps away and surrenders to the line, still fairly long. As she waits, she wonders how Jenny really feels about being a minister's wife. Someone that pretty could have been any Charleston man's wife, save maybe Palmer's. But Jenny White picked Warren. She *picked* him. Blissfully buried in the brown-and-green hills of Northern California, Hannah never considered this possibility, but of course that's what happened. Jenny picked Warren in high school, probably while they were still chatting on the Nelsons' beach-house porch, during the time Hannah still thought he was hers. It's all so clear now. Suddenly any guilt she felt about the book thing dissipates. Jenny White isn't stupid. She never was. If anything, Hannah muses, I was stupid for underestimating her.

It's her turn now with Reverend Meyers. He smiles at Hannah carefully.

"Hi," she says. "That was a nice God talk you gave."

"Thank you."

"So? Here I am at services. Even had the pleasure of talking to your wife."

"Great."

"She said she'd never read your book, by the way. Is that true?"

Hannah is pleased to note that she has succeeded in making Warren lose his saintly composure for the moment. He twirls a curl with his finger. "You told her about the book?"

"I just mentioned it. I thought she would have read it by now."

"No," he says. "She hasn't."

"Well, I don't get it. Why don't you show it to her now?"

"I . . ." He clears his throat. "Did you like the sermon?"

"I just said I did. Warren, what's going on?"

He puts his finger under his collar. "I never showed it to her because it was bad. Anyway, thanks for coming. It's always nice to see a new face in the crowd."

He looks over her shoulder, as if to beckon the next member of the congregation along.

"Wait. Who's this person you said could help? And please don't say Jesus."

"It's my mother, since you ask. I thought she might be able to talk some sense into you about letting this thing go. But now I've got to explain to my wife why I published a book and never told her about it. So, you know, thanks. Thanks for that."

"No offense, Minister, but you're the one who lied." He glares at her. "Anyway, I've already talked to your mother. As you know."

"I think—" He squares up, looking over Hannah's head.

"Hello, Warren." Daisy has breezed past the line and come to stand next to them. "What a nice, calm sermon."

"Thank you, Mrs. DeWitt."

"So we have Hannah home for a spell. Isn't it a treat?"

"It sure is."

As Daisy smiles, Hannah can't help but marvel at how pretty she is—even in Goodwill Elvis lapels. Pretty, Hannah ponders. Jenny's pretty. Mom's pretty. Why am I not pretty? But now her mother's face has become considerably less pretty. She's still smiling, but it's a frightening smile. Her eyes are too wide, and her teeth are slightly clenched.

"Mom?"

"Oh, look," she growls. "Virginia."

"Hi, there." Virginia appears in an Indian silk tunic, white pants, and feather dream-catcher earrings. "Hannah, good to see you again. Daisy, it's been a while."

As they stand there, the four of them, Hannah can't help but notice the way they're positioned—she is across from Warren; Virginia across from her mother. A perfect, awkward square.

"Mom," Hannah finally mumbles, "I was just going to catch up with Virginia and Warren for a while."

"Ah." A visible look of distaste. "Well, fine, then. I suppose you can walk home?"

"Sure."

"Watch for nails, dear," she says. "Don't want to have to extract any more metal from your head, at least for the moment. And, Virginia, it was lovely to see you. Such a brave color."

Virginia purses her lips. "Thank you."

"Well. I'm off!"

They watch as Daisy strides purposefully away, a sleepy gathering of pigeons and squirrels scattering on either side of her path.

"Good Lord," Virginia mutters.

"I'm going to find Jenny," Warren says. "You two catch up."

Virginia looks at Hannah. "So?" she asks. "Warren said you have something to ask me?"

Whenever Hannah is about to learn something she doesn't want to know—which, lately, has been too often—she experiences a distinct physical sensation. A prickle. Like now: even though it's warm out, the hair on her arms goes vertical.

"It's about a party," Hannah says.

"What party?"

"The Nelsons' party."

"The Nelsons?" Virginia snorts. "Who talks to the Nelsons anymore?"

"I mean, a long time ago. The one party you, Mom, and Dad were at together."

Virginia shrugs. "I don't know."

"I found a picture. You're in it, and so are my parents."

"Well, sweetheart, we went to parties."

"But DeWitt's in it. And my mother said she didn't know him then."

Virginia regards her cautiously. "Well, I don't know anything about that."

"I guess I'm trying to figure things out."

"Do you have it? This picture?"

Hannah reaches into her bag and finds the envelope. Virginia takes it, glances at Hannah, and looks at it again.

"Well. Weren't we pretty," she says.

"Yes. You were. But what about DeWitt? Do you know why he was..."

Hannah doesn't finish, because for a very brief moment, something has come over Virginia, as if she can't help it. She brings the image closer and closer, until the picture is nearly touching her face.

"Virginia?"

Virginia shakes her head.

"Sorry, Hannah. I—" She composes herself and hands the photo back to Hannah. "I don't remember."

"Warren thought you might."

"Well, Warren was wrong," she says quickly. "Listen—I'll see you later, all right? We'll get a drink or something. I've got to run." She rushes off, disappearing behind the church.

Hannah watches her go, her mind clicking and grinding like the inner wheels of a clock. Of course, she thinks.

Virginia and Buzz were together when they were younger. Hannah always knew that. Everyone knew that. But now it's clear: Virginia never got over him. *Warren's mother was in love with Hannah's father.* It's not the whole picture—she knows it's not. Still, she feels the truth getting closer.

Hannah raises her hand to Warren and Jenny, then heads home through the graveyard. She doesn't bother to look to see if they're waving back.

16

Something Else Hannah Just Remembered

I N THE CAR very late on a weekend night. The road was empty because everyone else was somewhere better. In their houses. Warm and safe in bed.

Palmer's head on Hannah's shoulder. Palmer was sleeping; Hannah was pretending. This was before everything. They were all smaller.

Virginia's were the best parties. The children were left unsupervised, and there were always costume themes. Gatsby (all whites, champagne in a makeshift fountain); King Arthur (the dining table dragged out to the garden); Woodstock (headbands, clouds of bitter, earthy smoke). That night Daisy had gone out dressed as a man, while Buzz wore a tennis dress of his wife's. The hair on his legs scared Hannah, made her cry.

It was wilder than usual. She and her brother had spent the night in the garden, fighting with the Nelson boys.

Let us kiss you for a dollar.

No!

Let us—

No!

Palmer chipped his tooth for her.

It's just ridiculous, her mother said.

What now?

These parties. You're unbearable.

Why?

I might as well come with a phantom. That's what it's like. I'm always alone.

How are you alone? I'm with you.

Off in the corner.

I'm cornered?

You know who I'm talking about. You'll go back to her. I know it. Might as well get ready now. You'll leave me someday.

We're just friends, Daisy. I keep telling you.

You and your corners.

You're drunk.

Do you know what it's like, being your wife?

A constant party?

Ha.

A warm bath.
No.
Then what?
It's like being married to air.

A car approached and passed, flooding the family's space with a pause of light. Buzz turned around to look at his children. Hannah shut her eyes as quickly as she could, feigning sleep. Soon enough, it claimed her.

17

Warren, Again

IN HER NEW life, the first person Hannah sees every morning is Mr. Mitchell. Everyone else is always gone. Even DeWitt
has vacated the premises by the time she rises, and he doesn't
even really have a job, other than visiting his various properties to
make sure other people are working. But she's been sleeping late.
She sees no reason not to. At first she made an attempt to fit into
the routine, but the truth is, she has no routine. So it serves her
well to pass as much of the morning as she can in bed; that way,
she's closer to afternoon, which is closer to night, which means
another day here has come and gone.

The thing is, Hannah's not a sleeper. By ten, she can't stand
it anymore—the light streaming in the windows, the insistent
rustle of the magnolia leaves outside. Every morning, the same
thoughts drive her out of bed: It's a nice day, and here you are,
an adulterous lazy blob. The world is moving on without you.
Get up.

This morning she descends the staircase in a pair of high school flannel pajamas printed with various images of Madonna. Her body is roughly the same size as it was then; apparently her mind also.

"Good morning," Mr. Mitchell says, watching Hannah fumble with the coffee. It's become their unspoken tradition as of late to have coffee together. He seems to like Jon's rigid French-press recipe.

"Hi."

"Another big sleep?"

"I was reading."

"Mmm-hmm."

"Hey, how are your kids?"

"Good. One of the grandkids went to Harvard. He's a doctor now."

"Congratulations."

"So you doing OK, then?"

"Sure, I'm great." Out of the corner of her eye, she catches a glimpse of herself in the hall mirror. Her hair is standing three inches off her head, and her bandage is frayed and dirty. "You know."

"Sure."

"Mr. Mitchell," Hannah says, "you knew my father, right?"

"Sure. Dr. Legare. My sister's doc and my wife's, too. Best doctor in town."

"So you remember what he looks like?"

"Sure."

"You ever see anyone in town who looks like that?"

Mr. Mitchell drains his cup carefully and puts it down. "Can't say that I have."

"Maybe out on Johns Island?"

"I haven't seen your dad since he died."

"Since he disappeared, you mean."

"Yeah, I haven't seen him since then." He says this pleasantly. "Have you?"

"Thought I did a couple of times, but it wasn't him."

"Well, we see what we want to see."

"You think I'm crazy?"

"I think we all have ideas. Personally, I think your dad's in heaven."

"I don't believe in heaven."

"Well, that's too bad for you." He picks up his toolbox. "All right. I'm going up. Somebody's comin' up on the porch. Why don't you go see."

He leaves the room. Hannah wrestles her hair back into a ponytail and peeks out the French doors. Warren Meyers is standing on the piazza, dwarfed by the marble columns. She tries to dart back before he sees her, but either she's too slow or he's too quick.

"Hannah," he says, knocking on the window. When she opens the door, he looks her up and down with an uncharacteristic expression of amusement. "I remember those pajamas."

"Yeah." She steps aside to let him in. "Seems I'm stuck in a different era in multiple ways."

Warren doesn't answer.

"You want some coffee?" Is this my life now? she wonders. Sitting around her parents' mansion in her Madonna pajamas, offering people coffee?

"Sure."

She decides to make a fresh pot, mostly because she doesn't feel like talking just now. He sits at the table silently as she grinds, boils, and stirs. Even during the three-minute steeping process, they say nothing.

"Let's go to the solarium," she finally offers, breaking the silence.

Much as Hannah dislikes this house, she's always enjoyed being able to say that. *Let's go to the solarium.* It's not even her favorite room — it's hot and bright and no one looks good in all that light — but she enjoys working it into sentences, along with "cupola" and "hothouse." Thus, when people come over to visit Hannah, they tend to find themselves in the least comfortable parts of the house.

She leads, holding their cups. Coffee sloshes on the floor. They sit on sofas across from each other, surrounded by her mother's jungle of exotic plants. There was a time when they would sit together, draped over each other, nested in books.

"I guess I'll talk first," Hannah finally says. "Can you believe the size of that rubber plant?"

Warren frowns. "I just wanted to come by and apologize for being short with you yesterday. About the book and Jenny."

"That's OK."

"I should have shown it to her."

"Probably."

"It was just — back then I was still really pissed at you."

Hannah pulls her knees up. "Glad to see you're not anymore."

"No, I'm still pissed. Just not as much."

"That's good, I guess."

"But I didn't want her to know that I still thought about you. I wrote an entire novella about you, for Chrissakes."

"Aren't ministers not supposed to say things like that?"

He doesn't answer. They hold their coffee cups aloft, like little shields.

"Are you going to show it to her now?"

"I threw out all the copies."

Hannah almost says, Oh, wait, I have a copy with me. But then he would know how pathetically much it means to her. And, worse, he might give her copy to Jenny White.

"Anyway," she says, "sorry I brought it up."

"Well, sorry I was rude."

"Stop being so Southern. It's fine. You were feeling rude, so you *were*."

"Yeah, well. What's done is done, I guess."

"You know," she says, "I've never gotten that expression. That, and 'It is what it is.' What 'it' are they even talking about?"

She can tell he thinks she's being difficult now. Well, people are difficult, Warren. Sorry. Deal with it. She lies back on the sofa, arms over her head, wrinkling her nose at the smell of old coffee and sleep.

"So I talked with your mom," she says.

"Yeah?"

"We barely talked at all, really. I just showed her the picture."

Warren plays with a succulent on the table. He breaks off a leaf and kneads it between his fingers.

"I didn't know that she was in love with my dad."

Warren looks up, surprised. "Is that what she said?"

"No, I just figured it out."

"Huh."

"Why didn't you ever tell me?" Hannah asks. "Don't you think it's kind of screwed up that you didn't tell me?"

He grins. His teeth are startlingly white against his tan. He's wearing the old uniform today—faded jeans, boots, a flannel shirt. She feels the urge to reach out and touch the cloth. "What's done is done," he says. "It is what it is."

"If it's true, then that's just sad."

"Why?" Warren is indignant. "It's important to love some-one."

"Even if you can't have that person?"

He destroys another leaf. Then another.

"This plant needs water."

"It's a cactus."

"It's not prickly, though."

"It's in the cactus family."

"I think caring for someone is never a bad thing, even if the situation you idealize, I don't know, doesn't happen for you."

"You sound like a self-help book."

"I think anything that gets people through the day is a good thing."

"Like God?"

"Like God."

"What happened to you?" Hannah asks. "How can you believe in all that?"

His leg jiggles. Up. Down. He pushes the plant toward her.

"I don't care if this is a cactus. It's still dying."

"That's a shame," Hannah says. "It's really a very nice plant."

So they end up alone together in her closet.

This is not Hannah's fault or even her idea. Usually it would be—she knows she's entirely capable of such things. But today all she does is say, "Wait down here. I'll go get more photos of your mom. There are some good ones in a box upstairs." And so she leaves him in the solarium, where he is supposed to wait, but then she takes too long. She changes her clothes (necessary) and puts some makeup on (vanity) and then discovers that there are not just one or two pictures of Virginia but scores of them. She turns on the lantern and starts to shuffle through and edit them, and then there he is, saying hi and ducking through the door.

"I thought you were downstairs," she says.

"So it really *is* still here."

"Yeah. Nowhere is still here."

"I forgot you called it that."

He nudges the pillows with his foot. She slides the pile of photos over. "Look." She spreads them out, a fan of images. In most of them, his mother's not even with anyone. She's alone.

"You know, I always sort of prayed you'd be back in here someday," she says.

"Ha." He taps her knee with his foot. "So you do pray sometimes?"

"Fine, OK. You got me."

"Should I sit?"

"I don't know."

"Me neither."

"Well, probably not," Hannah says. He bends over closer to the photographs. "We could bring these downstairs."

But Warren is suddenly entranced by the pictures of his mother. "Oh, look, Hannah. Look at these."

"I know."

"Can you turn up that light?"

"Of course."

He sits.

* * *

It's a tricky substance, the familiar. Resilient as tar. Hannah thinks of Palmer and Tom and her mother and DeWitt. Their familiar routines have almost become their religion. They wake up, have the same breakfast, drive or bike or walk the same way to work. DeWitt checks the stock market on his computer and eats his bacon; Daisy plans a new way to save money; Palmer grooms himself or tends to his plants.

Hannah's father had no familiar. He seemed to reject the entire idea. Sometimes he would be around, sometimes he would not. He would forget birthdays, then bring home roses or toys on an afternoon of no remark. When it was time for dinner, they would listen for the door. Would he be here tonight, making them laugh with stories of his patients and turning his napkin into a puppet and feeding Tucker at the table even though that was *against the rules?* Or would it be a quiet, fatherless meal, plates of disappointed beef, their mother snapping at them to keep their elbows off the table? You never knew. That's what made it interesting. Sometimes bad interesting, sometimes good. Every day was devoid of prediction.

Now she and Warren are in their familiar place. He sits on his old pillow and leans over to look at the pictures by the lamplight. His brows knit in concentration. He is excavating, his knee just inches from hers.

"Look at this one," he says. His mother is laughing, her knees drawn up.

He should never have come, she thinks. I should never have let him in the door. What was she thinking? Oh, she knew exactly what she was thinking. She knew he would follow her. She came to Nowhere, because.

He doesn't look at her when he does it. That's what she means by the familiar. It's a trap. I'm sorry, Warren, she wants to say. But it's inevitable. You don't want to do it, but you have to. Even if, while it's happening, you're so guilty you can't even look over. You have to look at pictures of your own mother as your hand reaches up under your old girlfriend's shirt. You have a wife, you have daughters. Still, you put your palm flat on my waist, as if you're pushing open a door. You have to make sure it still feels the same way. Does it? It does, it does. Thank God it still does. We are both still here, not too old, still alive. Familiar.

Still it's wrong, somehow. All wrong. She's with Warren, and it's delicious. He's kissing her just like he used to. But it just doesn't fit anymore. The person she wants to be with here is her husband. Jon. Where is Jon?

"Stop," she says.

"I'm sorry."

"No, it's OK. But you don't want to do that."

"Oh, God. What am I doing here? I can't be here." He gets up too quickly and knocks his head. The smack shakes the roof. Holding his temple, he hurries out into the bedroom, where the light blazes in.

Back out here, they are old again. Graying. Pale. Thinning skin pulled to the ground by insistent gravity.

"Nothing happened," she says.

"I think my head may be bleeding."

"But you and I shouldn't be together. Seriously, we shouldn't even see each other at all. I'm a real fuck-up, Warren. I'll fuck everything up."

"Fucking hell." He looks at the bit of blood on his fingers.

"I'm sorry."

"It's my fault for coming over."

"We didn't do anything. Pretty much. You don't have to worry."

"God."

"You rubbed my back. We kissed. Something you'd done a thousand times already. Just lump it into the high school stuff."

He shakes his head.

"Look, whatever happened in there—which is nothing, sort of—just know it's my fault."

"Hannah."

"It's true. I—" Hannah puts her hand out and moves it back and forth, as if it is a fish swimming. "I wander."

"No."

"I ruin things. I don't even know why. I have a problem with faith."

Here Warren starts laughing. In fact, for the situation they are in at the moment, Hannah believes he's laughing inappropriately hard.

"What?"

He takes the photos he's still holding and tosses them into the air. Images of Hannah's family and Warren's mother rain down on the bed.

"Hannah." He puts his hand on her shoulder and points to the photos, randomly scattered, a collage of her memory. "Look at these. You've hidden this shrine to your dad for over twenty years. Twenty years. Jesus fucking Christ."

"You really need to stop swearing like that. One day I'll tell on you, and you'll get fired. Which I secretly think is a good idea. But still."

He picks up one of the pictures—his mother on the beach—and pockets it.

"You're troubled. I'll give you that. But don't think you're unfaithful, Hannah. I mean, think about it. I'm a little jealous, actually. You're the most faithful person I know."

He twirls a curl on the back of his head. She knew he would. Familiar. He stumbles down the stairs, leaving her alone again.

See you later, then, maybe, Hannah thinks to herself. See you. My lovely, fallen priest.

18

Palmer and His Sister

THE DOG KNOWS something is wrong. Palmer has never taken a huge liking to Rumpus; since Tucker, he hasn't allowed himself to get attached to an animal. His profession has trained him to see them as specimens to be spayed, euthanized, or, for a little while at least, healed. Rumpus is a nervous dog, and odd. But she's not stupid. Sensing discord, she runs around in circles, emitting her horrible, mute bark. She has also left a neat pile of shit in the bedroom, an act that usually would infuriate Palmer, if the dog hadn't pointedly done it next to Tom's side of the bed.

In an effort to erase all of Tom's remnants, Palmer cleans. The house isn't dirty. It can't really even be described as slightly dingy. It couldn't be; Palmer has a maid named Jolie who scrubs the house every week using a near-lethal combination of Ajax, ammonia, and Pine-Sol. Usually she does a good job, but the later the night gets, the more Palmer notices the spots she has missed. There is a speck of green mold around the sink faucet. A fine layer of dust coats the area behind the television.

He pulls out the rags and the bucket and mops the floors, sending Rumpus to her area under the kitchen table. He vacuums the sofas, washes the windows, strips the bed, even though the sheets have already been changed. When the landline rings at ten thirty, Palmer has just begun a reorganization of the linen closet. Pillowcases should be at eye level, not above! And where are the labels? He needs to buy Jolie a label maker. How can anyone cope?

"Hello?"

"So you see that I got my things out," Tom says.

"Yes."

"I left some toiletries, but you can set them aside for me, can't you?"

"Of course."

There is a pause.

"I'm only calling to tell you that you're an asshole. Not only that. You're just sad."

Blankets up top? Or the extra pillows?

"A sad, sad man. I'm glad you ended things. I can't be with someone as emotionally closed as you."

"Where are you living?"

"Always practical, aren't you?"

"Where?"

"I'm moving in with Naomi."

"Why?"

"We're sort of friends. I'm thinking that I might do this kid thing anyway. I have the money."

"Naomi is a hippie pothead loser. She's a *checkout* girl, Tom."

Tom gives a sad laugh. "You know, I saw you at the deli. I saw your car and I thought, I should go over there."

Palmer doesn't reply.

"And then I realized, no. No! I always go over. I always make the effort, and I'm so sick of it."

"I'm sorry."

"Why didn't you just come over, Palmer?"

Flat sheets *above* fitted.

"Palmer?"

"You drove away before I could get to you."

There is a crackling sound, as if Tom has just opened a candy bar. Palmer is suddenly hungry.

"You're really staying at Naomi's? It's a little pathetic."

"Really? Pathetic? Me? Well, let's see. I'm about to dine with a nice woman and have an interesting conversation about the declining state of our country. And you are . . . what? Off to watch *Top Chef* alone? With that fucked-up dog?"

"I—"

"Good luck, Palmer. Good-bye."

Palmer puts the phone down and stares at the closet for a good five minutes. Then he goes in the living room, puts Rumpus in his lap, and calls his sister. The dog wriggles away.

"Hi," she says. "Don't be mean to me. I've been really nice to everyone today and have done nothing wrong."

"What are you doing?"

"Hiding. Drinking wine in my room."

"Want to come over? Have a drink?"

"I thought you said I was supposed to do a cleanse."

"Tom moved out." The words echo off the walls. There is the

sound of rustling sheets on the other end of the line. "Are you really drinking in bed?"

"I'm no liar."

"Gross."

"You're such a dickhead." She sighs. "OK. I'll sneak out of here and take the Earth Cruiser. Just give me twenty minutes."

He hangs up and cleans some more. Rumpus sits in the living room, staring with determination at the back corner.

"The door, Rumpus. If he comes back, it'll probably be through the door."

"Palmer?"

Hannah has let herself in through the back. Before he can get to the kitchen, he hears an enormous clatter, and comes in to see that she has excavated a large bottle of vodka, vermouth, and olives and is now rummaging through the newly rearranged and polished glassware.

"Make yourself comfortable."

"I didn't lock my bike. It's in the back. But it's an ugly piece of shit, so I think it'll be OK."

She throws ice and vodka into the shaker.

"I don't really drink hard liquor," he says.

"You asked me over for a drink."

"I meant wine."

"Palmer. This is an emergency."

"All right."

He watches his sister shake, swish, and pour. She's surprisingly graceful at this. What else is she good at? Palmer wonders. I seem to have missed most of my sister's life.

She slides him a drink without spilling.

"So what happened?"

"I don't know. I just wasn't feeling it. You know?"

"Not really. I feel everything." She takes a long gulp. "Is it this baby thing?"

"It's more than that. He says I'm not emotionally open or something."

"And this is news?"

Palmer wipes the counter down. "You think I'm not emotionally open?" he asks.

"You're a Southern male with the clamps on. Plus you're a Legare. Plus you're sort of a DeWitt. Of course you're not open. You've always been like this. Honestly, I was proud of you for lasting this long."

"So you think this failure is my fault? Again?"

"If you want to be with someone like Tom, you're going to have to open up a little. Yeah."

"Like how?"

"Play his game. Go to yoga with him."

"Screw you."

"Therapy."

"I'm going to vomit."

"Don't vomit. Drink more. It's the Southern way."

"You know," Palmer says, "the weird part is I saw him the other day. I was really going to get him back. But I couldn't. Literally, I was frozen to the spot."

"The clamps. I told you."

"Maybe it's for the best."

"Not if you love the guy," Hannah says, thoughtfully chewing a toothpick.

"I don't know if I do," he says. "I love some things."

"Like what?"

"The way he plays tennis. His taste in furniture."

"Palmer, that's not love."

"Right, so. Better to let it go, right?"

Hannah responds by finishing her drink.

"He'll come back," she says finally. "Just don't call him."

"Is that what you're doing with Jon?"

"Of course not. I call him every day. But you don't see him here with me, do you?"

"Good point."

"That's what I'm telling you." She's beginning to slur slightly.

"But I would never call him in the first place," Palmer says. "Why would I call a man who doesn't want to talk to me?"

"See, that's the difference. That's the difference between you and me."

Palmer lifts up the shaker. There's a little bit more. He pours it in her glass.

"I think there are a few other differences between us besides that."

"I know. Sometimes I wonder if we're even related at all."

"We are, though."

"I know."

Palmer watches, slightly disgusted, as she jams her hand into the olive jar. He takes his drink and goes out to the living room. She follows. He sits in a large burnt-orange chair he's never much liked, and she flops on the suede couch, propping her feet on the coffee table.

"Can you at least take your shoes off, please?"

"Anal bastard."

Palmer flips on the television. The Dow: a jagged red line,

sliding downward. Images of terrified bankers and Bush looking blankly from side to side. Palmer flips it off.

"This economy. We're all so screwed."

"Are you guys going to be OK?"

"Sure. People always need animal doctors, right?"

"Right."

"Though people are leaving their pets in their houses when they foreclose. We've had four turned in this week."

"That's sick." She puts her glass on the ground. It falls over. "Jesus. I don't even like animals, but that's really sick, just leaving them like that."

Palmer thinks he sees a hint of tears, which makes him uncomfortable. He changes the subject.

"Tom might be in trouble, though. A lot of his projects are on hold."

"See? He'll be back if you want him. He'll have to. This crash could be good for you."

"Always the delusional optimist."

"Shut up."

"What about you? What's going to happen with your business?"

"Oh, people always need exorbitantly priced sex toys. Right?"

"So you're screwed, too."

"Probably. We have the apartment, though. It's all paid off."

"Well, you can't sell it now. What are you going to do, build a wall down the middle and split it?"

"Totally. A soundproof wall so I don't have to hear the sex."

Palmer laughs. "You're funnier when you're drunk."

"You're nicer."

"Do you think DeWitt will be all right?"

"Sure. The really rich people always make out OK."

She stretches her arms over her head and closes her eyes. Her shirt is ripped, revealing some of her bra. It's purple, trimmed with a bit of black lace. Her brown hair is wiry and electric. Her mouth is too small, and her nose is crooked like their father's. Her eyes are enormous. They are observant to the point of prying. Lying on the couch with her spectacular limbs splayed, she looks like a Terry Richardson interpretation of an eighteenth-century courtesan: sad, homely, seductive, and slightly dirty. He's hit by a pang of love for her. A feeling only understood between a brother and a sister. She has to be the most irritating woman on Earth. He often hates her, truly. But if he could gather her up and lock her in a safe to keep her away from anything else that could possibly damage her, he would.

Her eyes snap open. "Do you know what they did with Dad's boat?" she asks suddenly.

"What?"

"Dad's boat. I never knew what DeWitt did with it."

"It's still in the carriage house."

"Really? Still there? Have you ever used it?"

"No. Well, once. I took it to the Rockville Regatta in college. But it wasn't a good idea. It felt—"

"Wrong."

"I don't even know why we still have the damned thing."

"I'm glad, though."

Palmer braces himself. They are three and a half drinks in, the perfect time for Hannah to bring up her awful theory. Instead she rolls over and looks at Rumpus.

"Men are such fucking dogs," she says.

"What do you mean?"

"I don't know. Assholes."

"Who?" He is surprised to hear his voice rising. "What do you mean?"

"Dad, leaving us. You, being an ass to this guy who clearly loves you. Jon, screwing Denise."

"I work with dogs, Hannah. I work with them all day."

"So you should know." She makes an imaginary gun with her fingers, points it at Rumpus, and shoots. "Dogs."

"Men are not dogs." Palmer feels himself growing too warm again. "Look at that one. She's been sitting there, waiting for Tom for hours. Tom doesn't even like her. Then he leaves, and she just sits there, thinking of nothing else except When is my owner coming back? You can club her in the head, she'll still wait. You can be shot in the head, and your dog won't run away. It'll just sit there with you, waiting to—"

"Die," she says.

"I don't know. I just don't think it's a very appropriate saying. A bad idiom. Men can be assholes. But there's nothing more faithful than a dog."

"That's funny," Hannah says. "Warren just told me that I am the most faithful person he knows."

"Well."

"Well, woof," Hannah says. "Get me more vodka."

"Don't throw up. This is a five-thousand-dollar couch."

"Just get it."

He goes back into the kitchen. As often happens with vodka, his mood has gone dark.

I should just tell her, he thinks. I should tell her everything. It's me, Hannah. Dad drowned because of me.

He already regrets the hangover he will have tomorrow. So

what is the point of being drunk? Still, he mixes the drinks. He is not as good at this as Hannah; his martinis come out full of ice chips. Tom would laugh, he thinks. It doesn't matter. By the time he brings them back to the living room, his sister's eyes are closed.

"You asleep?"

"Room. Spinning."

He puts the drinks on the table and pulls the cashmere blanket over her.

"No, tha's OK. I'll just wait a minute and ride the Cruiser home."

"Don't be an idiot."

"The pink Cruiser." She giggles. "Someone blew up her tires."

"Shut up. Sleep."

He watches her for a while as her breath slows.

"Do you think we'll be fucked up like this forever?" she whispers.

"Sleep."

He takes the drinks to the kitchen, dumps them in the sink, turns out the lights, and uses the remote to switch off the gas fireplace. He whistles for Rumpus, but she's back in her corner, where she clearly intends to stay.

19

Jon, Again

HANNAH WAKES UP to the phone ringing. The air is cold. She opens her eyes, greeted by suede fabric and fish swimming in the fireplace, and begins a mental list.

Things I Need to Stop Doing

Drinking
Sleeping on sofas
Waking up in drool
Avoiding work
Kissing old boyfriends
Drinking

She covers her eyes. Some people merely get nausea when hungover. Others, crippling headaches. Hannah gets both of those things, as well as a feeling of deep remorse and anxiety, inevitably resulting in the laughable resolution to never drink again.

Reluctantly, she leaves her horizontal position and takes an investigative walk around. Rumpus is missing, as is Palmer. Her poor brother must be at work. She stumbles to the bathroom to wash her face, smearing on as many of the expensive products as she can: Kiehl's, Jurlique, Malin + Goetz. She goes to the kitchen and helps herself to some sparkling water. She makes a cappuccino in the shiny machine—one of three caffeine-producing devices—and walks around the house. She looks at the steam shower with the tiny blue sparkling tiles, the plunge pool, the media room. God, she envies Palmer. Such a comfortable, ordered life!

The coffee is not helping much with the anxiety. Fresh air. She needs it. She staggers out to the Cruiser to start her ride. The alcohol makes her mind tricky. Things that are not usually amusing to Hannah suddenly become hilarious. Her reflection in the barbershop window, so funny. A man jump-starting his car: *Ha.* And then there are these old, speed-walking ladies, their heads like fluffy Q-tips cased in plastic visors, an entire new plateau of laughably absurd.

Because it is her opinion that she currently looks and feels like a used piece of Kleenex, Hannah takes the back way home, behind the supermarket, where the train station used to be. Now there are cruise ships back here, huge cities of people waiting to float to the next scenic little town. How much does it cost to ride? Is anyone on there happy? When the economy tanks, will they be empty? Will they just blow them up, or sink them, or—

A sudden jolt. Hannah is hurtling forward over the handlebars, rushing toward the pavement, and now she is on her hands and knees, her wet, raw palms bitten into by a thousand sharp gravelly nails, her knees one with the pitted, crumbled street. She has fallen off her bike. She is not eleven; she is not thirty-five; she is ninety years old and dying. She looks back and the Cruiser is there, still upright, mocking her from the groove of an old train track. Somehow, the fat tires have gotten wedged in.

It takes a while to hobble to the house. She hopes no one will be there. The only remedy for the pain is a shower, three Tylenol PMs, and a day in bed. But opening the door, Hannah is greeted by an unexpected hum of activity. She hears Daisy, she hears DeWitt, but there's someone else in there, a presence that at once terrifies her and produces a splitting surge of joy.

It's not supposed to happen this way. There is meant to be a warning when your husband finally comes to save you, so that you can shower and get a bikini wax and wear something appropriate, perhaps a virginal yet formfitting jersey dress that says, *I've been repenting. I am a serious, loving, interesting wife who is thirty-five and still manages to look good in jersey.* Instead, she reeks of used vodka and is bleeding in ugly clothes that she slept in.

"Oh, here she is." Daisy sighs. "Tried to ride home on your tricycle, did you? Well, home has come to you."

"Hi." Hannah's husband stands up from the breakfast table. He, naturally, looks great, in gray dress pants and a pressed blue shirt. "Surprise."

"Hi."

"You're bleeding again."

"It's a habit."

"Oh, Hannah-Fanana-Louisiana," DeWitt says. "You make the girls at the Wild Wild Joker look clean."

"Why have you been to the Joker, you dirty man?" her mother asks. "And, Hannah, where have you been?"

"I was at Palmer's."

"And he let you get yourself in this condition?"

"He's not a saint, Mom. He was drinking last night, too."

Daisy clearly wants to tell Hannah she doesn't believe this at all, as her son is the most perfect specimen of male ever to grace the Earth. (She has never been reticent about having a favorite.)

"I'm taking a shower," Hannah says to Jon. "You want to come up and talk?"

She can see that he doesn't, really, but the alternative — more time with her parents — is even less appealing.

"Sure."

Daisy waves them away, and they begin the climb together.

"I forgot about this place," he says. "It's so *Brideshead Revisited* in here."

Jon visited with Hannah when they were first married. It was a Gothic, giddy visit. They drank her stepfather's ancient scotch and had sex in all of the weirdest spots in the house. They even managed to copulate on the roof at dawn one morning. It wasn't comfortable; Jon had to scrub the bird excrement from her back with a brush.

When they reach her room, they look at each other blankly. "Wait here. I'll get the blood off."

Hannah goes into the bathroom, strips off her clothes, and showers, hoping the steam will clear at least some of this hangover away. It helps mildly, but the soap is like acid in the new wounds. She swears lustily as she peroxides and bandages her palms and knees, then reenters her room wrapped in a towel. Jon is sitting on her bed, looking at some of the photos she's left out. She sits next to him. When he doesn't move, she puts her wet head on his shoulder.

"I'm really, really glad to see you."

He emits a small grunt, indicating that this makeup process will not be in any way simple. She tries again.

"Seriously, Jon. I love you."

"Right."

"You're everything to me. My whole life."

Nothing.

"OK, how far into the cliché bag do I have to go, here?"

"Stop now and save yourself some dignity."

"I have dignity?"

"Hannah, I got here last night. You just forced me to endure *two* consecutive meals with your parents."

"I'm *sorry*. I didn't know you were coming. If you had called me back—"

"I didn't call because I wasn't sure coming was a good idea. But I knew talking to you wouldn't help, so I just got on a plane. Your messages made you sound like a total strung out psychopath, by the way."

"I am strung out. I wanted to talk to you. You're supposed to be my husband. And you wouldn't call me back."

He gets up and paces. There is no better pacer than Jon. Before she knew him, she thought pacing was just a stage direction, something Clark Gable did to compete with Vivien Leigh when she was upstaging him or giving him an especially hard time. But Jon paces with fierce concentration, as if he is actually trying to wear a groove into the floor.

"Seriously, I'm sorry for everything. You probably think I was off with someone else, but really I was just with Palmer. Tom's leaving him, probably, and he..."

Jon kicks the door shut with his foot. It slams.

"What are you doing? Mom will—"

"Just be quiet," he says, and rushes her.

Before, Hannah and Jon used to have nice sex. Thoughtful sex. The type you have when your partner is—for lack of better words—a grateful nerd. Today, the sex is different. Jon is angry. He bites and pushes and slams. It's like sleeping with a completely different man. She loves it, but she also sort of misses her husband.

It takes a while. Afterward they are exhausted. They roll away from each other and lie side by side. She takes his hand and squeezes it. He pushes hers away.

"I need to tell you something," he says.

"No, you don't. I don't need to know anything."

"Listen to me."

"No, no. I don't care. That Denise person? Heroin? Crack to get you through the hard times? Really. It's OK."

"Ignoring the problem won't work this time, Hannah."

"I'm not as bad as I look. I've been doing really, really well here. I swear. Last night was just a slipup. I was helping my brother out. You can ask him."

"I'm not here for that," he says. "I'm not here to check up on you."

"Just sex, then?"

"Hannah." He presses his lips together. A firm, red line. "I'm filing for a divorce."

She's falling off the balcony. She's hurtling over her handlebars. There are knives downstairs, Jon. Cut me open, why don't you? Throw some rusty fishhooks in my eyelids, then string me up.

"But you're naked. You're telling me you want a"—she can't even get her mouth around the word—"divorce, and you're naked in my room. You just had sex with me."

Jon gets up and pulls his boxers on.

"It's not fair."

"Hannah, I have every right to divorce you. Any judge will grant me that. Adultery, mental abuse—"

"Excuse me?"

"But we don't need to go there, do we?"

Hannah opens her mouth, then snaps it closed.

"It's just not working, sweetheart."

"But you're not even giving me a chance."

"I gave you four chances. Remember those? The guy from Cisco, the yoga instructor, the—"

"But *this* time."

"I don't want to do this anymore, Hannah."

"Jon."

"No, listen—I know we *can*. We can squeeze some pathetic years out of this. I just...don't want to."

She won't cry, she vows. Tears annoy Jon.

"It's bad. We're bad together."

"We are not."

She gets up and opens an old drawer to pull on some clothes. She's not crying, but she still can't seem to see anything. She ends up in a very small plaid skirt—seventh grade? eighth?—and a Bangles T-shirt.

"You know what? I won't let you divorce me. You were unfaithful, too. I'll just hire a fucking awesome lawyer and take everything."

"That's another thing, honey."

"Stop calling me honey. You can't come in here, screw me, ask for a divorce, and call me honey. Hasn't anyone ever taught you about mixed messages?"

"We're broke."

"We are not. We're doing fine."

"We *were* doing fine. That was before the stock market Hiroshima."

"It's not a permanent thing, Jon. The election will happen and then—"

"No, Hannah. I don't know how the hell you haven't noticed this, since the business side is your damned job. But these last three quarters cleaned us out. We operated at a four-hundred-thousand-dollar loss this year because of that advertising campaign—"

"Your idea!"

"Well I thought I had the money. You *told* me we had the money, Hannah, and I'm beginning to realize you had no idea what was going on. Wait, what are you doing?"

"This skirt is too small. I'm changing."

"Anyway, I've got no one to borrow from, not four hundred thousand, at least. . . . I can't talk to you like this. You have no pants on."

"Just hold on." She fishes the Madonna pajama bottoms from under a heap.

"Everyone's out."

"Shit." Hannah puts her hands on her hips. "And Mom?"

"There's no way we can make this work, Hannah. People don't want to buy six-hundred-dollar vibrators. They can't even make their rent."

"You should have let me stay involved. I could have marketed—"

"It wouldn't have worked. Trust me."

"What about what we owe?"

"Bankruptcy."

"What? No. DeWitt will help us."

"I wouldn't let him."

"But we can't just give up."

"Bankruptcy isn't giving up. It's acknowledging the situation is beyond our control."

"I won't just stop like that," she says. "I won't let it go. We've been at this for years. No."

"Hannah, there is no money," he says. "Look, I used to find your dogmatic ways endearing, but come on. Haven't you been reading anything? Paying attention at all? Bankruptcy is in. It's like a new Coldplay song."

"You like that song? The one about Israel?"

"You think it's about Israel? I thought it was about Mexico."

"Coldplay?"

"I was making a reference."

"God, it's that Denise woman. Is she living with you? What, are you going to Burning Man with her this year?"

"It's not Denise. Look, none of this is Denise."

"Do you promise?"

"Of course."

He's not lying, she can see that. It's one of the many reasons Hannah married Jon. He doesn't lie. He edits, but he doesn't lie.

She opens the window and puts her feet out. This is not a dangerous move; it's a dormer window that opens out onto a large, only slightly sloped section of roof. In middle school, she used to sit there for hours, looking for a boat that might have her father on it.

"Divorce?" She wraps her arms around her knees. "Really?"

"Yeah."

"It's actually sort of a pretty word."

"I guess."

"We'll be divorced people."

"Us and forty-something percent of adult America."

"Great." She throws a pebble off the roof. It bounces off her stepfather's truck and into the street. "All that work, and we can't even fail in a special way."

Jon stays for a few more days. They kill the time as best they can. They decide not to break the news to Daisy while Jon's here; too much drama. Even though they are divorcing and penniless aside from the paid-off apartment (they put it in Hannah's name to avoid losing it in the bankruptcy process), the mood turns oddly light. They make bad jokes and drink beer in the morning. They wander around town, looking at strange antiques and buying things with the company credit card since the bill will soon be expunged. Hannah buys dresses for parties people can't afford to have; Jon buys a Civil War–era gun, and they go out to DeWitt's plantation and shoot it. It all feels overly giddy and sentimental, much like the last week of camp.

And then there's the sex. Three or four times a day, he approaches her or she climbs on him and they remind themselves of the old spots they'll soon miss. They do new things, too, trying SweetJane products they never bothered with in the past. It's amusing for a while, but the last time they do this, Hannah cries at the end, so she rolls away and doesn't touch him anymore.

*   *   *

The night before Jon's plane leaves, they crawl out onto the roof and split a bottle of $150 wine. (A last SweetJane company-credit-card gift.) The moon is out, a perfectly round, gently scarred orb, illuminating the entire harbor, Sullivan's Island, Folly Beach, the jetties.

"See those rocks?" Hannah points to the mouth of the harbor. "That's where they found my dad's boat."

"That's way out there."

"They think it went out even farther, but the tide pushed it back in."

"Huh." Jon is pretending this is news, but he has heard this story many, many times before.

"I'm beginning to think that maybe everyone is right," she says. "That maybe he's not alive."

"Interesting." He pours her more wine.

"What do you mean, interesting?"

Jon has always been on Hannah's side about her father. Sure, he said to her when she first told him her story. It was on their first date, when they were drinking in their kickball uniforms. He could have swum to shore, Jon theorized, or masterminded some big hoax. Hell, he could be a modern-day pirate. Or maybe he's being held hostage as a slave worker on a pot farm.

"What I'm saying is," he says now, "interesting that after spending more than a forty-eight-hour expanse of time at home, you change your mind."

"Do you think I'm being brainwashed?"

"I don't know what I think." He sounds tired.

"Hey," Hannah says, "will you come look at something with me?"

"Sure."

They climb back inside, bringing the empty bottle with them. Hannah has never shown Jon her closet before. It never seemed appropriate, somehow. The only other person who's been in here is Warren, and the closet was their place. It's stupid, though. It's not as if he hasn't taken Jenny White-Meyers to their places, like to the end of Folly Beach or to the Bowen's Island oyster bar.

Still, she's a little excited. "Get ready," she says, taking his arm. They duck through the dresses and the sweaters, and she crawls in ahead of him and turns on the light.

"Hey," he says. "A fort."

"Isn't it cool?"

"Sure." He sneezes. "A little dusty."

"I used to hang out in here all the time."

"You must have been a very pale kid."

"But don't you like how the fabric makes it look like a tent? And the pillows?"

"Sure. Very accomplished, for a seventh grader." He leans over to turn up the lamp. "Why are we here? Oh, we haven't had sex in here yet, have we? You want one last go-round in an even weirder part of your house?"

"No." She picks up the shoe box of pictures. "I need your help."

"Can we go back in your room? I'm dying in here."

"Fine."

I hate you, she thinks. I hate everything.

They go back into her room, and she dumps the collection, spreading the photos out so they can both see them. Jon begins sifting through the pictures and holding them up.

"Who's this woman?" he asks, pointing at Virginia.

"My old boyfriend's mom, Virginia."

"So? What's with her?"

"Oh, she had a crush on my dad. They were friends when they were little."

"Friends?"

"She was always around. It's sad, really."

"Hannah." He picks up another one of Virginia. Then another.

"What?"

"Don't be an idiot."

"Excuse me?"

"Do you see how many photos there are of her?"

"Yeah, there was a whole box of them. I told you. She was around a lot."

"Sweetheart...," Jon says.

Hannah feels the cold prickle coming on. That, paired with a wave of extreme frustration at not being able to figure something out. She finds it much like trying to solve the bill at a group dinner, when one has gone over it fourteen times and gotten money from everyone, but still is $78 short.

"What?"

"Who do you think took these pictures?" he asks. He is forming his words very slowly.

"Don't talk to me like I'm an ESL student. I'm right here."

"Why are there so many of... what's her name again? Virginia? Why aren't they of Daisy? Or Palmer? Or you?"

"What do you mean?" Hannah says. "What are you talking about?"

"You said your dad took these, right?"

"Yeah. I mean, he must have. I found them back in high school with all the old photos. They were in DeWitt's basement with our stuff."

Jon looks her over. He puts his palm out and runs it over her hair, her face, her knees, her feet.

"Let's go to bed," he says, standing. "My flight's at seven in the morning."

"Tell me what you're talking about."

"Hannah, I have to get ready to leave."

I have to get ready to leave. She carefully puts the pictures away. She takes a long time doing it, letting him stand there, waiting. After a very long while, she gets up.

"Are you all right?"

"You're not sleeping in here." She shoves his suitcase toward the door with her foot. "Fantasy Fun Camp is over."

"OK. If that's how you want it."

"It is."

"OK."

"We've got seven guest rooms. Go find one."

"Sure."

Still, he hovers.

"Out."

"Hannah..."

"I'll have my lawyer contact you."

"I was thinking we'd use a mediator. It'll be a lot cheaper for both of us."

"Whatever. We can use a meter maid, if that'll make you happy."

"Is that a joke?"

"I don't know."

"That makes no sense."

"Get out, Jon. I don't want to talk to you anymore."

"Stop yelling."

"I. AM. NOT. YELLING."

"All right. OK. I'm sorry, OK?"

"I said good night. The cab number's on the fridge."

"OK. OK, so." He shuffles out and she shuts the door. He's still standing out there, though. She can tell.

"She's not the one who was wandering, Hannah," he says through the wood. "I'm doing you a favor here, OK? That's what it means. The pictures. The ones of the other woman. Your dad took them."

"Screw the pictures."

"It's just that you're missing the point."

"There is no point."

"You're obsessed with your mother and your stepfather, when it really seems like your dad was—"

"I'll be in contact."

She listens as he shifts on his feet a couple of times. After a minute, he leaves, dragging his suitcase to the next floor. She throws the pictures into the trash. She needs to get rid of the wine bottle so her mother won't find it; brush her teeth; wash her face; change her Band-Aids, but she can't leave the room. Not until he's gone.

She tries pacing. Once she starts, she can see why her almost-ex-husband likes it so much. She walks back and forth for what must be hours, because she's still moving when his taxi comes. Only when she hears the door slam and watches the car pull safely around the corner, out of sight, *away*, does she finally allow herself to lie down.

The sheets smell of Jon. He's not a cologne wearer, but there is a shaving cream he likes with rosemary in it, and it's still there somewhere, haunting the threads. Hannah rips the sheets off and throws them in the corner, then curls up on the musty stitched upholstery of the bare mattress.

Missing the point, he said to her. Missing the point? How could anyone miss the point while lying alone on a dirty mattress? After the person who taught you how to properly make coffee drives away, never to come back? Oh, Jon, she wants to say, I get the point. I've gotten it for years. She ignores it sometimes. Other times she thinks she's gotten past it, pushed it all the way under. But look, it's still here, pressing in her side now, sharp, insistent. It's here even as she closes the morning out by squeezing her eyes shut and praying—*Ha, so you do pray sometimes? Fine, OK. You got me*—for a long, cool shadow of sleep.

20

Hannah's Last Whispers to the Ceiling

SATURDAY. JON HAS just gone. Hannah has nothing left to remember. And if she does, she doesn't want to anymore.

She stays where she is for an entire day. No one comes to get her. No one calls. She doesn't look out the window or to the side. Just up.

She's never looked up this hard before.

The ceiling is full of cracks. There's an old rosette molding in the middle. It looks like the sort of thing a chandelier would hang from, but there is no trace of a light fixture. The plaster bulbs and flowers are shaded in with dust. Somebody should really clean up there.

There was a time when Hannah would talk to the flowers on the ceiling at night. She made up a story that her father had installed a camera in the middle. Even when she was about to go to college, she believed it.

Whispered, secret messages. She liked to think he could hear her.

Hi, Dad, school's OK. Made an A in social studies.

Hey, Tucker died. I'm sorry.

I'm going to the prom with Warren Meyers. I could send you a picture—

But things are almost always better anyway when there are fewer words, aren't they? No words, and you can make what you want from it. Like when you tell someone you love them. If they say nothing, it might mean, I don't love you. Or, I like you all right. But it could also mean something else. For example, I love you more than I can explain.

That's what Hannah's always squeezed from it. That's the nothing she's listened for.

Yet it seems that she is the only fool here. She's the only one who's waited and believed, and nothing's exactly what she's gotten. No call or letter. No good-bye note. And now what? Her father, it turns out, was an adulterer. No better than herself in her very worst moments. I looked up to you, Dad, and you lied and cheated and then left nothing for me but a professor's nose. And you didn't even mean to leave that. So if you want to know how I'm feeling, just listen to the answer I'm not giving you. Or else put your ear here, on the ceiling. Get a ladder if you want to. The answer is in the cracks.

21

What Palmer Finds

AFTER ELEVEN DAYS without Tom, Palmer cries. He's cutting peppers to go in his omelet and thinking of what Naomi's house must look like. Tapestries? Incense-stick holders?

This is when he cuts his finger. It's not a bad cut; it doesn't even hurt. Still, it's a bleeder. It's the blood that frustrates him — so hard to get out of everything. It's all over the counter and the cutting board, and even after two Band-Aids, it won't stop. It's on his jeans and in the eggs and on poor Rumpus's forehead. So he's dealing with this, he is *dealing*, when he happens to glance out the window and see that the basil he's forgotten to rotate has withered, and here it comes, oh, shit, alone in the kitchen — tears.

It is clear now that Tom is never speaking to Palmer again. The breakup is perhaps Palmer's most successful yet. As promised, Tom came over to get his things while Palmer was at work. The rest they will divide, or at least Palmer will pay Tom back for the materials installed. It's become a problem, of course, the renovation. Palmer should have seen this coming. They should have used more of a Legoland approach, so that items could be dismembered and carried away. How to cut apart the chandelier? The built-in cappuccino machine? He could pry the fish tank loose, but where would it go? And what of the fish?

Palmer was surprised at first by the funk brought on by the breakup, but after a day, he embraced it. He skipped the gym. He drank a bottle of wine a night. He watched movies starring Matt Damon. He watched *Top Chef.* He made great mixing bowls of fluorescent-orange macaroni and cheese from blue boxes and ate them on the couch next to Rumpus. He called old boyfriends and had phone sex. He gave $5,000 to the ASPCA.

At work, at least, everything is more or less normal. It's easy to pretend that all is as it was before, because Tom never visited him at work in the first place, and Palmer rarely talked about him. Certainly he does not tell Jenny. He can't stand the fawning that will ensue, or the inevitable flash of hope that will cross her face. He is able to concentrate just fine anyway, maybe even better, because now he does not have to be bothered with calling Tom over the course of the workday. (A forgotten call back would induce hours of frosty wrath.) No, now he can just be in the office, *present,* as his old lover would say, right here, fully with the sturdy canines and the yodeling, pissing cats.

Hannah, it seems, is too characteristically self-absorbed to call and check in. He hasn't heard from her in almost a week. Probably because Jon has been visiting. Palmer thought about going to say hello, but Hannah's husband was there either to break up with her or to reunite. Palmer didn't want to be around for the aftermath of someone else's bust-up — his own being bad enough —

and he sure as hell didn't want to witness the bliss that would result if they didn't.

Five days, though. His sister is a highly vocal person, and her silence can mean nothing good. She must be wallowing, just like he is.

He spends the morning watching the presidential campaign. He will vote Democrat, of course, but for some reason finds no joy in watching his candidate speak. It's not that the man isn't articulate or good-looking; he moves with the grace of a dancer, exuding almost supernatural ability — exactly the sort of person you want to meet as your captain when boarding a plane. But as Palmer listens to the commentators, their faces visibly crusty with makeup, it occurs to him that he has no faith in his choice. It's rather like beginning a new relationship, he thinks, pouring an eleven a.m. glass of chardonnay. You start with hope, then end up disillusioned. He's a gay liberal Democrat living in South Carolina. He's been beaten into submission.

What he needs, he realizes, is a project. Palmer is a big believer in the positive virtues of projects. Back in the Tom days, projects were shared and usually centered around the house — finding the right ottoman or searching for a camellia bush of the correct shape. One thing that has eluded him for a very long time has been the perfect bench for the small garden behind the pool.

I could build the bench, he thinks as he throws away old macaroni. How hard can it be? I can just build it. It's Saturday, after all. The perfect day to build something. And so, with almost a spring in his step, he showers, puts on a shirt that seems appropriate for working with one's hands, takes out a notebook, and sketches the dimensions. A simple bench: four legs and a top. A bench. A bench of wood!

There is a lumberyard north of the city that he decides to visit. Tom has mentioned it when talking of his work. He sometimes goes there with his builders. Palmer looks up the address—it's way out in North Charleston, a vast plain of superstores and conference hotels near the airport. He prints the directions and heads for the BMW. He hasn't turned on his stereo in days, so he reaches down and flips the knob.

Eckhart Tolle's soothing voice fills the air, telling him to live in the *now*. Palmer squints with confusion, then realizes he's listening to one of Tom's CDs. What the hell does that *mean*, Eckhart? he wants to ask. If all that matters is now, why, exactly, am I still so fucked up from yesterday? He presses eject and throws the disc out the window, watching as it sails behind the car and bounces into the road. He gives a loud yawp into the October air. He is free, he is a man, he is a *woodworker*.

Pulling into the parking lot of the lumberyard, he is pleased with what he sees. Despite being dwarfed by the neighboring Costco, it is an honest-looking sort of place, with a wooden door, a hand-painted sign, and a few large trucks in the gravel parking lot. The yard itself is enormous. On the left, a large hangar filled with long planks of wood, meticulously stacked and organized. On the right, a small building labeled OFFICE AND PURCHASING. Following the lead of the other capable-looking, directed men, Palmer pulls a huge metal dolly out of the stall.

It feels good, buying things from a store like this. He walks up and down the aisles, admiring the pine, the oak, and the mahogany. He frowns. Which woods are environmentally friendly? Which are hardest? Why are some planks $12 and others $145? After much deliberation, he chooses pine and oak. Pine, because he likes the smell, and oak, because of his memories of the moss-glazed oak tree behind his house on Atlantic Street. Oh, this will be a good bench. This bench will save him, will pull him out of heartbreak and lethargy into a better place where he will meet new people and buy a better house and find a less-troublesome lover who does not insist on babies and *feeling* all the time. Maybe after this bench, he will make a table, chairs, a sofa. Perhaps he'll fill his new house entirely with wood furniture made by his own hands. It will be practical. Easy to clean. Good for Rumpus.

He enters the office, dragging his half-loaded dolly behind him. No one's at the counter. Palmer is usually patient and polite at empty counters, but today he is feeling antsy. He's wasted so much time finding his purpose. Suddenly nothing else on Earth could be as important as making this bench.

"Hello?" he calls out.

He hears movement in the back office. A moment later a large man in a flannel shirt and baseball cap comes out — just the sort of man you'd expect to work at a lumberyard.

"Hi, there," Palmer says. "I'd like to pay for these."

"All right." The man begins punching numbers into the computer, barely even glancing at the wood.

"Will it be an extra charge to have these cut?"

"Oh, we don't cut," the man says. He looks at Palmer and suppresses a smile. "No, no. We don't cut."

"But I saw a band saw out back."

"Well, we cut for *big* jobs. Sure, we'll cut for those. But not four pieces of wood."

"Wouldn't it just take a moment?"

"Ain't you got a saw?"

Palmer, who already does not particularly like this man, now finds himself falling into a dangerous zone of contempt. Is a saw *necessary* for manhood? Does a gentleman *need* a saw over, say, a cum laude degree from the Citadel, or a veterinary medicine MD from Emory University?

"Sure—but, I mean—isn't there any way I could pay a little extra and have this done here?"

The man shakes his head. "Don't have the manpower. Not on Saturday." The man is giving him an unmistakably condescending look. It's the same kind of look given by the straight men who bring him their pets. *I screw women and you don't,* the look says. When this happens in his office, Palmer does not get angry; instead he lets his hand or the sleeve of his white coat brush a body part of the person in question, causing the perpetrator to blanch with fright.

"You know," Palmer says, "I can see the band saw out there through the window. I could use it myself. It would only take—"

"You?" the man barks. "Think we got the insurance for that?"

"Look, is there someone I could speak to? A manager, perhaps?"

The man now folds his muttonchop arms into a surprisingly neat square.

"Perhaps." The word, spat. He disappears into the office. Palmer is left to wait several minutes. He hears laughter seep in from the back room. But just as Palmer decides to screw this place anyway and take his money to Home Depot—he wasn't going to, but now he gets why franchises with enforced customer service really *work*—a manager emerges. He's a tall, lanky man with a droopy face and tired eyes partially hidden behind wire glasses. He wears a polo shirt tucked into a pair of jeans. Palmer

cannot stop looking at the jeans. The jeans are not terrible, which is surprising. North Charleston has the potential for truly bad, acid-washed, high-waisted jeans. These are only moderately bad—what Tom would call dad jeans.

The man hesitates and then puts out his hand. "Hey, Palmer."

"Shawn," Palmer says. "Hi."

What does Palmer remember about Shawn?

I remember you used to hiccup before you laughed. You swore that celery gave you a fever. Your freckles turned almost blue if you swam too long in a pool. You twisted the pillow when you slept, and sometimes, when you sat in a chair, you tucked your feet under your body, as if you were a resting bird.

The band saw, of course, is no problem. Shawn won't let Palmer do it himself, but he does let him watch.

"I discourage it," Shawn explains. "I cut for one person, and I'll get all sorts of crazies back here asking for custom-cut things. Some old lady'll ask me to cut her a stopper for the bathtub. Things like that. But I can do it sometimes."

"My boyfriend loves this store," Palmer says. "Tom Salinger?"

"Oh, sure. The architect. Man, he's a real stickler."

There is no sign of surprise from Shawn at Palmer's indirect announcement that he is openly gay. He must have guessed that Palmer would come out. Or perhaps he heard it; someone told him in passing. And then there is the more likely scenario—that Shawn doesn't particularly care.

"So, do you live close by?" Palmer asks, as friendly and non-committal as he knows how to be.

"I live in the Oats."

"Where?"

"One of the new developments off Bees Ferry Road."

"Oh, yeah. Those are nice."

The saw wails higher now as Shawn passes the first piece of wood through the blade.

"Got two houses, actually," Shawn yells over the noise. "One for me, one for the wife and kids."

"Divorce?"

"Yup."

"Kids, though?"

"Yeah."

The saw roars up again, almost immediately hitting an unbearable shriek. Still, Palmer is glad for it. He looks at the wood. The pieces are taking shape now, which excites him. He can see the legs in his head.

"You doin' this in oak?" Shawn asks.

"And pine. Oak and pine both."

"Pine's really soft," Shawn says. "Those are very different woods."

"All right." Palmer tries to keep the annoyance out of his voice. He doesn't want opinions.

"I'd go all oak if I were you."

"I'll work it out," Palmer says.

The saw wails again. Palmer hears a ringing sound in the inner sanctum of his ear.

"So, I never asked . . .," Shawn says, pausing. Palmer's heart begins to thrum. "Never mind."

"What?" Palmer asks, trying not to seem too eager. Could it

be possible that Shawn is still in love with him? Does he really have that power?

"I was just wondering. It's a little — oh, fuck it. Coach ever come after you?"

Palmer blinks.

"Coach?" he repeats.

"Yeah. *Man*, he would not leave me alone."

Palmer tries to picture the coach, vaguely remembering a large, red-faced man with an oppressive laugh.

"About soccer?"

"No, Palmer. Not about soccer."

Other information is coming back now. Something about a scandal, after they'd graduated.

"What do you mean?"

"I mean what you think I mean." Shawn takes the next piece of wood and runs it through. Palmer waits for the noise to stop. The smell of wood sap has suddenly grown overwhelming. "Guy was a perv."

"God, that's awful," Palmer says. "Wasn't he the one who —"

"Yeah. He got fired a few years after because some other boys told on him. That old, tired lion's ass licker."

As horrific as it is, Palmer can't help but smile at the old habit of profanity.

"Don't worry," Shawn continues. "I never let him do anything. I would have reported him, but..."

"God."

"Yeah. It's all right. It was actually sort of funny."

"It doesn't sound funny."

Shawn gives a hollow laugh, then goes quiet again. "I guess not. Anyway. I always wondered if you were in the same boat."

"No."

"Really screwed me up for a while."

"Shawn. That's terrible. I'm so sorry to hear this."

Shawn shakes his head and puts another piece of wood in the saw.

"Wait, but why didn't you tell anyone?" Palmer yells to be heard.

"I couldn't," Shawn yells back. "He said he'd tell. You know, because of what he saw."

"What he saw?"

Shawn shrugs.

"What did he see?" Palmer asks slowly.

Shawn's mouth works itself into a shape resembling a sideways semicolon.

"He saw something?" Palmer says again.

Shawn turns off the saw now and puts his hand on his hip. "You know what he saw, asshole."

Palmer shakes his head.

"Through the window?" Shawn says. "That day after the game?"

There have been several instances, as Palmer has grown older, when he has been certain that time is folding like a bedsheet. For example, when his mother mentioned in passing that she'd been married to DeWitt for twenty years. Palmer couldn't believe it. Had it been that long? It seemed no more distant than the previous Christmas. He was so determined that she retrieved the marriage license out of her files to show him. It was the same now: the soccer game happened years ago, but he could swear it was last week. That's how clearly he remembers it.

"You're telling me it was *Coach* in the window?" The words

come out at a higher pitch than Palmer would have chosen. "Are you sure?"

"Sure, I'm sure. That gecko-dicked platypus-fucker was after me for the rest of school. Why?"

"I just—thought it was someone else," Palmer says, placing his hand over his face, processing the information.

"Nope. It was Coach, all right. It wasn't—well—he must have taken it easy on you, what with your dad and all. I mean, let's face it, who's gonna go after you with something like that going on?"

"You're right," Palmer says, opening his eyes again. "Who?"

The wood is done. Palmer pays the bill, and together they tie the larger pieces to the top of the car. Palmer admits to Shawn that he knows nothing about making furniture, so Shawn explains how to sand everything, what stain to use, and the basics of joinery. As he goes on, though, Palmer drifts farther and farther away from the project. He can actually feel his interest disappearing, like sand trickling through the fingers of a cupped hand.

"Well," Shawn says, "good running into you."

"Yes."

"Well, I should—"

"Wait, Shawn. I haven't really asked you about yourself. Are you all right? I'm just...pretty shocked about all of this."

"I'm fine, Palmer."

"And you—you had a wife?"

"Yeah." Shawn looks toward the building nervously. "It didn't work out."

"And are you—"

"I don't even know. After that Coach thing, you know. I went off it."

"I'm sorry. It must have sucked."

"It did."

Palmer is quiet for a moment. "Do you blame me?"

Shawn nods. "I did for a while. But it wasn't you. It's just what happened."

Palmer rubs his thumb over the grain of the wood.

"You know," he says, "all this time I thought it was my dad in the window. I thought he saw us and got upset and then went out in his boat."

Shawn shakes his head and laughs a little. "Well, *that's* kind of a stupid theory."

"Excuse me?"

"I always heard your dad was a really cool guy. Everyone on Atlantic Street talked about him like a martyr."

"Well, sure. He did a lot of great things."

"Right. So I doubt seeing his son doing his natural thing would've set him off like that. I mean, come on. He was your dad."

"Well. It was all a long time ago."

Shawn tightens the rope around the wood once more. "Palmer, I'm not even that good of a dad, but if I saw my kid fooling around, I'd just tell him to quit and move on, you know?"

"Yeah."

"You can't blame a kid."

Palmer nods. "OK, well. Thanks again." They shake hands and say good-bye. As Palmer drives away, he takes one last glance in the rearview mirror; Shawn is back at the saw, scowling up in concentration, dwarfed by the huge stacks of wood.

That night, Palmer looks up Shawn Cohen in the phone book. There are two listed in Charleston County. He takes down the numbers and then calls from his blocked landline. Shawn answers on Palmer's first try. A television is blaring in the background. Palmer immediately hangs up.

The second has an answering machine. *This is Dorothy Cohen, we're not here, leave a message.* Palmer takes down the address. The next day he drives to the house. He doesn't knock, just looks. It's a nice house, an older two-story on a good street in the suburbs. There are bicycles in the yard. Palmer can't see them, but he can hear Shawn's children. He sits out front for as long as he dares. Seven minutes, maybe. Ten. He closes his eyes, concentrating. He draws on the lilt of their voices.

22

Hannah Tries Again

SOMEONE IS TRYING to invade Hannah's world from downstairs. She's been mostly in her room since Jon has gone, leaving only to eat and shower. She's dragged a television in and set it up on the floor; the bed is now a nest of magazines and crumbs. She's taken to spending her mornings watching the squawking women on *The View*. Hannah's adopted a particularly violent hatred of the blond one. An easy target, almost too easy. So bleached, so shrill, so gleefully *wrong*.

"Birth begins at conception!" she screeches. "Obama is surrounded by a terrorist circle!"

Hannah is throwing candy wrappers at the woman's pixilated face when she realizes the annoying, repetitive sound interrupting her target practice is her mother.

"Hi," Hannah calls back, coming out to hang over the banister.

"The morgue called," Daisy says, today sporting a red '80s *Working Girl* power suit. "They wanted to know if they could come collect the body. Seems the neighbors think you're dead."

"I'm just really busy. We have a big shipment to deal with."

That's what Hannah has told them she is doing. Work. Jon came to get me on track with the business, she replied to her parents' curious inquiries, and now I have an "incredible" amount to do. It's surprising to her, how easy it is not to say anything about the divorce or the bankruptcy. She doesn't tell them the first day, then the second. Now it's been more than a week, and it's just too awkward to bring up. Maybe I won't mention it at all, she muses. If I ignore my divorce, will it just go away?

"I want to talk to you about the private sale. The one we said we'd have for my friends. They're all *very* interested."

"But I didn't agree to—"

"How about dinner tomorrow? At Fish, maybe?"

Hannah considers this bribe. She does love dinner with wine at a good restaurant, but she is skeptical of her mother's motives.

"Sure, I think I can make it."

Her mother's face shrinks into a scowl. "You *think?*"

"We'll go." Hannah sighs. "Tomorrow."

"All right. I'll make the reservation. Also, please bathe before coming downstairs. Your stench is creating a fly problem."

Hannah shuffles into her room and takes her position back in front of the television. She falls into a lace of light sleep during the segment about purging, then wakes to the sound of DeWitt's reverberating voice.

"BANANA!" he booms.

"Hi."

"It's like the Batcave in here!" he says cheerfully, ripping open the curtains. "Lord Almighty! What a view! Aren't you a lucky girl!"

"Extremely."

"You look like a vampire, Louisiana! You know we like our girls tan in the South, right? Tan, blond, and buxom!"

"Guess I should make an appointment with the plastic surgeon."

"Oh, you've got a fine figure."

"Gross." Hannah squints into the light. Dust particles move frenetically in the sun.

"Especially for your age. Only the slightest signs that you're gettin' on."

"What do you mean, signs?"

"Hey, why don't you come out with me to the plantation?"

Hannah shakes her head. "No, that's OK."

"C'mon. I've got some errands to run out there. Need the company. You can earn your keep."

She tries to think of an excuse. Work? No, she can't face work. She shrugs, puts on her shoes, and follows him out to his behemoth truck. As soon as they pull away, she regrets her mistake. It's a long ride to River House, DeWitt's plantation. Last week, when she went out there with Jon, the ride was light and easy, full of shared jokes. Now in the car with her stepfather, she can actually feel the precious moments of her life dripping away. They kill the hour by listening to Kenny Rogers on the cassette player. DeWitt sings every word, despite her protests. But on the return trip, after his forty-five minutes of "work" — Hannah spent the time communing with the goats at the petting zoo — he seems to feel the need to bond, because he leans over and switches the radio off.

"No more Kenny?"

"A man can only sing to 'Ruby' so many times." He drums his fingers on the wheel. "It's a damned good *day!*"

"Are you always so relentlessly cheerful?"

"Why not? I'm wealthy and healthy."

"For now."

"Also, think the wife puts happy pills in my food. Hey, you need anything from Costco?"

Daisy was the one to turn DeWitt on to Costco. Ever since the store opened, she's been shopping for the family there as if the Apocalypse is nigh. Now DeWitt isn't allowed to get groceries anywhere else, even though he could afford to buy the entire inventory of Whole Foods.

"No."

"'Cause I'm thinking of going to Costco on the way home."

"OK."

"They have great meat there."

"All right."

Another minute of silence.

Hannah nods absently, trying to resist an irrepressible urge to nap. She looks out the window at the trees. The pines seem dissatisfied, as if longing for proper seasons.

"So, how's it going? The plantation and everything?"

Although DeWitt's main source of income is the interest generated by his inheritance, he also sells admission to tours of River House. However, as he leaves most of the running of River House to his managers, his main job, as far as Hannah can tell, is to walk around the property once a week and have lunch at the restaurant.

"Good, good. African Alley really boosted ticket sales. That was a good call on your part. People love it."

Hannah nods. African Alley is River House's "replica" of a slave community built after a tantrum Hannah threw on her one visit home for Christmas during college, when she denounced DeWitt as a racist. (She had just completed a course at Stanford entitled The Culture of American White Supremacy: Then and Now.) Unfortunately, instead of hiring a historian to oversee the development of the project, DeWitt, when complying with Hannah's request, used an interior decorator. The result, Hannah fears, is not a little misleading to impressionable young minds: the stockades were skipped in favor of a boiled-peanut demonstration, and instead of lectures on slavery, reenactors in period dress lounge in cute cabins, singing spirituals and hoeing cabbage and serving fragrant corn pone. It's not that it's not attractive, but it has little to do with reality. It's so cozy, one might imagine Hobbits happily curling up in African Alley for a nap.

"Glad to hear it."

DeWitt glances longingly at the bird tapes resting near the stereo. "So? Any last plans while you're here?"

"I thought I might go see Virginia, but I probably won't."

"How come?"

"I've seen enough people."

"She'd love to see you. I know her, you know. I know that she likes you."

"Mmm-hmm."

"But if you don't want to . . ."

"I don't, really."

"Though maybe by seeing her you'll wrap some things up."

Hannah adjusts the air vent so it's not blowing in her face. "What do you mean?"

"Well, Bobana, it seems like you're on a bit of a search."

"What?"

"Talking to the walls—"

"I don't do that anymore."

"Hiding in the closet, mooning over old pictures.... Wait a cotton-pickin' second!" The truck screeches to a stop.

"You didn't really say 'cotton-pickin',' did you?"

"Is that an orange-crowned warbler?"

"What?"

"I've got to spot this, honey. Hang tight."

"What are you talking about?"

"There." He points to a tree, but Hannah doesn't see anything. Cursing, he begins to root through the car for his binoculars.

"You know about the closet?"

"Sure, Pollyana. It's my house, you know. I'm a damned good snooper. Damned good. I know you and that reverend—Virginia's kid—were back there the other day."

He gets out of the car and peers through his field glasses.

"We were just looking at pictures."

"I think the little bugger's in that tree there."

"Pictures of you and Mom in the same place, before you were married."

"Damn it to hell! DAMN. Missed him."

His huge shoulders slump with disappointment.

"Can't you just put it on the list anyway?"

DeWitt sighs in exasperation. "Well, that'd be cheating, Bobana."

"I'll back you up."

"Naw. *I* have to know I did it." He scratches his head.

"Don't you care?"

"Hell, yeah! I've wanted that goddamned warbler for *years*."

"I mean about the pictures. Don't you care about those?"

"Hannah, there are more important things to care about than what's gone. Do you see what I'm saying?"

"Not really."

"Ah. Well." He sighs and carefully puts his field glasses back in their case. His red forehead is beaded with sweat. "You got to know it to see it, lady. No! I mean, 'Know when to hold 'em, know when to'... Aw, you get it. Don't look at me like that, Bug Eyes. All right. So. Costco?"

When they get back, safely tucked away in their respective pockets of the mansion, Hannah realizes, with great annoyance, that about this one thing her stepfather is right. Going back to San Francisco without giving Virginia at least one last try at the truth would render this already miserable trip utterly pointless. It would be like spending years dreaming of building a rare, intricate miniature schooner, setting out all of the tiny sails and masts and glue, then just getting up and moving to another house and leaving it all on the table. Or like hearing a warbler singing in the next room and just saying, Screw it.

And so, shamed into action, Hannah showers, dresses in holeless jeans and an ironed floral shirt, and walks slowly to Tradd Street. When Virginia answers the door, Hannah notes that she does not look nearly as happy to see her as the last time she was here.

"Hannah," she says, frowning. "Come in."

The rich smell of cooking meat. Hannah looks at her watch. It's five o'clock.

"Are you cooking dinner?"

"We just finished. The girls eat early. Join us."

Standing on the porch, she can see the dining room through the window. The entire Meyers family is looking at her, seated

238

around large plates of roast beef and quivering yellow mounds that Hannah remembers as Virginia's Yorkshire pudding.

"That's all right. I just came by to chat with you."

"Well, come in and say hello." She turns and walks into the house. Hannah realizes she has two choices. She can be a complete crazy woman and run away, or she can summon her manners. For once, she goes with the latter.

"Hannah." Warren stands slowly, as if he is pressing up on something extremely heavy with the top of his head. "What are you doing here?"

"I just came by to say hi."

"Hi," says one of the girls.

"Missed you in church today," Warren says.

"Oh, I don't really go. I was just, you know."

Jenny puts her fork down. She is staring at her plate.

"Anyway. I don't want to keep you from your dinner. I just . . . well. Virginia? Do you have a minute?"

"Sure." Hannah has to hand it to her; if she's at all ruffled by the fact that her son's high school ex-girlfriend, daughter of her disappeared lover, is crashing her Sunday meal, she doesn't show it. She takes her glass of wine from the table and gestures for Hannah to follow her to the sunporch. "Y'all finish up," she calls back to the rest of them. Safely sequestered, she takes her favorite position in the cushioned chair, feet tucked up under her, hugging an ugly woven cushion.

"OK, Hannah. What now?"

"So." Hannah takes a breath. "So. About Dad."

"Yes?"

"I take it you two had an affair?" She tries to control the anger in her voice.

Virginia gives Hannah a sympathetic look. She leans over, opens an intricately inlaid lacquered box, and extracts a crumpled pack of American Spirits.

"No, honey," she says. "Of course not."

"Really?"

"We had a friendship."

"That's it?"

Virginia lights up. "Do I have a reason to lie?"

"I don't know. Do you?"

"Don't be snippy. Of course I don't. We were together in high school, yes. Everybody knows that. And, yes, we were close. Like Warren and you were close. Jesus, I thought you would eat each other alive. But you know how it's over between you two?"

Hannah nods.

"It was the same. Long over by then."

"What happened?"

"Well, relationships change. Grew up, fell out of it. You know the drill. We went all the way over and came back out as friends. Your father was very helpful to me during a hard, hard time. Being alone with a son, you know. Your mother always thought we were fooling around, though. That's because she's crazy."

"She's not that crazy," Hannah says, experiencing an uncharacteristic jolt of loyalty. She reaches over and takes a sip of Virginia's wine.

"The woman was obsessed. We both tried to talk sense into her." She looks out the window. "I shouldn't tell you this, but she was driving him away. We all thought he was going to leave her."

Take her to China. I don't care.

Virginia laughs sadly. "But he didn't leave, did he?" It's not a question but a bitter statement. "He drowned first."

"You know, I've never thought he was dead."

She frowns. "I do know that. Warren told me. I think Daisy told me, too."

"Right."

She shrugs. "And why do you think that?" she asks.

"Dying just doesn't seem like something he would do."

"Well, he did die," she says curtly.

"I just don't know, Virginia. The whole thing is so unclosed. The boat. The dog. No note. No—"

"He died." Her voice goes up a notch. Hannah looks over in surprise. "He wouldn't have just left all of us." Embarrassed, she looks away.

Hannah is quiet for a moment. So I'm not the only one, she thinks, that needs to believe something about my father.

"So what about DeWitt? Why was he at that party?"

"Oh." Virginia sighs. "Well. That is the question."

"What question?"

"We used to be together."

"What?" Hannah shrieks. "You and *DeWitt?*"

"Yes. Me and DeWitt. We got together twice."

Hannah pauses, taking this in. "When?"

"Once shortly before your father died." She hesitates. "And once about ten or eleven years before that."

"Hang on." Hannah shakes her head. "Wait. *Wait.*"

"Now, don't rupture anything."

"Will is Warren's father?"

"Oh, no!" Virginia laughs. "Good Lord, no. No, that was Ralph, my pathetic ten-month husband. I actually left him for Will, and things were going well. I think I loved him, even. I won't lie. I had some dreams of the mansion myself. We were on and off for years. Boredom, mostly. It just wasn't there. Then I took him to the Nelsons' party, and he took one look at your mom and flipped his lid."

"Is that why you don't get along?"

"Of course. Can't have two Southern ladies fighting over the same man."

"Did they get together at the Nelsons' party? The one the photo is of?"

"No, Hannah," Virginia says. "Your parents were very, very in love. I really don't think Daisy noticed Will that night. But he sure as hell noticed her."

Hannah nods. Her mother is difficult not to notice.

"Your father was my best friend. He . . . he really was a good man."

Hannah's eyes sting momentarily. She fights for control. "You know," she says, "there are some pictures of you . . ."

Virginia frowns. "What pictures?"

"I found them at our house. A box of them. I thought they were Dad's."

"Oh," she says. "No. Those were definitely Will's."

"Huh." Hannah looks out the window. "Why the hell didn't Warren just tell me about you?"

"Oh, I never told Warren about Will. He was a baby the first time, and the second time was just that party. I never bring a man to the house unless it's serious. Which, by the way, is an excellent rule of thumb."

Hannah nervously pulls her hair back. "So all of my theories about my parents were completely wrong?"

"Probably." Virginia grins.

"I can't believe it."

"Face it. Your parents were a boring, semi-happy married couple. End of story."

"And I still don't know why he left."

"He went fishing, Hannah," Virginia says, tapping the ash.

"I just really feel like I need more of an answer than that."

Virginia sighs. "But I just don't think you're going to get one, sugar." She tucks a curl behind her ear. Her eyes are still glassy. "Don't you think it's time for you to go home? Fix that marriage of yours?"

"It's too late, I think."

"Have a kid, maybe? It's that time. Maybe——"

Hannah shakes her head. "No."

"What about your career? The sex stuff?"

"No. That's not going to work out either. We're bankrupt. I don't know. Really. I don't."

"That's too bad." She looks at her cigarette as if she's surprised to see it, then delicately stubs it out. "We've all got to hang on to something."

When they come back into the house, Warren's family has drifted into the other rooms. The girls are on their knees facing each other, playing patty-cake. Hannah had no idea children still did this. The percussive thuds their small hands make is comforting, somehow. *Slap, slap, slap.*

"Well," Hannah says, "I think I'll leave you all to it."

Jenny emerges from the kitchen, drying her hands on a bright-yellow dish towel. For some reason, Hannah feels a twinge of fear. Actually, she knows the reason, and fear is highly appropriate.

"Hannah." Jenny's smooth cheeks are flushed pink. Her lip is trembling slightly. "I just wanted to say something to you."

"OK."

Virginia wisely disappears into the living room.

"Will you come back out here with me?"

"Sure." Hannah reluctantly follows her outside to the sunporch. Jenny looks at the used ashtray and wrinkles her nose. "It wasn't me," Hannah says quickly.

"Oh, it doesn't matter. Well, that's not why...anyway." She squares her shoulders. "I think...oh, God, how do I say this? Hannah, I think you are a bad *person*."

"What?"

"I just want you to stay away from us." Her voice is shaking. "Can't you just stay *away* from us?"

"I live in California, Jenny."

"But you're *here*. At Sunday *dinner*." The tears arrive. "Excuse me. I cry a lot."

"I heard."

"How? Warren?"

"My brother told me."

"Oh."

"Tom thinks it might be your birth control pills."

"Maybe. I'll see. Wait—this is none of your business." She wipes her eyes with her sleeve. "Look, I can't talk to you, OK? I *know* Warren went to see you."

"Jenny, you're being hysterical."

"He wrote a whole *book* about you."

"Did you read it? It's really not very nice. Hardly the sort of book one wants written about herself. Trust me."

"I can't read it. I don't have it."

"I can —"

"You are a *threat*." She sobs.

"Jenny, come on. Really."

"He won't talk to me."

"Warren doesn't talk. That's his thing."

"It's awful," Jenny says. "All I want is someone in the house who's nice. Who talks. Like your *brother*."

"Wrong tree, Jenny."

"What?"

"You're barking up the wrong tree."

She shakes her head, blows her nose.

"It's an expression."

Jenny is the type of person, Hannah observes with annoyance, who manages to be pretty even while crying. When Hannah cries, her nostrils actually grow, pouring forth ancient reserves of thick green mucus.

"You just don't know what it's like."

Hannah has to admit, she really doesn't know what it's like. She's never thought about that before. She's fantasized for years about what it would be like if she had married Warren. But it could very well have been absolutely terrible. All that quiet seemed so alluring once, but over a decade it might just be boring. What if he wasn't who she thought he was? She'd always assumed he was a deep, complex well. What if, one horrific morning, she got a good look inside and discovered the water was only a few inches deep?

"I'm sorry," Hannah says. She *is* sorry. Hannah is sorry that, like the rest of them, Jenny Meyers wants things she can't have.

Jenny has not stopped crying. In fact, she is crying harder now. Her face is a dangerous shade of purple.

"Really, I am. Please calm down."

"Jenny?" Virginia says, appearing in the doorway. She comes in and puts her arm around her daughter-in-law. "Hannah, what's going on here?"

"I—"

"It's all right, honey. Don't cry."

"Jenny?"

"Mommy?"

And now they are all there. Warren, the girls, Virginia. They gather around Jenny, whispering and tending to her, stroking her hair.

"Hannah, I'm sorry, but you need to leave."

Where, Virginia? Hannah wants to ask. Where would you like me to—

And then, suddenly, she knows. Of course. She's been so stupid, wasting all of this time on accusations and pointless rooting through memories. The way to get the answer is just so obvious.

"Hannah, did you hear me?" The Meyers are circling their wagons.

"Sorry," Hannah says. "It's OK. I'm leaving, I'm leaving." It's a relief to say this, as it's a promise she can make good on. Especially now that she knows exactly where to go.

23

The Legares' New Emergency

P ALMER IS DISCOVERING a new stretch of morning loneliness he cannot master. The rest of the day will be all right. There will be a stack of patients waiting for him; he will go to the gym; maybe tell Jenny about the breakup, which will make her cry. Still, there is this empty place at which he arrives when opening his eyes in the morning. In an effort to ward it off, Palmer has started to allow Rumpus in bed in the morning. He calls for her, but the dog is still hiding somewhere. She's been acting strange due to the disruption of the household, wedging herself behind the sofa and under the guest bed.

The shrill ringing of the landline at an ungodly hour causes him to rise slightly from the low place. The phone is too far away to get to, so he lies in bed and waits for the machine to pick it up. It is his mother. She wants him to come to the DeWitt House.

"It's an *emergency*." Her voice is rendered into static fuzz from the machine. "Your presence is *required*."

He dresses for the chilly morning and drives over, wondering if there'll be breakfast. He is always dubious about coming to meals here. You may sit at a Chippendale dining table, but at the DeWitt House, you will be served Bi-Lo chicken, at best.

"Mom?" he calls, walking in. There is no sign of life in the ballroom or the parlor. He is not surprised. Despite having twenty-plus rooms to lounge in, his mother and stepfather use only the living room, kitchen, and bedroom. Basically, they inhabit a cottage encased in a mansion.

"Hello?"

He pokes his head in the dining room, but the table is not set. There is no evidence of cooking. It doesn't matter. He is glad the house is quiet, because he has much to talk to her about. Her advice as to how to split up a $6000 aquarium set, to start.

"Did you walk or crawl? I called an hour ago." Her voice is coming from the solarium. Palmer frowns. She is not in her usual impeccably strange dress, opting instead for an old-fashioned, Joan Crawford–worthy bathrobe.

"Hi. Are we eating?"

"There's coffee."

"All right."

Palmer goes in the kitchen, helps himself to a cup, and returns. "Where's DeWitt?"

"Looking for Hannah."

"What?" Palmer succumbs to a wave of annoyance. Can't something, just for once, be about him? "Did we lose her?"

"Unclear."

"Should we make breakfast?"

"Palmer, I know the stomach rules the mind, but aren't you at all curious as to the situation?"

"Sorry." His belly growls stubbornly.

"We need your help. I didn't want to alarm you over the phone."

"What's happening?"

"She's missing."

"What do you mean?" Palmer glances at a row of plants. They are thirsty to the point of expiration.

"She's off somewhere. She didn't come home for dinner last night, despite the fact that we had plans to go out to Fish."

"She missed a free meal?" Very unlike his sister.

"She didn't even call."

Palmer drums his fingers. "Is she out with...I don't know. Friends?"

"Friends?" Daisy snorts. He notices that his mother has no makeup on. Without it, her skin looks like blank tissue paper. "Who? Warren Meyers's wife? Your sister has no friends here."

Palmer puts his coffee down. "Wait. All right. Let's not panic."

"Certainly not."

"Did you call Jon?"

"Of course."

"And?"

"He doesn't know anything. Except that he's preparing to file both for bankruptcy and for divorce."

"Oh, my God."

"So she didn't tell you either."

"No."

Daisy looks into the bottom of her cup as if there is an answer there. "I thought I was doing the right thing, here, bringing her home. I knew she'd never agree to a real institution."

"She doesn't need to be institutionalized, Mom."

"You wouldn't call this a nervous breakdown?"

"I'd call this her midthirties."

"Your father, at least, had the decency to wait until forty."

"It's not the same thing."

"Let's hope not," she says.

He takes a sip of lukewarm coffee. "You know, it's not our job to fix her."

"Don't be ridiculous. I'm her mother. Of course that's my job."

The phone rings. Daisy rises to answer it.

"Hello. Oh, hi, Will. All right. So no one—" She puts her hand on her temple. "All right. No, I'm fine. She's not a child. I'm certain she's just off somewhere, spending your money. I know you gave her some—it's in your checkbook. It's called enabling, darling. No, I'm fine. Keep looking. All right. I love you."

She hangs up. It strikes Palmer then that he's rarely heard his mother tell Will that she loves him.

"Should we go to her room?" Palmer says. "See if she left a note?"

"I went up there but didn't find anything."

"Let's just look again."

"All right."

They climb up together and push the door open. The bed is made, but the room is disheveled, as if his sister was in a hurry to go to a party. There are photographs scattered in and around the trash bin. Palmer squats next to them.

"I wonder which picture it is?"

"Whatever do you mean?"

"Oh, she's been going on about this picture she found of you and Dad and DeWitt."

"What?" Daisy is distracted. She is playing detective, picking up Hannah's things and cautiously squinting at them. Watching her, Palmer senses a wave of regret. His mother had a family once. A mash of bodies at her breakfast table every morning. It wasn't a Chippendale; it was from Sears. It was scratched and cramped and stained from wineglasses and coffee cups. Still, they were all there. Mother, father, brother, sister. Dog weaving in and out of their feet. *Palmer, don't eat all the Tater Tots.* Left-handed Hannah marooned at the end for hitting elbows. The whole point of being a mother is to have a full table, isn't it? But all this family's ever done is leave.

He turns his attention back to the photographs. "This must be the one." He extracts a picture that is particularly frayed at the edges. Yes, it's just what his sister described. His mother, his father, and DeWitt all in one picture. They look so young! He stares at his father, at the likenesses to his own face.

"Let me see it."

Reluctantly, he hands it to his mother.

"Oh," she says after a moment. "Look at us."

"Yes."

"Well." Daisy purses her lips. "That certainly was a lovely time. And—you know, I'd forgotten Will was there."

"Mom," Palmer says impatiently, "you know that's one of the things that set Hannah off in the first place. You *told* her you and DeWitt hadn't met then."

"Well, apparently we had." Daisy shrugs. "I'm old. How am I supposed to remember these things? It's sort of nice, to have a picture of us all, isn't it? I think I'll frame it." She puts it in her pocket. "So would you like some pancakes?"

"What?"

"Well, you've been whining like a sick chicken about breakfast for the last hour. Now I'm offering some. Interested?"

"Well, I am pretty—"

"Good. Then come." Daisy spins around and descends the stairs, her Hollywood dressing gown flaring behind her.

Palmer shakes his head. His mother, as ever, has now moved on to the day's next activity. Why dwell on blame, or responsibility, or the minutia of the past? It's how she gets through things, he realizes. He supposes he's fine with it. We all have to get through somehow. And at least now he finally gets to eat.

24

Where Hannah Went

BEFORE HANNAH COULD go, she needed to steal Rumpus. So, around one o'clock on Monday afternoon, she went up to Palmer's house. First she tried both the front and side doors, which were locked. This neither surprised nor deterred her; no one as meticulous as her brother would ever leave a door unlocked. She'd seen a dog door that ran in and out of the kitchen—perhaps she could lure Rumpus outside through it, or, if necessary, squeeze in. The main obstacle was the privacy fence, but again Hannah wasn't discouraged. After surviving a three-story drop, a ten-foot wall was nothing. She dragged the neighbors' garbage can to the wall, climbed on top of it, and, giving a quick look back and forth, hopped over. As soon as she hit the yard, Rumpus appeared, tearing into her with a bark as soundless as it was furious.

"Hey, there," Hannah said to her. "Came just for you."

She leaned over to grab the dog, but Rumpus immediately darted away into the house. Hannah crawled in after her, grunting as she forced her hips through the small plastic dog opening. (Too much Charleston she-crab soup.) The next thirty minutes were a breathless chase, with Rumpus darting under the table and the bed, dancing away when Hannah would get close, and then taunting her with cold, beady stares. Only a finger smeared with Palmer's oily natural peanut butter finally slowed Rumpus down.

Taking the boat from the DeWitt property undetected was no small feat, but Hannah happened upon some luck that Monday. DeWitt had announced he would be away until nightfall, bird-ing—the warbler had set him off—while Daisy's day was com-pletely booked with the museum committee, a beginner's guitar lesson, and something else Hannah had not listened to. The DeWitt House staff always cleared out by three, so Hannah cal-culated she had a two-hour window to complete the preparations for her journey.

The scheme had come to her all at once while being chewed out at Virginia's house. It was clear that if Hannah wanted to know what became of her father, her approach would have to be more sci-entific. And so she would follow the exact footsteps her father had made, packing the same supplies, taking the same boat, putting in at approximately the same time of day, charting the same course. Not that she was going to find out anything definitive. But perhaps she might stumble upon a clue as to what happened. A perspective, which was a hell of a lot more than she had now.

With Rumpus safely stashed in the cab of Will's second truck (he kept an extra in the garage for "hauling emergencies"), Han-nah returned to the DeWitt House and backed the vehicle into the yard. She hadn't been inside the carriage house for years, and now, stepping into the dusty, mildewed gloom, she remembered why. From the dim shaft of light spilling in through the sliding door, she could just make out the form of the boat. Edging closer, she gazed at the shrouded object for a moment, then shoved away the easels; deflated, boxed beach toys; and old dining chairs barricading the vessel to free it of its filthy tarp with a snap. She peered inside. More or less the same as she remembered it, aside from a few cigarette butts, no doubt remnants from Palmer's college trip to Rockville.

Taking a deep breath, she walked out to the truck. Hitching it up wasn't nearly as complicated as she'd feared. Proud of her accomplishment, she pulled the boat into the yard and hosed it off. Rumpus was now alert and, nose pressed against the window, watched with interest as years of dirt and mold ran off the sides of the boat and onto the grass. Hannah walked around it, trying to remember everything her father did before trips, then paused and made a quick list.

Stuff I Need to Check First

Drain plug *(Securely in place?)*
Battery *(Working?)*
Lifesaving devices *(One for every passenger?)*
Fuel *(Adequately fueled? Leaks?)*
Food *(Have some?)*
Beer *(Yes?)*

She went through the items as quickly as she could. She had at least an hour yet; still, the last thing she wanted was her mother or stepfather coming home and politely asking what in God's name she was doing.

Getting the boat to the club was the trickiest part. The street was quiet, probably due to this grim fall afternoon, but driving with the boat was a more unwieldy task than she'd guessed. It took two tries to back out, and she cut at least one corner too close, barely missing a fire hydrant. She managed to get it into the water without submerging the truck, then tied the boat to the dock and loaded the supplies. Finished, she drove the truck back, parked it exactly where it had been before, then returned, dragging Rumpus behind her.

There was no sign of life anywhere. The club must have cut the staff when the cold came; even the bar seemed shut down for the duration. Taking the dog in her arms, Hannah descended the ramp and got into the boat. Rumpus hit the deck, limbs splayed. It made her uneasy, how quiet the club was, as there would be no log saying where she went.

"Enough," she said to Rumpus, who scrambled unhelpfully under a bench. Hannah lumbered about the boat, untying and coiling and pumping the gas line; once the lines were free, she pulled the cord. To her surprise and pleasure, the boat started immediately, but she couldn't remember exactly how the levers worked. The boat lurched backward, the aluminum hull making a horrible sound against the dock. A flock of seagulls scattered above while Rumpus shot out to the lip of the bow. Finally, coaxing the controls in the right direction, Hannah pulled away.

The huge expanse of harbor stretched out before her, terrifying and lonely. The chop was high, and an eerie mist hung over the creeks to her right. Bracing herself, she steered in the direction of the jetties, a huge underwater wall of rock built at the mouth of the harbor a century ago to prevent the storms from washing the islands away. This is where the authorities had always assumed her father had been heading; everyone knows it's one of the best spots in the harbor to fish.

It wasn't a short trip. She drove the boat slowly to stay reasonably dry in the chop. She could feel herself calming down. It felt good to pull away, to watch the houses shrink to the size of toys, the cars and people by now almost invisible. The DeWitt House loomed over all of the mansions around the Battery; even a mile out, she could see the window to her room.

The wind was merciless, and the cold numbed her hands and feet despite her layers of down and fleece. Should she have a sandwich? Too early. A beer? Too chilly. Should she put on a life jacket? No, no one wore a life jacket except for kids. She knew where they were, though. It was part of the checklist. Middle compartment—one for every passenger. One for her, one for Rumpus, four to spare.

God, this is stupid, she thought. I'm so cold. She tried to focus, to concentrate on the trip's purpose. All right. If he were going to the jetties, would he have headed left? There was a ship far off on the horizon. Could he have gotten caught in someone's wake?

Wake up, her mind chattered nonsensically. She began laughing.

"What am I *doing?*" The dog, still under the bow, shot her a look of contempt and turned away. Clichés began running uncontrollably through Hannah's brain:

Can't teach an old dog new tricks
Can't teach a new dog old tricks
Dog tired
Doggone

She shook her head, attempting to channel her father. Focus, Hannah, focus. What had it been like for him? Like this? No, almost certainly not. He left in April, after all, not late October.

A beautiful April night. She began to get angry. What had she *thought* would happen? Did she actually think she would find an answer out here? Be beamed up? Did she think she was going to meet a fucking pirate ship?

Rumpus climbed up on the bow, her body shaking with mute barks.

"What, Rumpus?" Hannah sighed. Maybe pirates after all. Peering just ahead, she immediately saw what the dog was barking at: a gray fin, slicing through the waves. She tried not to yelp. Had her father been eaten by a shark? But the fish was moving in humping arcs. It slowed down as if to get a better look at her and swam next to the boat, tipping its smiling face up briefly. It was a dolphin.

Rumpus growled, teetering dangerously close to the edge.

"Rumpus! *Stay.*"

The dog looked back at her.

"Rumpus, no. Seriously. Get back here."

Rumpus paused, as if politely considering Hannah's request for obedience, then turned and leapt into the water.

"Damn it!" Hannah screamed. *"Rumpus!"*

Knocking over the cooler and banging her knee on the middle seat, she ran to the front of the boat. Rumpus—surprisingly athletic—was paddling away at a good clip.

"Rumpus!"

The dog ignored her, bobbing up and down in the waves. Hannah began to panic. Coming home after this adventure was already going to be tricky: Daisy would be pissed off and confused; DeWitt would be disapproving; Palmer would be annoyed. She had weighed all of this, and already planned on doing a few backflips to get DeWitt to give her a bit of money and let her be on her way. But coming home after stealing the truck, the boat, and Palmer's dog, and then having to explain that Rumpus had drowned in the course of Hannah's spiritual journey . . . well. She might as well tie up and take a taxi straight to the Charleston/ Dorchester Community Mental Health Center.

Hannah kept the dog firmly in her sight, sighing with relief as she got the boat close to her. Hannah grabbed a sandwich from the cooler.

"Look, Rumpus!" she yelled. "Food!"

The dog slowed down at this, looking back.

"That's right. Stay, puppy."

Leaning gracelessly over the water, Hannah grabbed Rumpus's collar, heaving her up high enough to wrap her arms around the animal. She staggered. The terrier was light, but her vigorous squirming sent Hannah falling backward. Her balance was already challenged by the waves, and, arms full of wet, twisting dog, she was unable to brace herself. She heard a large crack that she recognized instantly as the back of her head. For a moment, the sight of one of her eyes went completely white.

"Rumpus," she croaked, riding the wave of pain. She tried to lift herself, but a great weight sat on her chest. The boat was still moving slowly, the engine humming. Hannah felt a sweetness coming that she knew was unconsciousness. She knew she should fight it — whenever people passed out in movies, their sidekicks would slap their faces and yell, *Stay with me!* But this was not a movie, this was happening, and she really, really wanted to sleep.

Feeling a wet snout on her face, she opened her eyes to see Rumpus hovering curiously above. She turned her head a little to look past the dog at the sky. Already the last watery light of the cold, wasted day was giving way to nightfall. She was alone.

All this trouble, all this *effort,* and the only thing she had discovered was the fact that her father was not coming. No one was. But, strangely, Hannah was no longer scared. In fact, her last thought before succumbing to the blackness was that she couldn't recall feeling so completely calm before. Not even in her youngest memories, or the most elusive trenches of her dreams.

25

Someone Is Coming

W HEN HANNAH WAKES, the darkness is relentless. No stars, no moon. She wonders how long she's been out. It seems to be well past sunset. She sits up gingerly. The pain. Rumpus, who, taking Hannah's cue, has been curled up against her legs, lifts her head and quivers her nose.

Everything seems to be working, basically — her head, neck, and senses. It's suspiciously quiet. The only sound is the water slapping against the metal of the boat. After a few moments of enjoying the peace, Hannah realizes that the engine has died. She fishes the flashlight out of the bag she brought and crawls to the stern to investigate. There is still a bit of fuel sloshing around in the tank, so that's not the problem. She pulls the engine cord. Nothing happens. She pulls it again. No, something is wrong. It's broken. She leans in with her light and inspects the machinery but, knowing nothing about engines, finds this a completely use- less act. She tries to yank the cord once more. Nothing.

She sits down to try and think, then remembers her phone. She takes it out and sees, to her surprise, that it is four in the morning. Could she really have slept that long? There are seven missed calls from her mother. She looks at the screen, considering. If she calls her mother at this hour, she will be seen as nothing more than a crazy, incompetent mess — again. There will be screaming ... possibly the police. Hannah just doesn't know if she can take that right now. But if she waits until later in the morning, she might be able to get just DeWitt on the line and make a joke out of all this.

Oh, the things that will be different when she gets home. She'll change. They'll see. She will not obsess over the past, she will be more focused, she will be a selfless wife and family member and friend. She will volunteer and work in soup kitchens and animal shelters. *A new Hannah.*

She squints into the wet darkness. From the lights onshore, she can tell she's somewhere in between Fort Sumter and James Island. The boat appears to be in some kind of current, drifting out toward the open ocean, but Hannah takes heart in the fact that movement is slow. The only other ship she sees is far out on the horizon, lifetimes away.

She sits on the bottom of the boat. At least it's not raining. Things aren't so bad. She knows the thing to do is not to panic. Rumpus wriggles and stretches next to her. Hannah pats her head. She fishes in the cooler for a beer and a sandwich. She is suddenly ravenously hungry. And really there's nothing to _do_ anyway but eat. She finishes one sandwich, then takes out another and a bag of chips. After giving half the second sandwich to Rumpus, she digs into the potato chips, nibbling around the edges and then sloshing the crumbs around her mouth with sips of beer. She becomes bored. It's the main thing about being adrift, isn't it? She could try and sleep more, but she isn't tired. In fact, she can't remember being so awake.

She begins to play a mind game with herself that she often enters into when freezing on ski lifts, waiting out the rain when camping, or in other situations where she finds herself in physical discomfort. *If I could be anywhere in the world, where would I be?* Bali, maybe? In bed with Jon, the *New York Times,* and some coffee? She takes a sip of beer and looks out at the horizon. With mild interest, she notes that the ship that was so far away before is getting closer. Could she be drifting that fast? No, Hannah realizes, what's happening is that the boat—ship, actually—is coming toward her at what is clearly a rapid speed. Worse, there's probably no way for this enormous tanker to see or detect her, meaning if she doesn't figure out how to get out of the way, she and Palmer's dog will very likely be plowed over.

Hannah sternly tells herself not to panic; all she has to do is make herself seen. She turns on her flashlight and waves it from side to side in a wide arc for a few minutes, which discouragingly elicits no reaction. If anything, the ship seems to be speeding up. She yanks open one of the doors and grabs an orange flare box, thick with dust. The ship is closer now—close enough for her to see that it is a Carnival cruise ship, probably the same one she was staring at when she fell off her bicycle. Its brilliant lights illuminate the water around it, and from the glow she can just make out the cheerful logo and the name painted in garish letters on the side: ELATION. Hannah fumbles at the flare box and pries it open. Inside is an orange pistol; she grabs it, holds the gun over her head, and pulls the trigger. Nothing happens—cursing, she claws at the box and finds what must be the shell and jams it in.

"Please work," she whispers. "Please, please, please just *work*."

Holding the gun above her head again, she pulls the trigger. She hears a charged, whizzing sound above as the flare traces a beautiful arc, raining pink sparks that illuminate the water around her.

She looks over at the cruise ship, which is still churning toward her. Her mind rages ahead. All right, OK, this flare thing isn't working either. She'll get the life jackets—one on her, one on Rumpus. They'll jump in together like doomed lovers. Sure, it'll be cold as hell, but she'll call her brother first, then he can call the police or something. . . . Oh, God, she thinks. I really am so truly screwed.

She reloads the flare gun, shoots again, then waits, her heart thrashing. Is this what happened to her father? It strikes her suddenly, watching the *Elation* charge toward her, that his fate could have been determined by, literally, a million things. A ship, a shark, a gun, a wave, pirates. Or maybe he just left and moved to Florida with a woman named Trixie. The point is, he's not here now. Whatever happens is utterly up to her.

A sob escapes from her throat when she sees that the boat seems to be veering a little to the left. She shoots another and waits, scared to breathe. Then, suddenly, the air is pierced by a long, shattering horn blast. A few people come out to the deck in their pajamas, emerging from warm-looking, brightly lit cabins. Hannah can see them clutching the railing, can hear tinny music tinkling anemically from the disco. She lowers herself to the bottom of the boat and grabs Rumpus, who is shaking uncontrollably. Together, they watch the enormous vessel pass as the little johnboat tips dangerously in the *Elation*'s massive wake. Hannah puts her head down, pushing her nose into Rumpus's fur, and grips the side as the boat rocks violently for what feels like an hour. She can hear items splashing over the side and full beer cans sliding. Finally, the moving subsides. Everything grows quiet.

Hannah looks up slowly. Her face is wet; she is surprised to find that she is crying. The boat is a mess of littered cans and wrappers, she almost drowned, and she still has no answers. But what, exactly, was she expecting to find out here? There is a squad of people onshore, a whole team safe in their beds, who have bent their lives to take care of her. Her mother, her brother, her husband, her stepfather. Virginia and Warren. Jenny White, even. And yet she is in the middle of the cold harbor, chasing the final ghost. Still waiting faithfully with the dog.

Hannah has to let out a small laugh.

She is alone at sea, because.

The coast guard boat comes at five o'clock in the morning. Even when she spots it from far away—just a tiny white speck on the horizon—she knows it's coming for her. Vaguely surprising, though, as it's so early she hasn't yet called anyone. The vessel, white and proud as a nurse in a starched apron, motors without hesitation to her boat. She can see a figure standing at the railing: DeWitt, bundled up in a down coat and hunting cap. The vessel comes alongside the johnboat and ties up.

"Hey, Tropicana!" her stepfather yells over the noise. "You really wanted to go boating, you could've just *asked*."

"Hi," Hannah calls back. "You found me."

"Wasn't all that hard."

Men in white uniforms leap down onto her little boat and

maneuver it into towing position, paying little attention to Hannah herself; indeed, after a rather brisk medical examination, they seem annoyed that the affair hasn't proved more dire. At last, Hannah hands Rumpus up to her stepfather, then climbs aboard.

"How'd you figure out where I was?"

"Well," he says, wrapping her in a blanket, "you didn't come home, so I looked in town all night. Finally searched the house and saw that the boat was missing. Called the coast guard, and they said there had been reports of a woman in a fishing boat shooting a flare gun at a cruise ship. Figured that crazy lady could only be you."

"I wasn't shooting *at* the cruise ship. I was just signaling so it wouldn't hit me."

"Word is you scared the hell out of the passengers."

"I was going to call," she says. "I was just waiting until an appropriate hour."

"That's mannerly."

"Anyway, thanks for being here."

"Well, of course." DeWitt takes off his hat and scratches his head somewhat furiously. He seems almost irritated, but Hannah can't be sure. "Of course I'm here."

Hannah experiences an uncomfortable yet warm feeling. Here he is, her stepfather, all 250 plaid pounds of him. Sure, his jokes make her cringe, and he's loud and a little bit of a redneck. But he's always *there*. She knows she should say something to him; this would be the correct Hallmark moment. For instance: Thanks for everything. Thanks for coming now, and before when Mom needed you, and all of those times you bailed our family out. Thanks for being here when the other one wasn't. You've actually always been a really good stand-in dad.

And she would tell him those things. Really. But she's a little too cold right now, so she just says thanks again. DeWitt nods, still looking vaguely uncomfortable. He's not so great at this either.

"Well." DeWitt looks down at her father's old boat, littered with flare cartridges and sandwich wrappers and beer cans. "Looks like you had yourself quite a night."

"I did."

"So, I don't want to..." DeWitt shifts from foot to foot, then gestures at the water. "Guess what I mean is, you all done out here?"

"Yes." Hannah nods and wraps another towel around the shivering dog. "Thanks. I am. I'm all done."

26

What Buzz Left Behind

WHEN PALMER FIRST heard of his mother's sex-toy party, he was beyond horrified. He couldn't fathom what could possibly be spurring her to hold a vibrator sale at the DeWitt House, and loudly refused to go.

"I am supporting your sister," his mother hissed at his inquiries. "She's obviously going through some strange phase. But she needs our moral support, and the money won't hurt either."

Palmer grimaced. It was just so *her;* rather than taking Hannah aside for a heart-to-heart, his mother arranged an event. But curiosity won in the end. Who could miss this spectacle? And so, on Tuesday, a week after the coast guard towed Hannah in, he dons a pair of chinos and a crisp white shirt and—after stopping at the high school to vote, as it is Election Day—drives over to the DeWitt House.

He has taken care to arrive late, so already there is an impressive gaggle of women gathered around Hannah's wares. Entering quietly from the doorway, he sizes up the situation, and it is nothing short of alarming: Mrs. Nelson turning one of the platinum vibrators on and off and waving it at Daisy; Mrs. Jones loading porn in the DVD player while Mrs. Walters and her friend Georgia try out a pair of handcuffs.

"Palmer!" his mother chirps as soon as she spots him. "Come in, come in! Isn't this *fun?*"

"It's something."

"Look at this wand thingie. You just press this button, and the head begins to—"

"Right. Got it. Wow." Ever since Hannah's rescue, his mother has returned to her determinedly cheery self; as a practicing repressor himself, he thoroughly respects this strategy. Today she is dressed for the party in typical '70s finery, in a bright red, white, and blue–print pantsuit.

"You look very patriotic."

"Well, I wanted to make a statement. It is a day for patriotism, after all."

"Where's Hannah?"

"Upstairs. If you go up there, tell her she needs to come down. Everyone brought cash, but she wasn't particularly clear about the prices of things."

Palmer nods, pours himself a glass of champagne from the bar that has been set out for the occasion, and climbs up to Hannah's landing. The door is shut. He enters without knocking and finds that his sister is sitting on her bed, checking her flight time on the Internet.

"All packed?"

"Almost."

"You're missing the party."

"I know, I know. I was there for a while, but when Mrs. Nelson starting telling Mom about the difference between G-spot and clitoral orgasms, I had to leave."

"God."

"They all brought cash, though. I'll probably make a thousand dollars or something."

Palmer collapses onto the bed.

"It's nice of Mom to do it, actually," Hannah says. "I thought it was a stupid idea, but they're all having such a good time."

"True," Palmer says. "So, your head's OK?"

"Which side?"

"The inside."

"Oh. Yeah." She closes the laptop and lies back beside him. "The inside's OK, I guess." They stare at the ceiling together.

"It's really dirty up there," Palmer says.

"How's Tom?"

He tosses a pillow in the air. "Pretty good, actually."

After catching the amused, slightly confused report of Hannah's rescue on the local morning television news, Tom came to the dock to show his support for the family. By the time he arrived, they were gathered at the coast guard station, filling out paperwork. Palmer and his mother had come immediately, of course, as soon as DeWitt called. Palmer, for one, was not surprised to hear where his sister had been; in fact, the trip made so much sense that he was a little annoyed with himself for not guessing where she'd disappeared to. It was a bit touchy with the coast guard. After charging an astronomical fee for recovering the boat, the chief officer took DeWitt and Palmer aside and proceeded to lecture them on "keeping their women in check."

"I don't 'have' women," Palmer was in the middle of saying. "See, I'm a homosexual. Though" — he moved closer — "I'd love to keep *you* in check."

"Tom!" Daisy cried, elated to spy her son's lover hovering by the door. "How are you? We've *missed* you."

"Oh, fine, thank you," Tom said, his voice tremulous. His eyes darted over to Palmer. He was obviously terrified, and the women in the family immediately gravitated to his side. "How are you?" he ventured. "Is everyone all right?"

"Hannah's fine," Daisy said, waving her hand. "Just the usual theatrics. Have you been —"

"What are you doing here?" Palmer interrupted.

"Oh, well. I just thought..." Tom looked at the floor.

"We're *glad* you're here," Daisy said.

Palmer glared at his mother, rendering her mute for the moment. A long, painful silence followed.

Tom finally backed toward the door. "Well, I guess I should..."

"Wait," Palmer said. They all looked over, surprised. His pulse raced. It would be easier to just let Tom leave, Palmer knew. To promise to call him later, and then never follow up. It's always easier to let things lie, to stay in the protected box. But why is that better? Look at my sister, he thought. She makes everything hard as hell, but at least she *tries*. And trying is something, isn't it? If you're trying, you're moving. You're not in your perfect house, festering, just waiting for something to change.

"Tom," he said, reddening. *Can I do this?* "We are glad you're here. *I'm* glad. We're all just...glad." He shook his head at his pathetic attempt at reconciliation. Tom looked unmistakably dubious. Still, he hadn't left yet.

"Mom," Hannah said, "why don't you show me where the bathroom is?"

"Hannah, you just went to the ladies' room."

"Mother!"

Reluctantly, Daisy followed. Palmer turned to Tom.

"Really," Palmer said quickly before he could ruin things again. "Please. Will you stay?"

That was a week ago. Since then, things had almost returned to the way they were—although Palmer did permanently ban the baby idea. Tom agreed almost immediately, saying he would focus his affections on Rumpus instead.

"Has he moved back in yet?" Hannah asks now, propping herself up on her elbow.

"Pretty much. Now it's me, the dog, and Tom."

"A family," Hannah says.

Palmer grins involuntarily; he reddens at the show of emotion. "Well, we should go downstairs," he says. "All of these women want to buy your sex toys. And the election results are going to begin coming in soon."

"Hey," she says, sitting up. "Have you spoken to Jenny Meyers?"

"Of course. Every day at the office."

"Did she say anything about me?"

"Why?" Palmer looks at her. "Wait, you saw Warren. Jesus, did you—"

"No. I mean, we saw each other. And talked. But it was nothing, really."

"God. *Why* can you never just move *on?*"

"I just think if you've cared for someone . . . I don't know. Do they have to disappear from your life entirely?"

"Hannah."

"Palmer."

"Jenny's fine," Palmer says. "I wouldn't give it a second thought. Just leave. That's what she—" But he catches himself, realizing. "Sorry, I didn't mean that. We all love having you here."

"No, you're right," Hannah says. "I get it. It's time for me to go home."

The guests finally leave around seven. Hannah sits at the dining table and counts her money. It turns out she has grossed $2,300 — a sum Palmer is rather jealous of, given the current state of economic affairs. The family takes plates of leftover hors d'oeuvres and heads to the study, where the twenty-five-year-old Zenith sits hunkered on the old game table. Palmer, Daisy, Hannah, and DeWitt sip their drinks, watching the results come in and saying little. As Obama garners electoral votes, though, DeWitt grows increasingly restless.

"How can this be happening?" he growls. "He's just a damned whippersnapper!"

Palmer, who does not wish to argue today, concentrates on his crab cakes.

"You're just upset that he's black," Hannah says.

"Louisiana, of course I'm not upset he's black. I'm a redneck, maybe, but—Christ. I'm *glad* he's black. It means maybe we can get this out of everyone's system, for God's sake. Something to talk about at the Boat Club. What I *am* upset about is that he's twelve!"

"Oh, Will," Daisy says drowsily. "We're so old."

Palmer remains silent. They have never been a family to speak about politics or to watch television together; doing so now, he finds it's as if they are onstage in a play. It has been this way ever since Hannah's rescue. Daisy's cheerfulness has peaked near hysteria, while DeWitt has been insisting on group activities, including an extremely miserable early-morning birding trip. Hannah, for her part, has been uncharacteristically docile. Palmer can sense that his sister knows they are doing this for her, and that she is at once grateful and put out by it all. Everyone in the family, he suspects, is now aching for their separate, less complicated lives away from one another. Tonight he literally feels bruised, as if he's pulled a muscle in trying to be something he is not.

Still, he dutifully stays until the results are in, stays even past midnight to watch the people in Chicago scream and cheer as the president, with his shining, superhero face, delivers his acceptance speech. Palmer is so tired he can barely make out what the man is saying. Something about change and all things being possible. When he looks over, he sees that both Daisy and DeWitt have fallen asleep. Hannah, though, is watching intently, hanging on to every word.

"I'm going," he tells her.

"All right."

He kisses his mother, who wakes with a start and heads upstairs. DeWitt shakes Palmer's hand before following. Hannah walks him to the door.

"Be good," he says.

"Will you come visit?"

"Absolutely." The lie comforts him. They embrace a bit awkwardly, and he tells her that he loves her.

"A new president!" she calls after him as he gets into his car. "You think he can save us?"

She is looking at Palmer expectantly. He can see she is waiting for some wisdom from her older brother, some sort of ultimate sum-up. But he really doesn't have one. Suddenly he is almost too exhausted for words.

"We don't need saving," he says, and then, if only to fill the void, "We just need more *vodka*."

She stares at him. He's failed, and they both know it. His face darkens slightly with embarrassment.

"Right," she says after a moment. "Vodka." She smiles at him with what can only be called mercy, and lets her brother go.

There are 206 bones in the body. Miles of connective tissue. One and a half gallons of blood. Approximately 600 muscles. When you laugh, you use maybe 100 of those muscles. Less so when you cry.

Buzz Legare used to tell his children that the brain produces enough electricity to power three lightbulbs. We are born knowing how to breathe, he said. We inhale around twenty thousand times a day. But when Palmer is looking up at a plane or thinking about what kind of sandwich to eat for lunch, how does his body know not to crumple? That's the part Buzz never explained to them. Somehow when Hannah walks, her synapses know not to think about the steps she's taking. Instead, she has to trust herself. She has to just give up and float.

At dawn, Hannah is packed. She says good-bye to her mother and leaves a note thanking Mitchell for restoring her bike. DeWitt drives her to the airport, and they exchange an awkward, bumbling good-bye; as he drives away, she waves until he's around the bend, and thinks about all the fathers she's had.

Hannah uses the entirety of her frequent-flier miles to travel first class. Because it is so last-minute, the amount required is exorbitant. She knows she should save them — this many points would translate to four round-trip tickets in coach, and funds will be tight for a long, long while. But the waste seems appropriate, somehow. She still feels that she needs a little extra room.

The way back is long and jagged. She bumps through the bleak hours in Charlotte and Denver. On the plane, she takes a piece of notepaper out of her day planner and makes one last list:

Some Things About My Father

My father was a hero.
My father loved his wife.
My father saved a boy from a bee.
My father was someone I never knew very well.
My father wasn't here for us.
My father is always here for us.
My father did the best he could. It turned out to be enough.

By the time she finally arrives in San Francisco, it is late at night. She hasn't arranged for a ride, so she wheels her suitcase to the long queue of empty taxis and gets into the car at the front of the line. She gives the driver the address of the loft, but halfway there, she changes her mind.

"Upper Terrace, please," she calls up to the front.

She waits for the driver to ask where that is, because no one ever recognizes the address. But this one is different. No questioning look, no turning on his electronic GPS system. He just nods and acts like he knows where to go. Still, she's having trouble trusting and fears he may be taking her to the wrong place. She leans forward behind him, whispering directions he doesn't require:

"Up Fell. Left on Masonic, OK? Sorry, but keep going, then turn—just, yeah. Keep going. Keep going. Sorry, here's a twenty, keep the change. Don't have much more than that—we're bankrupt! I know, we're all in this together. So, anyway, good luck, then. OK, bye."

Is her husband home? He must be. She still doesn't have the new key, but his car's there, and this time she's got the right shoes for climbing.

She looks up the fire escape, considering. A wiser person, she knows, wouldn't do this. There are so many reasons not to. She's already mined this marriage bare; Jon has made that clear. There's a divorce on the table, and this could definitely be used against her. Plus, Denise might be up there ... or worse.

But what Hannah knows now is that she is gloriously and terminally faithful. She is someone who believes, even when others do not. If you're a dog, that means waiting for days in a boat for your owner to come back out of the ocean. If you're a woman, it might mean scaling a building to tell your husband you still love him, whether or not he's ready to hear you yet.

There won't always be a why, her father once called from the water.

She's climbing up high above her city. She's opening the door, shouting, turning on every light.

About the Author

Katie Crouch is the author of the *New York Times* bestselling novel *Girls in Trucks*. Her writing has also appeared in the *New York Observer*, *Tin House*, and *McSweeney's*. She received her MFA from Columbia University and was awarded a Walter E. Dakin Fellowship to the Sewanee Writers' Conference and a MacDowell Fellowship. She lives in San Francisco.